FOR ONE MOMENT WITH YOU

DEBBIE HOWELLS

B
Boldwood

First published in Great Britain in 2025 by Boldwood Books Ltd.

Copyright © Debbie Howells, 2025

Cover Design by Debbie Clement

Cover Images: Debbie Clement and Shutterstock

The moral right of Debbie Howells to be identified as the author of this work has been asserted in accordance with the Copyright, Designs and Patents Act 1988.

Every effort has been made to obtain the necessary permissions with reference to copyright material, both illustrative and quoted. We apologise for any omissions in this respect and will be pleased to make the appropriate acknowledgements in any future edition.

A CIP catalogue record for this book is available from the British Library.

Paperback ISBN 978-1-83703-736-0

Large Print ISBN 978-1-83703-737-7

Hardback ISBN 978-1-83703-735-3

Trade Paperback ISBN 978-1-80656-036-3

Ebook ISBN 978-1-83703-738-4

Kindle ISBN 978-1-83703-739-1

Audio CD ISBN 978-1-83703-730-8

MP3 CD ISBN 978-1-83703-731-5

Digital audio download ISBN 978-1-83703-733-9

This book is printed on certified sustainable paper. Boldwood Books is dedicated to putting sustainability at the heart of our business. For more information please visit https://www.boldwoodbooks.com/about-us/sustainability/

Boldwood Books Ltd, 23 Bowerdean Street, London, SW6 3TN

www.boldwoodbooks.com

For every reader who finds a little of themselves in these pages.

Only from the heart can you touch the sky.

— RUMI

PROLOGUE

If someone had told me twenty years ago, I'd end up living alone in Greece, I would have told them they had the wrong person. I mean, me, Tilly, going off and leaving her familiar life behind? No way, buster. You've got the wrong girl. But here I am. On the face of it, it sounds as though I've embarked on a wonderful adventure – which in a sense, I have. But there's no denying that I wouldn't be here at all if it wasn't for the devastating collapse of my marriage.

My plan wasn't to come to this tiny Cretan town as yet another tourist. I wanted to immerse myself in the culture, to experience how real life was here. And being part of life means helping your neighbours out. So it is that a couple of weeks after arriving here, I find myself setting off early for Michail's house. Michail is a gentleman of a certain age who last night had a fall I happened to witness, before he was whisked away to hospital. It just so happens he has a cat and chickens that need feeding, so yours truly offered to help.

After all, it's how the world works, I've always thought. People helping each other. It's meant getting up earlier than I've become used to latterly. Stopping to pick up a coffee along the way, I walk along streets that are stirring with faint sounds of Greek life, the sun rising above the rooftops. On reaching Michail's humble house, I unlock the blue-painted front door. But as I go through and into the garden behind it, to his chickens, it most definitely is not early and a positive chorus of squawking is coming from the hen house.

It stops as soon as I open the door and the birds come hurtling out. After throwing down some corn, I go inside to feed the cats – this morning, five of them have arrived for breakfast. It's true what they say here – there is never just one cat. Then as they eat, I cast my eyes around the place. In the low sunlight coming through the small window, I take in the unwashed plates and pans, the half-open packets scattered across the worktops, the general air of neglect that makes it clear to me that Michail isn't really coping.

I push up my sleeves, fill the sink with warm water and start washing up, before starting on the rest of the kitchen. Not once does it occur to me that it isn't my place to do this. After that's done, I clean the window, still humming happily to myself, then I scrub the floor and gather a bag of what is very obviously rubbish to take outside.

That done, I stand back and survey the results. A sense of satisfaction fills me. I mean, not just is it clean, but I like to think this will be welcoming for Michail to come home to. Stepping out through the back door, I stand there for a moment. While I've been cleaning, the blue sky has become obscured by grey cloud, the pleasant early morning warmth replaced by a cool breeze rippling through the air. But as my new friend, Nicos would say, it is October. I gaze around the garden, at the tree on which lemons are ripening, some straggly tomato plants, the similar houses on either side that hint at a simplicity of life here which as a tourist would simply pass you by.

It comes as a shock to realise I haven't so much as thought about Gareth, my soon to be ex-husband, for over two hours. Continuing this theme of distraction, I contemplate starting on cleaning the next room – just to give it a quick once-over, you understand. I mean, I wouldn't want Michail to think I've been judging him.

I turn to go back inside. But as I do, the steps catch me out and I trip, banging my knee against the door frame.

'Fuck,' I mutter, tears of pain filling my eyes. Then, glancing down, I notice one of my shoes is caked in chicken shit.

Standing there, I suddenly freeze. Exactly *why* am I doing this? I mean, I haven't come all this way to look after a stranger's chickens and cats, or to clean up their house, when I have a personal crisis of my own going on.

But that's the kind person of person you are, I tell myself. *You care. For frick's sake, wouldn't the world be a better place if more of us did?* It's what I believe – what I've always believed.

But this time, it's like I have another revelation – a massive one. You see, there's a reason I've always filled up my days doing things for other people. It stops me thinking about my own life; about the emptiness between the surface-level clutter. About the truth, which is that I've lost myself.

The thought is like a sucker punch, just as a gust of wind blows through the open door. I look up again just as rain starts to fall.

After closing up the house, I lock the door and pocket the key. Then, cursing myself for not bringing a jacket, I head back down the street towards the room I've rented. But with each step, the skies are visibly darkening, the rain falling in large, heavy drops that intensify just before the heavens open.

In no time, my sodden clothes are clinging to me. Even my sandals are soaked as the sloping narrow road becomes a stream. The little white houses suddenly look less welcoming as I shelter in a doorway and wait for the weather to pass. But as I stand there, alarm fills me as far from letting up, the rain becomes heavier, the stream down the narrow road by now a river.

Deciding to make a run for it before it gets any worse, I set off again, breaking into a stilted kind of run as I splash through the water. Once or twice I lose my footing, then I feel my feet go from under me. That's the last thing I remember as I'm pitched backwards: the rain, my feeling of powerlessness. Falling, before my head hits something.

A voice calls out that seems to come from far away. It's a voice I dimly recognise – or at least, I think I do. It's followed by silence.

I've absolutely no idea how, but the rain subsides. Then it's as though the years wind back until I find myself at the beginning – where all this started.

1

Those who cannot remember the past are condemned to repeat it.

— GEORGE SANTAYANA

Confusion fills my head. What's going on? I should be in Crete – shouldn't I? On my way back to my rented room in Andreas's house. Not in England, on a fine summer evening, watching a much younger version of myself just days away from making the biggest mistake of my life.

I remember thinking back then, *right then*, how much I bloody loved my life. I loved Gareth, too – not to mention my parents, for paying for our spectacular wedding that was coming up. The church wedding my dad wouldn't have considered any alternative to; the marquee reception in the picturesque grounds of a country house hotel. Lizzie, for planning the hen night I was dressing up for.

I watch myself study my reflection, my hand going to my face, smoothing skin that was faintly wrinkled last time I looked. I pinch myself. This has to be a dream. How else can I possibly be

here in Lizzie's flat again, the week before my wedding, watching
myself get ready for my hen party?

More to the point, *why?* I can remember how I felt that day,
the emotions that washed over me as I stood there. One that over-
rode the excitement and sense of anticipation I should have been
feeling. One that with my wedding looming, shouldn't have been
there. *Doubt*.

As I watch myself standing in front of the mirror, Lizzie came
bursting in. Emotion overwhelms me for the sister I've since lost,
who I miss desperately.

'Come on, Tilly! You're going to be late!' Wearing a cropped
psychedelic top and orange shorts that showed off her tan, her
fair hair subtly streaked, she was the essence of summer. She
thrust a cheap version of a veil at me. 'Put it on. Actually, on
second thoughts, I'll do it.' She snatched it back and fastened it
into my hair, then rummaged in my make-up bag and produced a
pink lipstick. 'You need this,' she ordered.

I looked vaguely ridiculous, but where Lizzie was concerned,
there was no point protesting. My sister satisfied, we stepped out
into the June sunshine, my veil attracting more than a few whis-
tles as we headed into town towards the bar where we'd
arranged to meet my best friend Jasmine and some other
friends.

Jasmine. We used to be such good friends. But life took us in
different directions; last I heard she was living in Dubai.

That day, as we made our entrance, my friends were already
making inroads into their second bottle of champagne and as
they saw us, a loud cheer went up that had everyone else's heads
turning.

'You'll get us thrown out,' I admonished them, taking the glass
of champagne that was pushed into one of my hands.

It was an afternoon of unbridled high spirits and hilarity, one during which after my initial tiddliness, for some reason I remained oddly sober.

'Drink this.' Lizzie thrust another glass at me. 'It's you who's supposed to be drunk – not the rest of us.'

'Thanks.' I took it, aware that for reasons I couldn't identify I just wasn't feeling it.

Later, Mum had joined us. 'Just for a while. Then I'll leave you young people to it.' She'd winked at me. 'I wouldn't want to cramp your style.'

But as afternoon became evening, my restlessness was growing. If it had been up to me, I would have settled for a Chinese takeaway and an early night, but I knew the others wouldn't have heard of it. And I got it. In the past, it would have sounded boring to me, too. I mean, whoever heard of a tame hen party?

It's strange, but I can remember exactly how I felt as I sat there. It was like I was detached in some way, observing everyone else. Lizzie, pink-cheeked, almost falling off the high heels she could carry off because she was so tiny. My lovely mum, in one of her printed cotton summer dresses. Jasmine, newly fake-tanned, in a golden dress that looked as though it had been sprayed on – Jasmine always had to outdo the rest of us.

I looked around at everyone – my family; the little group of friends I'd known since school. Then in a gesture that was out of character for me, I stood up. 'Thank you, so much, all of you, for being here today.' I gazed at each of them in turn, feeling my heart warm; knowing how much they were looking forward to our wedding day. 'Sound like a flipping vicar, don't I? But seriously, it means the world to me. Your glasses are looking very empty,' I joked, even though it wasn't true. 'How about I order us some cocktails?'

After much passing around and deliberation of the menu, I went to the bar to order the cocktails, and there he was. Adam

Cameron – except, in that moment, I didn't know that was his name. Nor did I know that he was the man who, in the space of a short meeting, was going to turn my life upside down.

'Looks like quite a party you're having,' he said amiably. 'Your hen party?' His eyes flickered over the veil I was wearing.

My hands went to it, straightening it, as suddenly I felt ridiculous. 'Bit of a giveaway, isn't it?' I gazed into his warm brown eyes that looked oddly familiar. 'Sorry about the racket. They're my family and my best friends.' I nodded towards our table.

'No need to apologise. We were... er, enjoying it!'

'Oh.' I frowned, wondering who the *we* meant. 'Who are you here with?'

'A mate.' He nodded towards a table where a man was sitting.

Relief filled me that he wasn't here with a girl – relief that made no sense when he meant nothing to me. 'I'm Tilly.' Impulsively, I held out my hand.

'Adam.'

As I took the hand he held out, the touch of it sent an electric shock through me.

Adam smiled. Then still holding my hand, he frowned slightly. 'Do I know you from somewhere?'

'I don't think so.' I gently let go of his hand. I knew we hadn't met before. There was no way on this earth I wouldn't have remembered him.

'It's nice to meet you, Tilly.'

I couldn't speak. It was the oddest feeling as he looked at me, like a powerful sense of déjà vu. The deepest sense of belonging, as though we'd known each other forever. As I stood there, a million thoughts had flashed through my brain. That I wanted to know more about this man, that I'd never felt like this about Gareth; that meetings like this were somehow fated. But a week away from the wedding I'd always dreamed of, that my mum had been planning down to the most carefully thought-out detail, it seemed the cruellest twist of fate that this was happening now.

My discomfort was growing by the second, and I did the only thing I could to break the moment. 'I should get back to everyone,' I said brightly. I nodded towards my family and friends.

'Oh. Of course.' He looked taken aback. Then he seemed to rally. 'He's a lucky guy,' he said softly.

'Thanks.' But any excitement I'd felt before had been all but snuffed out. I knew, in a way I couldn't explain, that sounded bonkers, even to me, that if I hadn't been getting married, Adam and I could have been something.

Carrying the tray of cocktails, I went back to the table, pinning on a smile as I sat down. Listening to everyone chattering and laughing, I felt strangely out of it, as beside me Lizzie nudged my elbow.

'You OK?' Her eyes searched mine.

'I'm fine.' I smiled brightly, wondering if she knew it was false. 'How could I not be?'

At that moment, the barman came over with a bottle of champagne and a tray of glasses. 'With the compliments of the gentleman over there.'

I watched him nod towards Adam, still standing at the bar, my heart missing a beat as across the room he met my eyes again.

'How lovely! Please say thank you to him.' After placing the tray in front of her, my mum started pouring the champagne, then passed me a glass. 'Don't you love how weddings bring out the best in people?'

* * *

I'd always been sensible. A black-and-white kind of girl. The girl who got her homework in on time, who was back from nights out at a most sensible hour – well, mostly. Perhaps it was unsurprising that my hen night wound up early, my pissed friends heading off to a bar, leaving Lizzie and me alone in the street together.

'You sure you're OK?' She'd definitely picked up on something.

'Of course I am. You should go with the others,' I said.

'And leave you on your own? I don't think so,' she said indignantly.

'Honestly.' I smiled at her. 'I think I'm going to head back to the flat.'

Lizzie stared at me for a moment. 'This is weird.' Then she hugged me. 'But OK. If that's what you want.'

As she tottered off after the others, I pulled off my veil and made my way back to the flat. Letting myself in, for once I had the place to myself. I went over to the windows, pushed them open and stood there.

Adam was somewhere out there. I sighed. What was going on with me? Restless, I put some music on. But I couldn't help thinking that the Universe had been sending me a sign. It made no difference that I didn't believe in signs – this wasn't like anything I'd experienced before. From the moment my eyes locked with Adam's, there was no going back.

Pulling myself together, I told myself what any person would have – that I was being ridiculous. I was in love with Gareth. Sure, he wasn't perfect, but who is? And we were getting married in six days. I felt a flicker of panic, then put it down to last minute jitters. I mean, everyone got them, didn't they?

* * *

By the time Gareth got home the next day, Adam had faded into the background of my mind – at least, that was what I told myself. As Gareth kissed me, his breath was beery. But he'd been on his stag weekend, I reminded myself, trying to respond, ignoring the fact that like my heart, my body just wasn't feeling it.

I remember that week. It was exactly as you would have expected it to be in the run-up to a big, carefully planned wedding. While Mum flapped around with seating plans and last minutes tweaks to the catering, I had the week off work in order to help her.

When the wedding had dominated my thoughts for months, now that it was almost here, I couldn't believe I was questioning it. Was I making a mistake? Was Adam a sign? Now, it seems more than purely coincidence when I bumped into Adam again, the evening after my hen party.

On my way back from my parents' house, I stopped at the local shop to pick up some wine. As I opened the door and walked in, he was coming out.

'Hi.' He looked surprised. 'Tilly, isn't it?' In blue jeans and a white T-shirt, he was every bit as hot as I remembered.

I felt my cheeks grow warm as I nodded. 'Hi.' I paused. 'I never thanked you for the champagne last night. It was really nice of you.'

'You're welcome.' His eyes appraised me. 'How's your head today?'

'Fine,' I said honestly. 'No hangover whatsoever – which is more than I can say for my sister.' I'd had a call from a very sorry-for-herself Lizzie on my way here.

He looked amused. 'I guess that's how hen parties go – not that I've ever been to one.' He paused. 'You must be counting down the days.'

'I am. It's hard to believe it's almost here,' I admitted,

suddenly uncomfortable. But at that moment, I didn't want to think about my wedding. I was curious to know more about Adam. 'Do you live around here? It's just I've never seen you before.' Realising how lame it sounded, I went on. 'I mean, it's a small town. And I've lived around here most of my life.'

'My place is about five minutes away.' He nodded in the direction of the park.

I frowned. When it was so close to where Gareth and I lived, I wondered how it had taken until now for our paths to cross.

'I moved here a couple of weeks ago,' he explained. 'I ended a long-term relationship. It felt like the right time for a change of scene.' He stepped back to let another customer into the shop.

'Do you think you'll stay?' I was making small talk, anything to keep him from walking away.

'For now.' He smiled. 'So you grew up here?'

I nodded. 'Near here. In a village – a couple of miles away. I moved into town a couple of years ago – with my fiancé.' As I spoke, I was conscious it sounded like I'd never done anything, or been anywhere. But the truth was, I hadn't.

'Cool.' He stood there. 'Well, I should probably let you get on.' He hesitated. 'It was really nice to see you again.'

I stood there, smiling. 'You too.' I was still standing there as he turned and walked away. That was when it hit me. It didn't matter how wrong this was, so close to my wedding, I didn't want him to go. But what could I do? Swallowing my disappointment, I went into the shop and bought a bottle of wine.

As I stepped outside into the evening sun again, I clutched the bottle, all too aware that seeing Adam, even fleetingly, had made me feel more alive than I'd ever felt. Fishing in my pocket for my keys, I walked back to my car. Then as I reached it, I heard footsteps behind me.

'Tilly?'

Even before I turned around, I knew it was him.

'I'm sorry.' Adam hesitated. 'Look, I know you're getting married. And you can tell me where to go, if that's what you want. You'd be completely within your rights. But I was wondering, if you had ten minutes, or twenty even, if I could buy you a coffee – or something?'

I gazed at him, at the face I barely knew but wanted to touch, hair I wanted to run my fingers through. Given the commitment I was about to make to Gareth, I knew this was the moment I should have been walking away. But even if I'd wanted to, I couldn't have. I looked at him, wondering if he could hear my heart starting to race. 'OK.'

He seemed to exhale visibly. 'I'm guessing around here isn't the best idea.'

I shrugged. 'I don't see why not. I mean, we're only going for a coffee.'

'You're right.' Looking relieved, he glanced across the road. 'There's a little cafe at the other end of the park – how about there?'

I left the bottle of wine I'd just bought in my car and locked it again, feeling oddly self-conscious as we start walking.

'Gorgeous evening, isn't it?' It was one of those balmy summer evenings, the air still warm, only the faintest layer of high cloud in sky of deepest blue. He gazed up at the sky briefly. 'It is.' He glanced sideways at me. 'I'm sorry. I suppose I did rather spring that on you.'

'You did.' I smiled. 'So, how are you finding it, living here?' I was trying to hide how out of my comfort zone I felt.

'It's good. It's a short commute to work – and I like the people I've met. So far, at least.'

As his arm brushed against mine, I felt a jolt of something. Taking it to mean it was me he was talking about, I felt my heart miss a beat. 'So what happened with your girlfriend?'

'It's a long story I won't go into. We probably stayed together too long. I suppose so much was still good between us. It made it much harder. She's a great person.' He shrugged. 'But the heart doesn't lie, does it? When it comes to love, I think it's simple. If you know something isn't right, you're with the wrong person.'

I stifled a gasp. Was it really that simple? If so, what was I doing with Gareth? 'All relationships go through rough patches, don't they? How did you know it wasn't just that?'

He was silent for a moment. 'I have a theory – it's only a theory. But I believe in soulmates. I believe we know when we meet them. It feels like nothing you've ever known before – in a way that defies logic. You can't explain it, but it's like you already know each other. You get each other, in a way other people never can.'

I was lost for words as he described what I'd never felt with Gareth, that I didn't want to admit I was feeling for him. 'And you didn't feel that way about her?' I wanted to be sure about what he was saying.

He shook his head. 'No.'

'Aren't you worried you might be looking for something that doesn't exist?' I asked tentatively.

'Not at all. I know it exists.' He pauses, looking at me. 'I've felt it, Tilly. Just once.'

I told myself it was probably a line he tried with all the girls. But then my eyes gazed into his. He was talking about us. I knew he was. But before I could speak, the moment was broken as a dog came running up. At the same instant, I glimpsed Lizzie across the park. Keeping my head down, I steered Adam away from her. 'My sister – in yellow running gear. Probably trying to run off her hangover. Don't look,' I muttered under my breath.

But it was too late. She'd seen us. She ran over and stopped in front of us. 'Tilly! What are you doing here?' Even pink and flushed from exertion, my sister looked stunning.

'I felt like a walk.' I shrugged. 'It's such a lovely evening! Believe it or not, we bumped into each other.' I glanced at Adam. 'You remember my sister, Lizzie, right?'

'I do. I'm Adam.' He held out his hand.

Now, I'd been counting on Lizzie not remembering. She'd been rather more piddled than I had that night – though clearly not as piddled as I'd thought.

Giving me a *what the fuck's going on* look, her eyes widened as she looked at me then back to him again. 'You're the guy from the hen party – who bought us champagne.'

'That's right.' He looked at her awkwardly. 'Well, a wedding's a special time, isn't it? I suppose you could say I'm a sucker for a happy ending.'

'Gosh.' Sounding slightly shocked, Lizzie met my eyes. There was astonishment in them; confusion, too.

'I should leave you two to it,' Adam said quickly. 'You must have plenty to talk about – with the wedding coming up, I mean.'

'Don't go on my account.' Lizzie glanced at her watch. 'Shit. I'm going out this evening – again, glutton for punishment that I am. And I'm going to be late. Nice to see you, Adam. And I'll see you in the morning, Tills. Don't be late.'

'The morning?' I frowned.

'The marquee,' she said impatiently. 'We're going to start decorating it – for your wedding – remember?'

As she carried on running, Adam turned to me. 'I hope we haven't put the cat amongst the pigeons.'

'We were just walking.' But instead of its earlier lightness, my heart felt heavy. If this was just walking, why this guilt? 'You know, maybe I should go back. You see, I'm not quite sure what we're doing here.' I gazed at him. 'I mean, I'm about to get married – and you and I are practically strangers.'

'You're right.' A look I couldn't read crossed his face. 'It's just that...'

My eyes met his. 'Just what?'

'Is it just me?' He hesitated. 'Because it doesn't feel like that, does it? Like we're strangers?'

Thoughts crowded my mind. Thoughts that didn't belong there, that I was struggling to make sense of. Emotions, ditto; feelings I'd never known before. 'It doesn't.' I felt a brief, delicious curl of something inside me, before guilt struck again. 'I really have to go,' I said quietly.

'You've done nothing wrong. We're just walking.' As he spoke, there was something about his voice.

'But we're not, are we?' This time, the words burst out of me. 'I feel something – something I shouldn't. Not when I'm getting married this weekend – to Gareth.'

Without waiting for him to reply, I turned and started heading back to my car, fighting the urge to look back, to see if he was still there, watching me.

Reaching my car, I got in and just sat there for a moment. What was I playing at? I loved Gareth. I wanted to spend the rest of my life with him – it had already been decided.

Even if I'd wanted to, when Mum had been living and breathing our wedding for the last few months, there was no way I could change my mind at this stage.

As memories come flooding back, I remember how conflicted, how out of my depth I felt. I watch the uncertainty ripple across the younger me's face. The truth is the dilemma I was in has been lost in the years that have passed. I made my decision. Since, I've mostly buried all thoughts of Adam; thrown myself into married life, until said married life spat me out again.

Now, however, given this window onto the past, I'm questioning myself. The way I'd rationalised how drawn I'd felt to Adam; why it seemed worse to cancel a wedding than to marry the wrong man. *What had I been thinking?*

But I'd believed I loved Gareth. It's easy enough with hindsight, though, to see how in marrying him, I'd made a mistake of monumental proportions. The gift of good old hindsight – and it was one that changed the course of the rest of my life.

When a part of me had always known Gareth and I were missing something, it's no surprise that ever since, our relationship had been so up and down. Even before we were married, the warning signs had been there.

It seems now that meeting Adam had been one of those signs; a gift, to jolt me out of the complacency I shouldn't have been so comfortable with. But instead of listening to my instincts, I'd blocked them out.

What if... I find myself thinking. What if I could go back... If I could have found my courage. Told Gareth it wasn't right between us; that there was no rush to get married. That we were young; I needed time. Had a conversation I would have absolutely dreaded with my parents. And OK, so my dad would have had plenty to say on the subject of commitment, but after the initial disappointment, I like to think they would have understood. And I would have been free – to be myself; to see where this thing with Adam would have taken us.

But if I had, I wouldn't have the twins, would I? Now, I can't bear even the thought of a life without Robbie and Alex. Even knowing what I know now, I'd marry Gareth again in a heartbeat rather than not have them in my life.

I feel myself sigh. Gareth and I were never soulmates. I doubt Gareth even knows what a soulmate is. Whereas Adam...

2

Back to the Future

I hear a distant voice calling my name. Then as the vision of my younger self starts to fade, a sense of panic consumes me. I can't leave her, not like this. And I need to understand why things happened the way they did...

'Tilly?'

The voice has an accent I don't recognise at first and as the image of the past disappears, I'm pulled back to the present; remember where I am. *Crete. The rain storm. Michail's house... Falling.*

Relief fills me. I'm fine. I was obviously knocked unconscious, but it's like I've come around from the strangest dream. I already know what I want to say. *Don't worry, it was nothing... I'm OK.*

I try to open my eyes, to form the words.

But I can't.

Fear floods through my veins. I'm alive. I can hear machines bleeping around me. I understand what's going on... It means my brain is working. But I can't communicate. Nor can I move.

'Tilly? We're taking you for a scan.' This time, it's a woman's voice with the same Greek accent.

I'm aware of my bed jolting slightly, before it feels as though it's moving. Suddenly I'm thinking of the boys. *Oh my God... Will anyone have told them?* But no one I've met in Crete knows about them, let alone how to contact them.

Panic fills me. I should have left an address with someone. No one will know that something's happened to me.

My heart starts to race, as the bleeping sound that seems to accompany me speeds up.

The woman speaks again. 'She's tachycardic. We must hurry.'

I'm not sure what tachycardic means, only that whatever it is, from the urgency in her voice, it isn't good.

'Has someone called her husband?'

No... I try to whisper. *You mustn't call Gareth. He's the last person I want here...* It's my last thought before the beeping sound grows louder.

Then everything fades again and my mind goes blank.

3

A Grey October Day at Selham Railway Station

This time, I find myself back at Selham railway station, that cold October afternoon just a few weeks ago, watching myself sitting on a rickety bench just moments before my life was about to implode. I like Selham railway station. It's like stepping back in time, one that's confined only by the limits of your imagination. You see, there are no trains here. In fact the last one went through several decades ago, making it the perfect place to sit, daydreaming about how things used to be.

I was lost in nostalgia that afternoon, gazing at the track overgrown with brambles, the platforms lost under banks of bracken; the air carrying echoes of trysts and assignations – if only I knew how to listen to them. Of course, I can see now, it didn't actually start that day. I mean, what happens in our lives is usually the consequence of everything that's gone before. And what was about to happen that day had so far remained invisible. It was also unexpected; filtering in like the softest whisper of a breeze – or something less perceptible than a whisper, because that afternoon, I was completely and blissfully unaware that anything in my life was about to change.

Don't get me wrong. I liked my life. But just for a moment, as I sat there, I wished I could peel back the veil of time, slip through it into a ghostly carriage of one of those trains and let it speed me back through the years to a time when nothing bad ever happened, when my mum and Lizzie were still here. Losing my mum was one thing. But three months ago, Lizzie died too, stranding me at a derelict station, without a signpost. That's what sisters are, aren't they? Guiding stars, signposts?

I knew what Lizzie would have said. *Stop looking back, Tilly! You can't change the past. It's about the future... Now the twins have grown up, you could have an adventure! Think about it. What do you really want from your life?*

Lizzie's belief in following her heart led her to embark on many adventures. But in my ordered life, responsibility won out over impulsiveness. And I was the one everyone needed. I was a wife and mother. My widowed father's helpful daughter. There was my part-time job as a legal assistant with a fairly smart law firm. In other words, I was one of those people whose role in life was to be a hub. The holder of many threads leading to other lives, which floated around me like vibrant, multicoloured balloons, as I liked to think of them. In my case, mostly male ones. Gareth's, for example. The twins, even though they were away at uni and hardly ever came home. My crotchety father's. But it gave me a sense of purpose in my life.

Since Lizzie's death, Rick had become another. Rick was her broken-hearted husband. He hadn't expected to lose his wife any more than I was ready to lose my sister, but men don't cope with loss as well as women do. My father was a case in point. His life locked down, never to evolve after my mother left this world. It meant that now, he depended on me. But it was kind of how it was meant to be, wasn't it? I mean, when our parents raised us, it was only fair that as they got older, we were there for them.

But while Lizzie was the shining star in his life, the looking-after role had fallen to me. I glanced at the dying bouquet abandoned on the platform, that was once a joyous declaration of love; the withered flowers a reminder. Nothing lasts.

Shivering, I pulled my jacket more tightly around me. Then as I gazed across towards the trees, the barely perceptible breeze suddenly became a powerful gust sending a swirl of golden leaves cascading around me, before they settled again and the first raindrops started to fall.

The rain rapidly became a downpour and as I drove home, I was still thinking about Lizzie. The bright, vivacious, go-getting one, she started an interior design business in her twenties that went from strength to strength; had a gorgeous husband who adored her. They'd never had children – Lizzie was younger than me; parenthood consigned to a future that neither of them dared to imagine wouldn't happen, both of them believing time was open ended.

But even the best planned futures could go off-piste. On reaching the house, I ran inside and closed the back door behind me. The rain was lashing against the windows and standing for a moment, I looked around our kitchen that was an homage to Lizzie's design skills with an artfully battered wooden table and pale floor tiles, the walls painted white, bold splashes of green and blue from carefully chosen pieces of china.

On the table were the scores of cards that had kept arriving since Lizzie died, holding anecdotes and memories of the sister I wanted to remember from before her illness; triggering memories of our childhood, our parents, how our lives used to be when we were younger.

Looking at them, I suddenly felt much older than my forties.

At least you'd never know how that feels, Lizzie... Being old and rather pointless. Though not entirely so because as I sat there, my mobile rang and Dad's number appeared on the screen.

'Hi, Dad. How are you?'

'I'm er... I'm not calling about me. It's the cat.'

It was Lizzie's idea for Dad to have a cat after Mum died. Another heartbeat in the house, was how she put it. And Dad was rather taken with Moses. He just wasn't terribly practical about cat ownership. A sense of alarm filled me. 'What's wrong with him?'

'He's had, um... a bit of an accident. On the carpet. I don't have a clue what to do about it.'

Can't you clean it up, Dad? But knowing he wouldn't know where to start, I don't say that. Forgetting my plans to start repainting the kitchen a bright and cheery shade of yellow, I sighed. 'Would you like me to come over?'

He paused. 'If you wouldn't mind.'

* * *

There was resentment in my heart as I drove through the pouring rain – for the second time that afternoon.

I wish I didn't, but I did fricking mind, so much... Driving fricking six miles to clean up my dad's cat's shit. In this shitty weather. When I'd rather have been at home sipping a cup of tea and leafing through Lizzie's cards again.

But in a million years, I would never have told him that. 'Hi, Dad.' My voice was bright when he opened the door. I kissed him on the cheek. 'What's Moses been up to?'

'I'll show you.' I followed Dad along the hallway into the small room that for as long as I could remember had been his study, the smell getting stronger with each step. 'There.' He pointed to the carpet where alongside what was clearly cat shit, there was evidence of sick, too, squodged into the carpet. He looked slightly apologetic. 'I think the door went over it.'

I went to the kitchen, gathered disinfectant and a bucket of hot water, then pulled on rubber gloves as I made a start.

But he wasn't even grateful; just stood there saying, 'You missed a bit,' as I scrubbed the fricking carpet, on my knees.

'Do you have time for a cup of tea?' he asked when I've finished scrubbing.

I had a brief cuppa with him, during which I suggested he made sure Moses spent more time outside.

'But he won't go,' my father said glumly. 'Moses doesn't like the rain.'

Which I understood; nor did I. But I liked cleaning up after him even less. 'Maybe you should think about putting down a cat litter tray.' I got up. 'Thanks for the tea. I should get home and change,' I said, the smell of cat shit still lingering in my nostrils.

Why me? I was silently fuming as I drove home. *Two hours of my life down the drain, cleaning up cat puke and shit that somehow ended up on me, too, so that now I stank, too, and so did my car.* Then guilt washed over me, for feeling so resentful.

But back at home, after a hot shower, I felt better. More so as I poured myself a restorative glass of white wine and started to make a risotto; for the hundredth time, wishing Lizzie was here as I heard the front door open, then close, before Gareth walked in. I pinned on a smile. 'Hi.' I tried to assume the bright demeanour everyone expected to see from me. But for whatever reason, today it felt false.

'Hi.' He stood there for a moment, his hair plastered to his head, his jacket damp from the rain.

'Hi,' I said again, cheerfully. 'How was your day?'

But he didn't respond, just glanced at the pile of sympathy

cards as he took his jacket off, a look of irritation crossing his face. 'Don't you think it's time you put those things away? It's been three months, Tilly. You must know every word by heart.'

Dragging my eyes away from the cards, I met his. 'The messages are beautiful. People wrote such nice things – it brings memories back. Three months isn't very long. In any case, I only got home a little while ago. Dad summoned me to clear up – after the cat.' I rolled my eyes for comedic effect.

But instead of sympathising, he sighed. 'It isn't just that.'

Something about the way he spoke made my blood chill. I watched him as he turned away. 'What do you mean?' Suddenly he had my undivided attention.

Coming over to the table, he sighed. 'I was hoping it had been enough time, Tilly – because we need to talk.' His voice was quiet, a note of sadness in it that tugged at my heartstrings. Pulling out a chair, he hung his jacket over it, then sat down. 'I've been waiting for the right moment. I thought by now...' Glancing at the pile of cards again, he shook his head. 'I thought you might have started to move on.'

The strangest feeling came over me. It wasn't the fact that three months was nothing when you'd lost your sister. It was more as though I felt removed; that in the most bizarre way, I was somehow watching myself. That I knew what he was going to say before he said it, as in his next breath, he told me he never meant it to happen. But...

I looked at him, stunned. *'You've met someone?'* The words sank in; snaking slowly, nauseously inside me.

Gareth's sigh was heavy, his face guilt-stricken. 'You have to believe I didn't mean to. It just happened, Tilly. But it's taught me about myself. And what I want from life.'

My skin felt cold, as though the blood had drained out of my veins. 'And you couldn't have stopped it? For fuck's sake, Gareth.

We're married. We have a commitment to each other. How could you do this?'

He had the grace to look embarrassed – for all of about two seconds. 'Marriages end, Tilly. I know it's painful. But sometimes, you just know, don't you? When things just have to change?'

4

The End

I remember that's how it felt, that this was the end. It sounds melodramatic. But in a sense, it was *the end*, of life as I knew it. It was an ending I wasn't ready for, that I'd spent most of my married life trying to prevent. And that was in spite of the signs – and there were many.

It was why, the following morning, instead of the shopping trip I'd planned, I was back at Selham station for the second time in as many days. Sitting on the platform, I was craving the quiet stillness of yesterday that had been replaced by the gale force wind driving icy needles of rain at me, as pulling up the collar of my jacket, I shivered.

It was only eight o'clock in the morning. Unable to sleep last night, I'd lain in bed as long, dark hours passed, going over what Gareth said, until eventually the first glimmer of daylight had appeared.

I thought about his so-called business trips, which most likely had been a cover for his extra-marital activities and in reality hadn't existed. Then I wondered what his girlfriend would think if she knew it was the first night that Gareth had slept in the spare room; that he was apparently spending the night in our house out of some misguided sense of responsibility. *To make sure I was OK*, was what he said – after telling me he was leaving me for someone else. I mean, pick the bones out of that.

Not wanting to face him, I'd stayed in bed listening to the familiar sound of him getting up, then going to work. Only as the sound of his car faded, had I got dressed and gone downstairs. Then, still reeling from last night, I'd driven here.

OK, so you wouldn't have described our marriage as exactly made in heaven. We'd had our fair share of challenges over the years. But everyone expected that – and we'd overcome them – until this point. But as I stared at the ring I'd worn for over two decades, I thought of the mental agony I went through the days before our wedding. The commitment I nevertheless made that felt like the right thing; watched my hands start to shake. *Marriages don't have to end – not if people want to make them work.*

Can you tell me what exactly is it we're hanging onto? Gareth had looked at me last night, bewildered. *Because truthfully, I'm not sure any more.*

Family? History? The tradition of marriage? I couldn't believe he needed to ask. As for love, surely that was a given? But how was it, neither of us mentioned love?

He looked exasperated. *In other words, you're saying it's about the past. You're obsessed with it, Tilly. Take those cards – they're a prime example.* As his eyes wandered towards the sympathy cards, his words were brutal. *The past is gone, Tilly. Forever. But you won't let it go, will you? You hang on, as if you think you can wish it back. You can't change what's happened. You have to move on.*

I'd gasped. It was as if he didn't even understand that I was grieving. *Lizzie's dead, Gareth. Don't you think it's normal I'd be upset?*

Sighing, he'd shaken his head. *It's like you've always been grieving. I'm not even sure what for. It's up to you if that's how you want to live. But I don't. I don't want to go on feeling stuck in a part of my life I can't change. I want to look forward. To the future, Tilly. Laugh. Have fun. Live.*

Laugh? I'd looked at him in disbelief. Lizzie was dead and Gareth was talking about laughing again? And of course, I was grieving. I still wasn't over losing my mother when I lost Lizzie, too.

His voice was defeated. *The last thing I wanted was to hurt you.*

Oh really, Gareth? Well, you have. Not just hurt. He'd killed – no, bloodily murdered, some vital part of me. *I don't understand. After all this time. When I've just lost Lizzie – why now?*

And that was when I knew my answer. The irony was he'd done it so soon after Lizzie because of Lizzie – because of the reminder that the older you get, the less you could take for granted how long you had. He was in the throes of a full-blown midlife crisis, one that in time, no doubt, he'd get over. I glared at him. *Don't you dare say life is short.*

His eyes were haunted as his hand reached towards one of mine. *But you know as well as I do – it is. Don't we owe it to ourselves to make the best of it?*

Snatching my hand away, I'd stormed up to our bedroom, slamming the door behind me then locking it, before collapsing onto our bed. The bed in which we'd lain next to each other for twenty-two years, where the twins had been conceived, shock giving way to loud, rasping sobs as I felt my entire world collapse around me. How could he do this to me? To us? To our entire family?

It was hours later when I sat up. Gazing tearfully around the room, I took in the photos, the pictures on the walls, the carefully chosen furniture, each piece of which had its own story, all of it suddenly meaningless. Most of our married life had taken place within this house. Then with just a few words, Gareth had wrecked all of it.

* * *

This morning, sitting on the bench, as the wind picks up, I tried to make sense of Gareth's accusations about how self-obsessed I was, my problem with nostalgia; how I should have been back at work, not noticing the damp seeping through my jeans. Instead, I was numb, replaying more words that proved it was all my fault. *You've been so obsessed with your sister's illness, Tilly. And now, this morbid fixation on her death... You have no idea how difficult it's been. Do yourself a favour and get back to work. We all have to go on. Life has to go on.*

I'd stared at this man, who was suddenly like a stranger to me. *Who is she?*

He didn't even have the decency to hesitate. *Her name's Olivia.*

Couldn't you just have had an affair? Got it out of your system?

Then he'd dropped the bombshell. *Olivia's just told me she's pregnant.*

As he went on talking, his words fell on deaf ears. I felt sick. You see, when I became pregnant, Gareth made it clear he didn't want children. *Not ever*, rather than *in a couple of years*, as he'd led me to believe. When he knew how important it was to me, it had caused a rift between us. It seemed the cruellest irony that he was leaving me for someone else because she was pregnant.

It was another twenty-four hours in which my life had taken yet another unimaginable twist. One that was out of my control. So what now? I asked myself the same question as yesterday.

As I sat there, my phone buzzed. For a moment I wondered if it was Gareth, realising what a mistake he'd made, wanting to apologise. I hesitated briefly, then pulling it out of my pocket, saw my closest friend Elena's face flashing up on the screen.

Elena and I met at Pilates years ago, our friendship forged over strengthening our cores and the glasses of wine that followed. 'Hey, El.'

'Hey! What are you up to? Come over – I haven't seen you in ages.'

I hesitated. 'It's not the best day, to be honest.'

'Are you OK?' My friend sounded worried.

'No.' My voice wavered, tears suddenly streaming down my face. 'Gareth's met someone else, El. He's leaving me.'

'Fuck.' She was shocked into silence. 'Where are you?'

'Out.' I wiped my face on my sleeve. The fact that Elena knew made it all the more real.

'He's a shit. Oh, Tilly...' Her voice was filled with sympathy. 'Do you want to come over?'

* * *

Elena's hug was warm and welcoming, as was her house. It was also messy, but between family life and work, she didn't have time to tidy. Unlike me, in the soon to be half-furnished, half-empty house that I was about to be living in, utterly alone.

'It's so lovely here.' Tears trickled down my face. 'It really is, El. You're so lucky.'

'It's a pigsty.' She looked at me as though I was mad. 'You know perfectly well you can't stand mess. Would you like tea? Or wine? Wine, I think.' She made the decision for me. 'But only one. We need to talk – and then, we need to make you a plan.'

I watched her get a couple of glasses, and then a bottle from the fridge. It's what friends were for, wine and sympathy, even at nine in the morning. 'What am I going to do now?' I said pitifully;

the question that was dogging me, mumbled through my tears. 'What about the boys? And the house? I can't afford to buy him out. I've only just lost Lizzie, and now I've lost Gareth, too.' My voice was growing more hysterical with every word. 'I have to tell the boys. How on earth do I do that, El? It's their home and I'm going to lose it. I'm going to lose everything.'

My friend placed two glasses of white wine on the table, then sat down opposite me. 'Tell me what happened.'

So I told her, about how there had been no warning. About Gareth's business trips that he'd obviously lied about. About how I was reassessing everything I'd believed I knew about him; about us.

'I feel like calling him and telling him exactly what I think of him,' she said furiously. 'I mean, does he have any idea at all how lucky he was to have you?'

'He doesn't want me.' I stared at the table. There was no dressing it up; that was what it came down to.

'He's a dick.' She followed it with a list of expletives.

'El, don't,' I said. 'It doesn't help.'

'Oh Tilly...' She was quiet for a moment. 'I know how shit this is,' she said sympathetically. 'And I know, right now, you'd give anything for things to go back to how they were.'

'It really is shit,' I said tearfully. 'After all this time, I've never imagined I couldn't count on us. Or he'd betray me like this.' I stopped suddenly. 'Maybe he'll realise what a mistake he's made. Maybe he just needs time.' Hope washed over me as I looked at my friend. 'I can't believe I haven't thought of this. I just have to be patient, don't I?'

'Tilly...' Elena hesitated. 'I completely get how you must be feeling. And I know you've had the most terrible shock, but we need to deal with the facts.'

I blinked at her. 'I know what Gareth's said, but we don't actually know what he's thinking, do we?' My mind was all over the place. 'Maybe it's because he's only just found out Olivia's pregnant. Maybe he's overreacting and he'll change his mind...'

'Hold on a moment.' Elena stared at me. 'Olivia's the woman?' When I nod, she went on. 'She's pregnant?' She sounded incredulous.

I nodded miserably. 'That's the whole problem, isn't it? He'll be feeling like he has a duty to be there.'

'Shit.' Elena looked stunned.

'It's complete shit.' I felt utterly wretched as I watched Elena take a slug of her wine.

'I can't believe this,' she muttered. 'Honestly. What is he thinking?'

'That he doesn't want me,' I said self-pityingly.

'Oh Tilly...' Elena sighed. 'Please don't take this the wrong way... But doesn't this show you what kind of man Gareth really is?' She frowned. 'But hang on. Didn't you tell me that when you got pregnant, he said he never wanted kids... Why has he done it again?'

'I don't know,' I say miserably. My hands are shaky as I drink a large mouthful of wine. 'I thought we were good. I honestly thought Gareth had changed,' I said sadly. 'Sometimes people do – and he's a good father.'

'He really is not,' my friend reminded me. 'He's a selfish bastard. Look at that ridiculous car he bought himself, when yours was falling apart – and you couldn't afford for the boys to go on that school ski trip. I still remember how upset you were. And it was you who took them to uni and carted all their stuff up flights of stairs, times two, because they're twins. Where was he those days?' I opened my mouth to speak, but holding up one of her hands, she silenced me. 'Gareth is all about Gareth. What's happening now is all the proof you need. We both know he doesn't give a hoot about anyone else.' Elena paused. 'He's a moron, Tilly. Surely you can see that?' She sounded irritated. 'This Olivia is probably younger and more glamorous than you, because she hasn't raised two kids or looked after a husband for twenty years,' she said. 'The bottom line is his ego's out of control, not to mention his... Never mind. He'll come crashing back to earth. I bet you anything it won't last – not once she finds out what he's really like. But it will be too late,' she said sternly. 'Because by then, you'll have worked out you really are better off without him.'

'But I'm not,' I wailed self-pityingly.

Elena gave me a moment. 'Oh Tilly... I know this has been forced on you, which really sucks. It's horrible and hurtful – and there's no getting around any of that. But you're you, Tilly.' Her eyes were filled with love. 'You're this wonderful, sparkly, strong person – if Gareth can't see that, it's his loss. Look.' She paused. 'You don't need him. And I'm here for you. You're going to be OK.' Her eyes searched mine. 'You do know that, don't you?'

'Thanks, El.' I wanted to believe her. But it felt like my entire world was crumbling around me. 'I'll have to sort the house out, won't I?' A lump stuck in my throat.

'At some point. When it suits you, though. Don't be pushed around by Gareth,' she said angrily. 'But after...' Her voice softened. 'You'll have money in the bank. You'll be free, Tilly. You could move somewhere new – or have an adventure.'

My mouth fell open. It was too similar to what Lizzie had said, as the thought fleetingly entered my head – *Could Lizzie have seen what was coming?* 'I don't want to move,' I muttered miserably. 'There's my job to think about, too. If I move out, how will I find somewhere to live?' An image came to me of a tiny house with a dingy sitting room; of mould growing up the walls, a pervading smell of damp filling the air.

'You don't even like your job,' Elena said gently.

'I know.' But this wasn't about my job. 'Gareth and I have been married for twenty-two years. It can't be over – just like that.' My voice wobbled. It was a long time to just give up on.

'Oh Tilly. Gareth's been a huge part of your life.' Elena's voice was kind. 'I know it must feel like forever.'

Which was nice of her to acknowledge, only from the way she said it, I was fairly sure she didn't mean it in a good way.

She sighed. 'But haven't you ever felt like you were missing something?'

Her question caught me on the hop. 'Not really. I don't know... I'm not sure I've thought about it. I like my life. Or at least, I used to.' More tears rolled down my cheeks, but in spite of them, I couldn't help noticing how lame it sounded, even to me. 'I guess I always thought he was the one.'

* * *

Hold on a moment. I can't believe I actually said that. Gareth was *the one*? But it was what I wanted to believe, even after meeting Adam. It was the only way to justify the choice I'd made to marry him – even to myself.

What a mess it was, Tilly, I remonstrate with myself. But Elena was right. That point in my life that was the end of something, as I went forward would also be a beginning. But back then, caught up in the moment, I was unable to see that. Though there was no question in my mind, that Elena got it. She completely got it.

* * *

Elena almost choked on her drink. 'TILLY. I can tell you this much, he most definitely is not *the one*. If he was, he wouldn't have done this to you. If I were you, I'd get that house sorted straight away. Then I'd move out and get as far away from here as humanly possible.'

'I can't do that,' I said stubbornly. 'Too many people rely on me.'

'Oh God.' Elena's patience disappeared as she rested her head in her hands. Then she added more gently, 'Gareth obviously doesn't.' She broke off. 'Sorry. I didn't mean to sound brutal, but try to forget Gareth for a moment. Maybe it's time to think about what *you* need. The twins are away at uni – and I'm sure your boss will understand if you want to take a break.'

'I'm already on compassionate leave,' I said wretchedly.

'I know – and maybe they'll let you extend it, especially if you explain why.' Elena paused. 'I suppose what I'm saying is that even though it doesn't feel like it, you do have choices. You could move out of the house today – if you wanted to.'

I gazed at her in horror. 'There's no way I could do that.' She was mad to even suggest it. I had the boys to think of. And my dad. And the home that was filled with so many precious things.

'OK. Maybe today is a bit extreme. But there's no reason why you couldn't pack what you want, find a divorce lawyer – ask someone at your firm, maybe. Then call Gareth and tell him he can sort out the rest. It's not really on, thinking he can fuck off to live with Olivia and leave everything to you.' She sounded cross again. 'Have you told your dad?'

I shook my head. 'Not yet.' My heart sank even lower. In my dad's eyes, marriage was till death us do part. In a million years, he would never get this.

* * *

'He's what?' My dad looked shocked. 'That can't be right. What's been going on, Tilly?' Almost as though this was my fault.

He's shacked up with another woman who's pregnant with his child, I wanted to say. 'He's been having an affair. For a while – I've only just found out.'

'You need to talk to him. Sort things out,' he said, as though it was that simple. 'Do the boys know?'

'I'm going to call them this evening.' I looked at him. 'I'm sorry, Dad.' Then I frowned. Why was I apologising for something I hadn't done?

My emotionally stunted father just shook his head. 'I have to say, I expected more of Gareth. Most disappointing.' His face was unreadable. 'Couldn't sort some washing while you're here, could you?'

I stared at him. I'd just told him Gareth was leaving me and he's asked me to do his frigging washing. 'I have to go, Dad.' I paused. 'Don't you think it's time you found a cleaner?'

* * *

As I drove home, I thought about what Elena had said. Brutally honest as they were, I was forced to admit her words made an odd sort of sense. The idea of going somewhere far away from here briefly pulled at me, but once I got home, inside the house, nostalgia had me in its grip again. Everywhere I looked, there were ghosts of family gatherings, the twins growing up, birthdays, Christmases... Not to mention those gorgeous curtains I had made just a year ago. The matching cushions, the year-old, state-of-the-art kitchen that Lizzie designed. The list went on. The thought of leaving it all behind felt like cutting off my right arm.

I put off talking to the boys, as that night, I stayed up late waiting for Gareth to come back, hoping we could talk, until

midnight passed, then 1 a.m., before I was forced to face the fact
that he wasn't coming home – not just tonight, but any other
night. Lying in bed, my heart twisted with anger before the green-
eyed monster of jealousy took me over as I thought of him with
another woman, torturing myself with images of them together,
before the deepest sense of sadness washed over me. We could
have tried, couldn't we? We still could – it wasn't too late. Maybe
that was what I should have said to him – that we should go to
counselling. To try and make things work – we were married,
after all. No one walked away without trying.

* * *

The following morning, I lay in bed until late. I'd like to have said
I was working out what to do next, but my mind felt like cotton
wool, while there seemed little incentive to do anything else. Nor
did it help that I was still in denial; in spite of what Elena said,
hoping Gareth would realise he'd made a mistake.

It was two o'clock in the afternoon by the time I got out of bed
and went down to the kitchen. After making a cup of coffee from
our brand-new coffee machine, as I sat at the table, my phone
pinged with an email.

It was from my boss. Opening it, as I started to read, my heart
sank. After the extended compassionate leave I'd had since Lizzie
died, it wasn't unreasonable that she wanted to see me. But the
thought of a meeting tomorrow, just to 'check up on how I am',
was the last thing in the world I felt like doing.

I pictured my misery like a particularly persistent, self-pitying
cloud, before berating myself for being melodramatic. After all,
no one had died – at least, not this time. But the end of a
marriage was all-consuming, I was finding. There was no short
cut. You simply had to feel it.

And I was definitely feeling it. After somehow getting through the rest of the day, in bed that night, under the cover of darkness, a sob came from me. Clenching my fists, I tried to stop it. But then it merged with the grief I'd stored up, for my mother; for Lizzie. How I wished they were both here, right now, when I needed them more than I ever had.

Eventually, exhausted, as my eyelids start to close, I became aware of a voice.

After all these years putting everyone else first, isn't it time you thought about you?

My heart started to race, my eyes springing open, because it was Lizzie's voice. But she wasn't here, I told myself, swallowing the lump in my throat.

The fact was, even three months on, it was still hard to grasp that Lizzie wasn't coming back. And for the most part, I'd blocked it out. I'd become adept at blocking things out over the years. But thinking of Lizzie again, I was suddenly remembering how towards the end she'd been distracted.

I know it's a cliché, but it's true. Life is far too bloody short, Tilly. Look what's happening to me. But none of us realise until it's slipping away from us. For all that's wrong in it, there's a whole big, beautiful world out there. Don't ever forget that.

I know, I remembered saying to her, even though the longest Gareth and I had been away together was for ten days to the Costa Blanca. *But there's Gareth's job to think about. And the twins need me.*

Her eyes had clouded over. *The twins are in their second year of uni – they only come home for Christmas and holidays. They have their own lives. You can't live the rest of yours around them, Tilly. And as for Gareth...*

There was something about the way she said his name. But as often happened towards the end, another wave of morphine had kicked in and Lizzie had closed her eyes. Whatever it was about Gareth that was bothering her, she never told me.

* * *

The following morning, I put on some make-up and pulled on clothes I hadn't worn in weeks: one of my smart knee-length skirts and a patterned top, my LK Bennett block-heel court shoes. I paused to stare at my reflection. On the outside, I looked the same as I'd always looked. Presentable, the dark circles under my eyes not quite hidden, my skin pale – done perhaps slightly for effect. But when I couldn't face going back to work yet, I didn't want Elizabeth to think I was fine.

As I walked into the premises of Harkness and Matthews, I tried to summon a spring in my step. I fantasised about them offering me a pay rise, as I imagined being able to keep the house – all of it totally ludicrous when I only worked part-time.

We've missed you terribly, Tilly. I hadn't quite realised just how much we all rely on you. Now, the partners and I have been talking... We'd like to offer you a promotion. How does this sound?

To my slightly scattered mind, it was a perfectly reasonable scenario. And for a moment, as I looked around, it was as though I'd never been away. A couple of clients I didn't recognise were waiting in the reception area; Maisie, the receptionist, gesturing urgently at me before the phone distracted her.

Noticing the time – Elizabeth was a stickler for punctuality – I went through the swing doors and made my way along the familiar corridor where her mahogany-coloured door was cracked open as it always was before a meeting, so that when I knocked, from behind her perfectly organised desk, she could see who it was.

'Tilly. Do come in. Close the door, will you?' Her voice was kind. 'How are you?'

Going in, I did as she said. 'Not too bad.' It seemed impossible that in the time since I was last here, my sister had died and my husband had left me.

'Why don't you sit down?' As always, Elizabeth oozed understated glamour, confidence. Her eyes were bright, her skin honey gold, her straight hair newly highlighted and neatly trimmed to shoulder length.

As I sat down, I felt, well, a little bit old, if I was honest. 'Thank you.' I waited for her to ask me if I was ready to come back to work. *Maybe two days a week to start with, if that would work better for you, but there aren't many people with your level of experience...*

But she was silent for a moment. 'The thing is...' Elizabeth looked untypically awkward. 'Word hasn't got around yet, but we're going to be making some redundancies. That's why I asked you to see me today. I'm under some pressure. But if you come back now, I think we can avoid your job being at risk.'

Shocked, I was swiftly realising things were going to change here, too; that people I knew weren't going to be working here any more. That I might have a job for now, but I had no way of knowing how long that would last.

Suddenly it occurred to me that if people I knew were leaving, I wasn't at all sure I wanted to be here. 'Could I take the redundancy?' I said on impulse. Then I stared at Elizabeth. *What the fuck had I done?*

She looked taken aback. 'Tilly, please. You've had a lot on your plate recently. You really don't need to do this.'

'Honestly. I think I do.' I gazed at her, already willing this to be over.

'If you're sure.' She paused. 'We've had a temp here while

you've been on compassionate leave. As it turns out, she's very competent. Of course, given the time you've had off, she's had to get up to speed with everything. More than that, she's suggested all this new software.' She paused again. 'I know things haven't been easy for you. If you're sure this suits you, maybe it's for the best.' A patronising smile played on her lips. 'There are times in all of our lives things have to change.'

God. How come I hadn't seen that before? All this time, I'd believed Elizabeth was sincere. But compassionate? She didn't know the meaning of the word.

Maintaining a composure I didn't feel, I got up. 'Thank you so much, Elizabeth. I hope it works out.'

She held out her hand. 'Good luck, Tilly.'

* * *

I don't remember leaving her office or even walking through the doors. Just that I was suddenly outside the building, standing there, wondering what the heck I'd just done. Not only was I husbandless, I was now jobless too – though I had only myself to blame for that.

As I watch myself stand on the street, I didn't seem to notice as the clouds parted and the sun broke through. In fact, I'm not sure what I was thinking as I stood there. All I remember is how as I contemplated never coming back here again, I was aware of a glimmer of my old spark, before my vision blurred and the streets started to fade. Then they were gone.

5

Every new beginning comes from some other beginning's end.

— SENECA

The closing of doors is generally a sign, I'm starting to realise. In my case, Gareth meeting someone else, then me leaving my job, albeit it being my idea, was all a huge great boot up the proverbial from the Universe – I can see that now. At the time, however, it was an unwanted turning point that felt as though it had been foisted on me. OK, so I could have gone back to work. But could I? *Really?* I can't help wondering if on a subconscious level – one that I'd managed to completely lose touch with – an inner part of me had known I needed to leave.

As I lie there, I'm aware of the electronic beeping sounds that are measures of my heart rate, my breath, such things that the essence of life boils down to. They sound steady, regular. But then fear has me in its grip again. My limbs are leaden and I still can't open my eyes. *What's happening to me?*

As the hospital sounds fade again, I find myself back in the past – this time, much longer ago, in the flat Gareth and I shared before moving to the family home we still own. The flat seems small and a bit on the untidy side, but back then, I just loved that it was ours.

I watch my old self walk in, as I work out exactly when this was and that I was carrying the bottle of wine I'd gone to buy before bumping into Adam. From his place stretched out on the sofa, Gareth barely moved.

Was he really that lazy? If so, why didn't I say something?

* * *

'I was about to send out a search party.' He flicked through the TV channels. 'Did you get the wine?'

'Yes. I bumped into Lizzie.' It wasn't a lie. 'It's a lovely evening. I hope the weather holds till Saturday.' But the flat felt claustro-phobic and I went over to the window and pushed it open. 'I'll pour us some wine.'

I went into the kitchen and got out a couple of glasses. As I opened the bottle, I felt my mobile buzz in my pocket. Getting it out, I saw the text from Lizzie.

LIZZIE

Is there something you're not telling me???? xxx

I replied:

TILLY

Nothing. Like I said, Adam and I bumped into each other xxx

She came straight back to me.

LIZZIE

I would believe you, sis, if he wasn't so
gorgeous!

But here, in the flat, I couldn't think about Adam.

TILLY

Please don't, Lizzie. Gareth's home. We can talk
in the morning xxx

I pressed send, then looked up to see Gareth standing in the doorway. 'Everything OK?'

'I was just replying to Lizzie.' After switching off my phone, I poured a glass of wine and passed it to him. 'It was about the marquee. We're going to start decorating tomorrow!' I put my phone away and poured myself a glass. Going over to Gareth, I chinked it against his. 'To us,' I said softly, willing him to respond. To say something that confirmed he *saw* me.

'Cheers.' He held my gaze for a moment that ended abruptly as he glanced around the kitchen. 'Have you seen the menu for the Chinese? I thought we could have a takeaway.'

That single exchange summed us up. I can't believe I hadn't noticed at the time, how unaware Gareth was. Not just of me, but of any kind of subtlety. Gareth thought about work, going to the pub, watching football, buying takeaways more often than was good for him. He'd chosen a suit for our wedding, but that was the extent of his input. He'd simply gone along with the rest – not in an *I trust you to make it lovely* kind of way. It was out of laziness.

I can guess what you're thinking. *How many men get involved in the minutiae of wedding planning?* And yes, I get that. But even when it came to the food and drink, Gareth had taken a back seat.

It had gone on to be the strangest evening. Me in the throes of a strange inner turmoil, Gareth completely oblivious as he made inroads into the Chinese takeaway on the table in-between us. It wouldn't have occurred to him to notice I barely touched it, or to ask if I was OK. Gareth's thoughts rarely extended to anyone else beyond himself.

That night, while Gareth slept, I lay awake for hours. I tried to remind myself what I loved about Gareth. How much fun we used to have, how handsome he was, eventually dozing off to dream I was walking down the aisle. Only instead of Gareth waiting for me, it was Adam who stood there. Handsome in a dark suit, he was looking at me as though I was the only girl in the world for him.

My eyes snapped open, the vision of Adam still crystal clear, the memory of how he'd made me feel with me, while beside me, Gareth snored. Sighing, tears filled my eyes. This was such a mess, one that could so easily have been avoided – if I'd chosen another venue for my hen do. But even if I had, it crossed my mind that if it was meant to be, maybe fate would have conspired to bring Adam there, too.

I lay awake until the first light appeared around the curtains, eventually dozing off and waking again to find Gareth getting up.

'Hey, sleepy head,' he said affectionately. 'I was trying to be quiet and let you sleep.'

I stifled a yawn. 'I'm fine. I need to get up. I'm meeting Lizzie.' I watched him pull on his jacket.

'Don't overdo it, will you?' Coming over, he kissed me.

It was what he always said. And I knew on one level, he cared about me. But it felt like surface level, which had always been enough. Suddenly, though, it wasn't; and it wasn't his fault, I just craved more. I put my arms around his neck, wanting to remind myself – both of us – of how we used to be inseparable. 'Do you have to go?'

'This time next week, I won't be going anywhere.' He disentangled himself. 'But you know what Eddie's like.' Eddie was Gareth's boss. 'See you tonight, babe.' After stopping to briefly check his reflection in the mirror, he was whistling as he headed for the door.

I listened as he opened it, then closed it behind him, then checked my watch. It was 7.30 a.m.

As I lay there, a memory of the dream of Adam was back. Suddenly uncomfortable, I got up and pulled on my running gear, then scraped my hair back into a ponytail. I needed exercise to clear my head and get my thoughts straight.

Going outside, I closed the door behind me, then headed down the street, breaking into a jog. My usual route was three miles – a far cry from Lizzie's eight. Hoping I wouldn't see Adam this morning, I ran faster, pushing myself harder, the words in my head matching the rhythm of my stride. *I love Gareth, we're getting married. I love Gareth, we're getting married...*

This time last week, I hadn't a care in the world. And to anyone who saw me now, everything looked the same. Inwardly, however, it was a whole other story. However crazy it sounded, there was no getting away from the fact that meeting Adam had turned my life upside down.

Repeatedly I told myself that there would always be chance meetings with other attractive men. That it didn't mean you were destined to become soulmates. The soulmates thing was something else, though. I'd looked it up. They shared a special kind of bond unique to themselves.

A bond Gareth and I had never had.

That morning, my determination to clear my head fuelled me to run an extra mile. Then back at the flat, after a shower, I got dressed and drove over to our wedding venue. As country house hotels went, it was a dream of a place, set in the most stunning gardens which was probably what had sold it to my mum, an avid gardener. Parking my car, I wandered around the side, following the gravel path edged with blowsy scented roses to the large area of lawn where the marquee had been put up.

Going in, I stood there for a moment, imagining the bare tables draped in white linen and festooned with flowers; there was a small stage at one end where the band would play, a dance floor for later on. My misgivings forgotten, I felt a thrill of excitement. Just five more days, and all our family and friends would be here.

'Hey, Tills!' Lizzie's voice came from behind me.

I watch myself turn to look at my funny, gorgeous, wise little sister, taking in her sassy shorts and sun-kissed hair, suddenly missing her more than ever.

Back then, turning, I smiled at her. 'Hi! I was just thinking about Saturday.' My excitement was already fading. I could tell from her expression she was going to ask about Adam.

'Is everything OK?' Her face was sober.

'Everything's fine.' Even to my sister, I couldn't admit that everything wasn't fine – far from it.

'It's just...' Lizzie hesitated. 'It's none of my business. It's just that since you and Gareth have been together, I've never known you look at another guy. Not ever.'

I sighed. 'It's complicated. But it's nothing. Honest.' I searched my sister's face. 'Don't we have a marquee to decorate?'

'You don't *have* to marry Gareth,' she said quietly. 'If you're having second thoughts, it isn't too late to cancel the wedding.'

I stared at her, shocked that she'd articulated what I was thinking. 'I can't.' I was shaking my head. 'Can you imagine Mum and Dad? They'd be devastated.'

There was worry in Lizzie's eyes as she took my hands in hers. 'You can't do this because of them,' she said. 'This isn't their lives we're talking about. It's yours. Tilly...' She paused. 'You owe it to yourself to be honest with yourself.'

My eyes filled with tears and I blinked them away. 'The wedding's going to happen, Lizzie. I made my mind up a long time ago.'

'I know you did. But if it really isn't right, it will catch up with you,' Lizzie persisted. 'I mean it. I know you love Gareth – and you've known him for such a long time. But...' She hesitated. 'It doesn't necessarily make him the one.'

'You really think there is such a thing? Because I don't believe in all that stuff,' I said carelessly. 'The only reason relationships work is if you want them to. You have to make them work, Lizzie. Gareth and I will be OK because it's what we both want.'

'Wow.' Lizzie stared at me disbelievingly. 'Don't take this the wrong way, but now I'm really worried.'

'There's no point.' There was a lump in my throat as I gazed at my sister. 'The wedding is going ahead.'

A voice came from outside. 'Cooee!'

'Mum,' Lizzie said under her breath as our eyes met. 'You're off the hook – for now. But we have not finished talking about this,' she added warningly.

'Oh girls.' My mum looked overwhelmed with happiness. 'Isn't this just wonderful? Did you see the roses? Now, I've been thinking about...'

As she went on telling us what she thought we should do today, and what would have to wait until nearer the time, I caught Lizzie's eye again. There was no going back – not without devastating my parents. Surely she could see that?

And that was the conundrum I'd found myself in. This glorious occasion planned to the last detail, my family around me, the man I'd loved for years waiting for me at the altar. Me, until that point, happy-go-lucky, floating through my life without so much as a care in the world – until Adam came into my life, just a few days ago.

By the end of that day, the marquee had sheer pale-pink drapes and hanging chandeliers, while some trees in pots had been delivered which Lizzie had adorned with tiny, glittering fairy lights – she had an eye for these things and I'd left it to her to decide what looked best.

Sitting on the grass, I closed my eyes for a moment, breathing in the rose-scented air and feeling the sun on my face. An image of Gareth came to me, a feeling of warmth coming over me. We met when I was seventeen and he was nineteen. Five years later, it was hard to picture life without him.

But my subconscious wasn't making it easy for me and a memory of that dream filled my mind, of Adam. Staring into the marquee, I knew I shouldn't, but for a moment I allowed myself to imagine us here together. That this was *our* wedding. Both of us knowing how right it felt; the happiest people in the world.

'Tilly?' Lizzie's voice startled me. 'You're miles away. Can you help? We're trying to decide where to put the cake table.'

'You decide.' I knew the cake had cost the best part of a grand, but in that moment, I honestly didn't care.

Coming out of the marquee, Lizzie fixed me with a look. 'Tilly, this is your wedding. Get in here now, and tell me where you want the table.'

* * *

Later that afternoon, Lizzie and I walked Mum back to her car.

Reaching it, she beamed at us both. 'You are coming for dinner, aren't you? Your father and I thought, well, it would be nice – it might be the last time it's just the four of us.'

'Of course we are.' Lizzie hugged Mum. 'Tilly and I have one or two more things to look at. Then we'll be with you.'

Mum glanced back towards the marquee. 'Do you need my help?'

'They're tiny things, Mum.' Lizzie winked at her. 'Go on. Dad will be wondering where you are.'

'Oh. Yes. Goodness.' She got in the car, started the engine and drove away.

But as I already knew, there were no tiny things to see to. Side by side, Lizzie and I watched the car disappear. 'You and I need to talk,' she said quietly.

Wandering across the garden, I found a bench under some trees while Lizzie went to get us drinks from the bar. Slightly apprehensive about being under her scrutiny again, I had no idea what I was going to say to her.

Minutes later, she was back carrying two glasses of icy Chardonnay. After passing me one of them, she sat down next to me. 'You know if I believed everything you've said, we wouldn't be doing this.' She paused. 'What's going on?' She stared at me. 'And don't say *nothing*.'

I sipped the wine. 'What it is,' I said carefully, sticking to the story I'd told myself, 'is I've met Adam twice. We get on really well. And that's all.'

Lizzie shook her head. 'I know you better than that. You looked different when I saw you with him. Your eyes were shining, Tills. I've never seen you look like that with Gareth.'

'I've never felt like that with Gareth.' The words were out before I could stop them as my guard came down. After all, there wasn't anyone else I could talk to about this. And I so badly needed to talk about it. 'What do I do, Lizzie? I hate myself. My wedding is in five days. Yet all I can think about is a man I met a couple of days ago.' There was a lump in my throat as I met her eyes. 'It's last minute nerves, isn't it? I mean, I love Gareth. It can't be anything else.' I faltered. 'Can it?'

'Oh Tilly...' My sister sighed. 'I'm not sure you're going to want to hear this,' she said gently. 'But it's like I said earlier. What if Gareth isn't the one? What if it's Adam? Or someone else? And this is some kind of wake-up call – before it's too late? You're twenty-two, Tills. You're really young. There's no rush to get hitched.'

'What about all of this?' I nodded towards the marquee, now resplendently and lovingly half decorated. 'I can't cancel the wedding – even if I did want to. It's too late.'

'I know it must feel like that.' Lizzie paused. 'One thing I do know is that if it was the other way around and Gareth was having second thoughts, he wouldn't think twice about calling it off.'

I gazed at her in amazement. 'No way would he do that. He loves me, Lizzie. He wouldn't be marrying me if he wasn't committed to me.' But I can't help thinking the truth lies somewhere in between; that what's more shocking is I had no idea she thought so little of him. 'I didn't know you felt like that.'

'That you're engaged to a man with little empathy or concern for anyone other than himself?' she said wryly. 'Really, Tilly, I sincerely doubt that.'

'Gareth cares about people,' I say defensively. 'He always has my back. And OK, so it might not be obvious. But if he was that uncaring, do you honestly think I'd be marrying him?' I stared at Lizzie again. 'You really don't like him, do you?'

Lizzie was silent. 'Seeing as we're being honest... It's not that I dislike him – really, Tills. I'm just not sure he's right for you.'

I remember feeling it was like the bottom had fallen out of my world. I'd always counted on Lizzie. It had never crossed my mind that she didn't love Gareth. Now, of course, I can see, she was asking all the right questions; that the problem was me, not wanting to hear the answers.

Lizzie went on. 'I do like him, Tills. He's a good laugh – I'll give him that much. But you're a giver. You have this huge, generous heart that has room for everyone you love. And you can forgive anything in the world. I've watched Gareth. All he does is take from you.'

This time, I gasped out loud. 'It isn't like that.' But I was reeling. Was that really how he was? The way I saw it, Gareth was just Gareth. Transparent – without pretention. A genuine, down-to-earth, what-you-see-is-what-you-get kind of guy. OK, so I was aware he took me for granted, just a little. But Lizzie was wrong – wasn't she?

'I'm so sorry.' Lizzie looked mortified. 'Me and my big mouth. I shouldn't have said any of that. I think I must have your wedding jitters.' Reaching out a hand, she grasped one of mine. 'Do you forgive me?'

'There's nothing to forgive.' I frowned. 'I'm just surprised. Do you really think he's like that?'

'Please, Tilly. Let's not go there.' Lizzie sounded flat. 'I don't want to character-assassinate the man who's about to become my brother-in-law.'

'I want to know. You and I have always been honest with each other.' I paused. 'This really matters to me.'

'I know it does. And it's your life,' she said quietly. 'It's up to you and no one else who you spend it with. If Gareth makes you happy, then that's enough for me.'

It was the end of the conversation. But I couldn't help thinking that if Gareth was the one, we wouldn't have been sitting there having this conversation in the first place; that I wouldn't have been remotely interested in Adam. I'd have been off my head with excitement, driving Lizzie and everyone else up the wall because I could only talk about one thing – my wedding. And I wasn't.

As the realisation hit me, I felt the bottom of my stomach drop. My all-seeing, wise little sister had seen what I hadn't wanted to. I stared at her. 'What do I do?'

'Only you know the answer to that one.' Her eyes gazed into mine. 'If I were you, I'd probably talk to Gareth. But if it was me, I wouldn't be able to hide it from him.'

But Gareth wouldn't notice if I wasn't myself. 'If I tell him I'm having doubts, it will be the end of us.' I stared across the neatly mown grass. 'I have to be really sure that's what I want.'

'You also have to be really sure if you go ahead, that you want that, too,' Lizzie reminded me gently.

* * *

Thanks to Lizzie, somehow I made it through that evening without my parents suspecting anything, nodding when my dad mentioned the church side of things and how he'd invited Father Peter, who was marrying us, to the reception. My dad was deeply religious – which felt like another pressure. If the wedding went ahead and if later on it all went wrong, I knew he'd be against us getting divorced.

But thinking about divorce before we were even married was making things worse and my head was spinning. Making my excuses, I avoided Lizzie's gaze as I left early. I drove down the lane, pulled over into a gateway and turned the engine off. Sitting there, I gazed across the fields, taking in the cattle that were mooching quietly, the swallows flitting around the skies, the butterflies hovering above the wildflowers. Everything seemingly so peaceful. If only I felt the same.

When I got back to the flat, Gareth was out. After throwing

open the windows, I cleared up the plate he'd left on the floor and picked up some empty beer bottles.

Sinking into the sofa, a sigh came from me. Lizzie was right – there was no point me telling myself otherwise. Gareth could be thoughtless at times – a petty example being those dirty plates he'd left on the floor, the washing up that sat on the side of the sink. Yet not once had I told him I didn't like it. And that was my fault, wasn't it? It wasn't fair to expect him to read my mind.

Sitting there, for a moment, I imagined us having a baby. We'd only vaguely talked about it, but suddenly I could see us: Gareth the adoring father, the hands-on dad and caring husband, loving that we were a family every bit as much as I did.

I heard a key in the door before it opened, then closed and Gareth walked in. When he saw me sitting on the sofa, a look of surprise crossed his face.

'I thought you were at your parents' house.'

'I was. I got back about twenty minutes ago.' I looked at him. 'Have you been to the pub?'

'Just for a couple. Thought I'd make the most of it.'

'What – being single, you mean?' The words slipped out without me intending them to.

Clearly I'd struck a nerve. Standing there, he had the grace to look uncomfortable. 'I didn't mean it like that, Tilly. It's hardly as though anything's going to change, is it?'

'We're getting married, Gareth.' I frowned. 'That's a pretty major change by anyone's account.'

'Yeah, but we'll still be living here, going to work, seeing the same people.' He shrugged. 'Our day-to-day lives will be exactly the same.'

For once, he was bang on. But if that was the case, why were we doing this? I stared at him, suddenly curious. 'Why do you want to get married, Gareth?'

He looked startled. 'What kind of a question is that?'

I shrugged. 'I want to know. I mean, I've always thought getting married is a big deal. If it isn't, I'm wondering why you want to do it.'

Coming over, he sat down next to me. 'What's really going on here?' he said gently.

'How do we know?' I searched the blue eyes that were so familiar to me. 'That we'll always feel like this? That what we have is enough?'

'We've been together for years. I love you, Tilly. I kind of assumed you love me too. Isn't love enough?' He looked hurt. 'No one knows what the future holds.' He frowned. 'Or has something happened?'

It was my perfect opportunity to tell him the truth. 'No.' I looked away, unable to do it. 'It's just that marriage is a huge commitment. There are things we haven't really talked about – not properly.'

'Of course we've talked.' He frowned. 'I don't know what you're getting at.'

'But we haven't,' I persisted. 'Not about children, for example. I've always assumed you want them. But until now, I haven't actually asked you.' I paused. 'Do you? Want children?'

'Of course I do. Doesn't everyone?' But he looked evasive. 'In time. We're young. There's no hurry. We've plenty of time to think about having a family.'

There it was. The giveaway hint that when it came to children, Gareth really wasn't that bothered about it. But I didn't want to believe it. 'I suppose we'd need a bigger place,' I said thoughtfully.

'Exactly,' he said quickly. 'See? A few years down the line, when we've bought a house, maybe, that will be the time.'

A few years down the line wasn't at all what I had in mind. But I didn't want to fight.

He frowned. 'Is there anything else?'

I folded my arms. I'd hoped that by expressing even a single concern, it would open up some honest conversation between us. But instead, there was an awkward silence that was far from satisfactory, while I knew if I pushed him, he'd only get angry.

He got up. 'Fancy a cuppa?'

'Thanks.' Sitting there, I watched him walk across the room, listening as he filled the kettle and switched it on. That he could just gloss over what felt like the elephant in the room, this close to our wedding, I absolutely knew it wasn't right.

It wasn't going to solve anything, but suddenly I needed to get out. As he came back in carrying two mugs, I got up. 'I just had a message from Lizzie,' I lied. 'She wants to talk to me about something. I'm going to meet her for a walk.'

'You've just spent the entire day with her.' Gareth sounded sulky. 'It can't be that important.'

'It's to do with the wedding.' I kissed him briefly on the lips. A kiss he didn't reciprocate. 'I won't be long.'

It would never occur to Gareth that there was no message from Lizzie. With hindsight, I should have texted her on the off chance he'd call her. But I knew he wouldn't. And I knew she wouldn't call him. Gareth and my sister had only one thing in common, and that was me.

As I walked along the street, I tuned out the traffic noise. I had the strangest sense of being at the centre of a life I was rapidly losing control over. There was this lavish wedding paid for by my parents. And that was the essence of the problem. If it had been some tiny do at a pub, it would have been so much easier to call it off. But a hundred people had been invited. They'd bought outfits and presents; planned their weekends around mine and Gareth's nuptials. Knowing that made it impossible to cancel it.

It meant I had no choice but to go ahead. Stopping at the end of the road, I waited for the traffic to clear before crossing it and entering the park. Surrounded by trees, I watched a group of kids kicking a football about. It wasn't helping that everywhere around me there were couples – younger ones, loved up, their hands entwined. An older one, arm in arm, an expression of quiet contentment in their eyes.

Would Gareth and I be like that? Our love enough to see us into old age? But how did anyone know? The fact was no one did. You had to believe in marriage, in each other, enough to want to take the chance.

'Tilly?' The voice came from behind me.

I froze for a split second, feeling my heart start to race, already knowing it was Adam as I turned to see him standing there. 'Hi.'

'You look as though you're carrying the cares of the world on those narrow shoulders.' He paused. 'Feel like sharing them?'

'I'm not sure it would help,' I said ruefully.

For a moment, neither of us spoke. 'Can I say something?' he said at last. 'Only, for someone who's getting married this week-end, you don't look exactly happy about it.'

I looked up into his eyes – warm, brown eyes – as I realised something. Unlike Gareth, Adam saw the real me. Actually *saw* how I was feeling. Suddenly there was a lump in my throat. 'Then it won't surprise you to know I'm having second thoughts.'

He breathed out slowly. 'And you feel terrible, I'm guessing.'

I nodded. 'My parents have paid for this amazing wedding. There are all our guests... Some of them are travelling miles, just to see me and Gareth get married. They've bought us all these presents... And I feel so guilty – and ungrateful.'

'This has nothing to do with gratitude.' Adam looked around. 'Why don't we find somewhere away from it all, where we can talk?'

'Like where?' The beautiful weather meant people were out in droves, all of them making the most of it. As far as I could see, there was nowhere.

Adam took my hand. 'I know somewhere.'

I let him lead me away from the park. I was unhappy enough not to care who saw us, or that a man I barely knew was holding my hand. On the other side of the park, we crossed the road and walked up a narrow street. After a minute or so, he stopped outside a terraced house.

'This is my place.' He hesitated. 'I was going to suggest we should go inside. But I don't want to talk you into doing anything you'll regret.'

Past caring what anyone else thought, I looked at him. 'Do you have gin?'

He pushed the gate open, then in front of the house, he unlocked the door and stood back to let me in. As the door closed behind us, I felt my body slump. Here, away from everything and everyone I knew, I no longer felt the need to hide anything.

'The kitchen's this way.' Adam started walking along a passageway.

I followed him into a bright, airy kitchen, freshly painted white, the only colour a row of perfect, miniature cacti plants arranged at intervals on a windowsill.

'These are cute.' Going over, I studied them.

'My cacti? How I ended up with them is a bit of an accident.' He got out a couple of glasses. 'I was given the first one as a present. After that, everyone seemed to think I was collecting them.' He got out some ice, then poured me a drink and passed it to me.

'Thanks.' I wandered over to the window, taking in the terrace on which a table and chairs had been set out; the stretch of grass that lay beyond; feeling strangely at home yet at the same time, wondering what the hell I was doing here.

Adam came over and stood beside me. 'I wish I could help you. I can see how difficult you're finding this.' He paused. 'This is about us, isn't it?'

As he said *us*, my heart leapt. 'It's hard to describe.' I owed it to him to try. 'Gareth and I get on, and it isn't that we don't love each other. But I think it's more like you said about your ex-girlfriend. There's something missing, and I've only just realised. Meanwhile, the wedding has an energy of its own...'

Adam was silent. 'Given what you've just told me, how can you go ahead?'

'How can I not?' There was a lump in my throat.

'I'm not sure I should be saying this...' He hesitated. 'But if you weren't getting married...' He stopped himself.

I turned to look at him. 'What? If I wasn't, I mean?'

His brown eyes gazed into mine. 'It probably isn't going to help. But I'd ask you out for dinner,' he said softly. 'That Italian that's just opened in town with tables outside. We'd order a bottle of chilled wine and tell each other our life stories.' He paused. 'I don't know why it is, but I have this compulsion to know every- thing about you. Your family, your childhood, your hopes and dreams...'

As he spoke, as I gazed into those beautiful eyes, my heart missed a beat. 'They're not exciting,' I said hastily. My dreams were simple – to live a happy life with the man I loved. Like I said, simple – yet from where I found myself at that moment, unbe- lievably complicated.

'I'd still want to hear about them,' he said quietly.

I was silent. I wanted to know everything about him, too. But a restless feeling filled me. There was no time.

'Where is your fiancé?' he asked suddenly. 'Because if I were him, I'd want to know why you weren't with me tonight.'

'I told him I was meeting Lizzie.' My cheeks flushed at my duplicity. 'I needed to get out. I couldn't think straight. Terrible, isn't it? Lying?'

Adam was quiet for a moment. 'Can I ask you something?'

I shrugged. 'Go ahead.'

'Why are you really here?'

Our eyes met and I couldn't look away. 'I don't know.' Given the reality of my life, nothing about this made sense.

'Then can I tell you how I've been feeling?' He paused. 'It's that I haven't been able to stop thinking about you. And however bad the timing is, I wish I could get to know you, properly. To make you laugh. To share adventures with you.' His eyes held mine. 'And it feels really important to me to tell you this.'

Wow. Just the thought was glorious. A small smile crept across my lips.

'That's better.' He smiled, too. Then it faded.

I sighed deeply. 'This is crazy. Isn't it?' I stared at him. 'I mean, we barely know each other.' A feeling of anguish filled me as I plummeted back down to earth. 'Once I'm married, I never will.'

He gazed through the window, then he turned to look at me again. 'What if I asked you to give me – us – one evening? Before you sign away the rest of your life?' He said it humorously but his eyes were serious.

My mouth fell open. 'You mean, this week?'

'I guess it will have to be.' He was watching me.

'I can't.' I'd never felt so conflicted. Or could I? No question, I wanted to. The thought of Gareth at home in our flat held no allure for me. Meanwhile, being here no longer felt wrong.

Already, I didn't want to leave. 'I don't know if I can.' The voice of reason taking over; the next days and hours having already been mapped out – which I hadn't minded – until now.

'Well, what if I said I'm working from home tomorrow?' He paused. 'I don't know what we do here. I'm on unfamiliar ground, Tilly. I've no idea what you must think of me, asking you this when I know you're getting married. And I swear I've never done anything like this in my life. I wouldn't be asking you if I didn't have a feeling you wanted it, too.' He paused. 'I could take the afternoon off – if you wanted me to?'

I had a silent battle going on with myself. OK, so I wanted to spend more time with him. I wanted to so much. But common sense was starting to kick in. I'd committed myself to someone else. This, whatever *this* was, happening when it was, it wasn't right. I felt powerless as I wiped away tears I hadn't known were there. But as I stood there, a recklessness took me over. 'OK.' My voice was husky. 'I'll be here.'

I left my drink unfinished. Adam walked me to the door, where I lingered a moment. We didn't speak. But we didn't need words. There were hopes, dreams, entire lifetimes in our eyes, promises as yet unlived.

I opened the door. 'Bye,' I said softly as I slipped outside.

I felt removed as I walked away. Displaced. The world no longer the familiar place it used to be just days ago. The sun was sinking, the park in shadow as I walked back. Reaching our flat, I could hear the football on the TV even before I opened the door. As I closed it, Gareth cheered loudly. 'You've missed a brilliant game,' he called out enthusiastically.

Going in, I watched him turn the TV off, then shuffle along the sofa to make enough room for me.

'You OK?' For a moment, he looked uncertain.

'Yes.' I tried to smile, my eyes taking in the predictable empty cans on the floor.

'Sorry, babe,' he said hastily. 'I must stop doing this. I'm going to change my ways, I promise you.' He leant down to pick them up. 'Can I get you a cuppa – or something stronger?'

'A glass of wine would be lovely.' Guilt flowed over me. Gareth meant well. And all I'd done these last few days was pick holes in him.

He came back holding a couple of glasses of wine. He sat down and passed one to me. 'To us.' He chinked his glass against mine.

'To us,' I murmured softly.

We actually talked that night – about our families and our wedding day; how one day not too long from now, hopefully we'd buy a little house. But in bed, while Gareth slept, my thoughts refused to settle. And not because I was thinking about my wedding. The only thing on my mind was seeing Adam.

The following morning, I was up and about early. Leaving Gareth snoring, I showered and dressed. As I made a mug of coffee, my phone buzzed with a text from Lizzie.

LIZZIE

How are you? I've been worried about you. Call me xxxx

I couldn't risk Gareth overhearing me. Taking my coffee outside, I closed the front door and called her back. 'Hey. Are you OK?'

'Of course I am.' Lizzie sounded impatient. 'It's you I'm worried about.'

'You don't need to be. Honestly,' I said. 'Everything's fine.'

'Have you seen him again? Adam, I mean?'

'Last night,' I said quietly.

'Oh my God.' Lizzie was silent for a moment. 'You do know don't you, that this would be the most romantic thing in the world, if it wasn't for the ever so slight problem of your wedding.'

I was silent for a moment. 'He asked me if I'd give him one evening.'

'Oh my God, Tilly. What did you say?'

'I said no at first.' I paused, swallowing. 'But all I could think was, what if I said yes?' I went on. 'I'm supposed to be seeing him this afternoon.' Suddenly I felt wretched.

'Tilly, you can't,' she said anxiously. 'I mean, you can. But this so isn't like you.' Lizzie paused. 'I'm worried about you. Imagine for a moment you do this. When you're standing in front of the altar with Gareth, don't you think the chances are you'll regret it?'

'You're right. I probably will.' In that moment, I really didn't like myself. And I didn't need Lizzie to tell me how selfish I sounded, that I was about to betray Gareth. 'But if I don't, I'll always wonder.' I paused. 'And the thing is, I don't think I can stop myself.'

* * *

It was a surreal morning – one when I'd imagined myself excitedly organising the clothes I'd carefully chosen for our honeymoon in Malta. In spite of recent chaotic events in my life, I liked to be organised. With a few days to go, I'd be putting together everything I needed for the big day itself, ready to pack up and take over to my parents' house.

Instead, I barely registered what I was doing. With one eye on the clock, I was going through the motions, while Gareth had gone to work, after which he was going over to his best man's house for one of their legendary barbecues.

Before he left this morning, he'd come over and put his arms around me. 'It's going to be good to get away – just the two of us. I wasn't going to say anything...' He'd faltered. 'But you haven't been yourself the last few days.' He looked slightly awkward. 'We are OK, aren't we, Tills?'

My heart had started to thump. 'Of course we are.' My throat was suddenly dry. 'I've had a lot on my mind – you know, the wedding and that.' I tried to make a joke of it. 'But I suppose, if I'm honest, I've been worrying about one or two things.'

Letting go of me, a wary look crossed his face. 'Such as?'

It was as though he'd completely forgotten the conversation we had. 'Having kids is a really big deal for me.' I watched his face. 'And I know what you said, about having them further down the line. But if you don't want to have them, I'd rather know. Now – before it's too late.' Realising as I said it, I was giving him a let out; that it would be far easier to say *Gareth got cold feet*, than the truth – that I had.

He froze. 'What are you saying?'

'I'm asking you to be honest. Once we're married...' I shrugged. 'I'd hate it to become this... this thing between us.' I didn't know how to describe it. 'Us having kids is really important to me.'

'Of course it is.' He looked awkward as he took my hands. 'And the answer is I do want them. I meant what I said. I just think it would make sense if we waited a few years.' He leant towards me to kiss me.

But I pulled back. 'How long is a few? I want to know if it's three, or ten...'

'Hey. Does it matter?' He frowned. 'We'll figure it out. We're young, Tilly. We have time.'

'It isn't about having time.' I didn't like that he was being evasive. 'Don't you get that? It's about us getting married and wanting the same things.' But I'd answered my own question.

Clearly he didn't feel like I did, or we wouldn't be speaking like this.

'Hey, chill, Tilly. Can't this stuff wait? We have a big week. Let's make the most of it. We'll work everything out.' He paused. 'You're feeling the stress, aren't you?'

'I suppose I am.' I knew it was the point when I should have pushed him, forced the issue. Yes, it would have caused a row. But it would at least have been honest.

He pulled me close again. 'Everything's done isn't it? Almost?'

I nodded. 'There are a few things to do, but not too much.'

'Take a bit of time for yourself.' Gareth looked concerned. 'It's a big day. An amazing day.'

I gazed into his eyes. 'You're right. Sorry. I do love you, Gareth.' I meant it. However scattered my mind was, I did love him.

'I love you, too.' He kissed me. 'I have to go.' After kissing me on the cheek again, he picked up his bag and stood there. 'I'll probably stay over at Pete's tonight.'

* * *

As I watch myself, memories come flooding back – of the shame I felt for the mess I'd got myself into, of my inability to be honest with myself, or anyone else. Even now, I can still remember how conflicted I felt; how I was wondering if it was possible to love two people. Then I'd berated myself, for putting *love* and *Adam* in the same sentence when after just a few days, I barely knew him.

That morning, I sat on our bed, listening as Gareth went out, whistling. Then, as he closed the door behind him, I felt a weight instantly lift. One that came crashing down on me again as I thought about our wedding. *I still had a few days,* I told myself. *Anything could happen. Gareth could still change his mind...*

* * *

Terrible, isn't it, that I thought it was OK to go ahead? But with the benefit of hindsight, I can see how lost I was. How frightened of rocking any boats, even though the signs were there, loud and clear. It was easier for everyone, easier for me to ignore them.

* * *

That afternoon, the sun was shining in a cloudless sky as I left the flat and walked to Adam's house. My hair was newly washed, and I was wearing a thin cotton dress I'd had for years. Excitement filled me at the thought of seeing him. I was also nervous. *And I was selfish*, I kept telling myself; going behind Gareth's back, imagining I could get away with this.

When he opened his front door, Adam looked nervous, too. 'I was half-expecting not to see you.'

I took in his faded jeans and grey T-shirt. 'I was half-expecting me to change my mind,' I confessed as I went inside.

I followed him through to the kitchen. The sliding door was open onto the garden, the room bathed in sunlight. It felt calm and peaceful; it was also a place where no one had any expectations of me, a feeling I wasn't familiar with – not that I recognised it at the time.

'Tea? Or would you prefer a cold drink?'

'I think cold.' I watched Adam go to the fridge and take out a couple of bottles.

He held one out. 'A beer?'

'Thanks.'

He opened them and passed one to me. 'Shall we sit down?'

Along one wall of the kitchen, the sofa was angled slightly

towards the garden. I sat down at one end, as Adam sat towards the other. 'Cheers.' He held up his beer bottle.

I clinked mine against it. 'Cheers.' For a fleeting moment, I had that *what the fuck am I doing here* feeling. But it passed. And I mean, quickly, as again I was overwhelmed by this feeling I had, of the connection between us; my words seeming stilted, reality hovering in the way of us. 'You've finished work for the day?'

He nodded. 'Work's flexible. I'm lucky in that way.'

I was curious. 'What is it do you do?'

'I'm partly a copywriter and partly a travel writer. It can be unpredictable – but the upside is I can work from anywhere. The travel writing is what I love, though.'

It was the first I'd glimpsed of this free-spirited side of him. 'You're away a lot?'

'A fair bit. I've just come back from some of the lesser-known Greek islands. Wonderful places off the beaten track – the kind of places I really like.'

'Wow.' While in one sense, I was envying him the freedom he had, on the other, it unsettled me. I couldn't imagine how it would be to live like that. But until now, I'd never known anyone who lived like that. 'I'm a bit of home bird,' I said.

'That's nice.' Adam's eyes were warm as they looked at me. 'I think I would be more that way, if I had someone to share it with.' He studied me. 'So how are you feeling?' he asked.

Obviously, he was talking about my wedding. 'All over the place.' I gazed into his eyes. 'Mixed up. Worried that whatever I do, I'll be making a mistake.'

'I don't envy you,' he said quietly. 'Usually, my advice would be to take some time out. But I guess in this case, you can't.'

'If only.' I was silent. 'So much work has gone into planning it. My mum is really excited about it – and it wasn't so long ago, it felt like my dream day. I mean, the venue is to die for. There are going to be flowers, literally everywhere. I have this incredible dress.' I paused. 'Up until my hen night, I couldn't wait. But now...' I broke off, my emotions in turmoil again.

He was quiet for a moment. 'Then why are you doing it?'

'I've asked myself the same question.' I shrugged. 'Gareth and I have been together a long time. We know each other's families and friends. We're comfortable together – and I love him...' All of it was true. 'It's probably last-minute jitters,' I looked at Adam. 'I mean, it happens, doesn't it?'

He didn't say anything for a moment. 'Have you talked to anyone about how you're feeling?'

'Only to Lizzie – my sister,' I said. 'She knows I'm here.'

'You haven't talked to your parents?'

'God, no,' I said with feeling. 'I couldn't. They'd think I was a terrible person.' I looked at Adam sadly. 'That's how I feel. This isn't the kind of thing I'd normally do – and what makes it a hundred times worse, is my wedding coming up.'

'Life can be messy, can't it?' he said gently. 'It's not like you planned this.'

'I planned coming here today.' Shame washed over me. 'I shouldn't have come here. If Gareth found out...'

'I don't know what to say.' A cloud crossed Adam's face. 'You're the only person who knows what's right for you. I suppose, in that sense, it doesn't matter what anyone else says. It's about you.'

It was almost exactly what Lizzie had said. 'I know.' I swallowed the lump in my throat. 'The thing is...' I hesitated, not sure how to say what I was thinking, without it sounding like I was blaming him...

'Go on,' he said.

I sighed. 'I suppose until the last few days, I've been going around with my head in the sand. Just going along with everything in my life. Then I met you...' I hesitated. 'It's made me look at things so differently.'

'I'm sorry.' He paused. 'Not sorry I met you, obviously. But I'm sorry it's caused you such a problem.'

'It isn't your fault it happened when it did.' I gazed out at the garden, at the shafts of sunlight dancing through the trees.

'The timing's strange, isn't it?' He sounded regretful. 'But I think sometimes people come into our lives for a reason. Maybe to shake our world up a bit – or to show us how to look at things a different way. At least, that's how it seems to me.'

I looked at him, slightly amazed, that I, Tilly, was capable of shaking up anyone's world. 'Is that what I've done? Shaken up your world?'

He smiled. 'Just a little.'

I felt my eyes widen. 'Oh.' I didn't know what else to say.

'The thing I find about signs,' he went on, 'is if we ignore them, they don't go away. They go on getting bigger – until we can't.'

I blinked at him. 'You think us meeting is a sign?'

He smiled again. 'I think it may be... You've certainly made me realise I did the right thing leaving my ex. No doubts, whatsoever. I should thank you for that.'

I was just a little bit speechless.

'The main thing here is what do you really want, Tilly?' he said gently. 'Is Gareth the person you want to share the rest of your life with?'

His words hung in the air. But we both knew, that if he was, I wouldn't have been there. I tried to imagine what I'd say to Lizzie in this situation, or to fast-forward a few years and imagine I was talking to my son or daughter. What would I say to them? But the answer was easy. I'd want them to be happy.

'It doesn't matter. It's too late,' I said abruptly. But the thought of having children had brought back the conversation with Gareth. 'I really do know how mad this must seem. And I'm not a bad person. I just hate upsetting anyone. In fact, I do anything I can to avoid it.' But even I could see the downside of marrying for the wrong reasons; that ultimately it had the potential to cause just as much upset.

'Why? You're not responsible for other people's feelings.'

I knew I wasn't. But I had this default setting to always smooth things over. 'The thought of being the cause of so much upset...' I broke off, realising this was the crux of my problem. I'd always done whatever it took to keep the peace. But it did nothing to change the fact that too much about my wedding felt wrong. 'Last night, when I told him I was going to meet Lizzie, he didn't think to ask how she was. But he never does.' I hesitated. 'There's also this other thing.'

He frowns slightly. 'What's that?'

I sighed. 'I want to have kids – I always have. But Gareth wants to wait – until we're more settled. But he was less than enthusiastic about the idea. We should have discussed it before. I suppose I never imagined it being a problem between us. But potentially, it is. And if I'm right, it's a really big one.'

'I can see his point. When it comes to kids, there's no rush, is there?' Adam frowned. 'Tilly, only you know how important that is to you. But after the wedding, you'll be husband and wife.' Adam looked at me. 'Don't you think you need to resolve this before then?'

'There's no chance of that.' I sighed. I was twenty-two years old, for crying out loud. Getting married was starting to feel like a trap.

'This is really hard.' He sounded hesitant. 'I'm trying to keep my opinions out of this. But...' He sighed. 'You're asking yourself questions you haven't asked before. Questions you want answers to, which isn't easy. But it can only be a good thing.'

'You think?' I was desperately seeking answers – he was right. I just wasn't sure I was ready to hear them.

'I've thought a lot about the timing of us meeting,' Adam said quietly. 'I think it was meant to happen – to make both of us look at our lives.' Time seemed to stop as he looked at me, then slowly reached out one of his hands and stroked my hair back. 'But also... I have this feeling you and I could be something.'

I stared at him, in that moment imagining calling the wedding off. The relief I'd feel, the freedom I'd have. I'd move in with Lizzie, go on holiday. Begin a life that had Adam in it. But then I thought of my parents, guilt crashing over me. 'I feel like my head's going to explode.'

'Can you imagine, though?' he said gently. 'If we'd met earlier?'

'It would have saved us a lot of trouble.' I shook my head. But maybe we weren't meant to. Maybe the timing wouldn't have been right, then, too. 'What if the reason it's happened now isn't to make me change my mind? If it's so that I go into marriage with my eyes open?'

'Is that what you really think?' As he moved closer, I could see the flecks in his eyes, the strands of his hair that were multiple shades of brown.

'I suppose it's one of those things we'll never know the answer to.' I tried to ignore the effect the closeness of him was having on me; how I wanted him to put his arms around me. To kiss me. I forced myself to break the moment. 'Tell me about your ex,' I said a little shyly.

He looked surprised. 'There's not a lot to say. Leanne and I were together for eighteen months, living together for about a year... On the surface, we had a nice life. But I'd always felt like there was something missing between us.' He shook his head. 'You won't believe how many times I questioned myself. I thought maybe we were too young. Then I started to think that I expect too much from relationships.' He paused. 'But meeting you showed me I don't.'

As he smoothed a strand of hair behind one of my ears, I felt my cheeks grow hot.

'You see,' His eyes gazed into mine, 'I haven't felt like this before. It's why I had to see you again. I needed to know if you felt the same.'

For a moment, I couldn't speak. It was as though I was standing at the biggest crossroads ever. In one direction lay my big fairy-tale wedding to Gareth, which meant spending the rest of my life with a man I was no longer sure about. While in the other lay a cancelled wedding and the unknown – but with it, freedom. *Freedom to see if Adam and I really were something.* I felt myself sigh. Was it worth risking everything I had for a man I'd only just met?

'What are you thinking?' Adam was watching me.

'So many things I don't know where to start.' This time, I sighed out loud. 'I know Gareth and I aren't perfect. But no relationship is – and we've come this far. Our wedding is in three days.' Tears pricked my eyes. 'It's everything I've always wanted. And now... I'm not sure.' My voice was husky. 'Maybe this is just me getting cold feet. So much has gone into making it a dream day. How can I cancel now?'

'A wedding isn't about one day,' Adam said. 'It's the start of marriage. It's about the rest of your life. If you did cancel, people would forget. It's incredible how short their memories can be!'

I knew he was trying to make me smile, but it wasn't helping.

'I bet some of them would think you're really brave,' he said. 'You can't be the only bride to question herself.'

'Probably not.' I thought about what he'd said. And the thing was, I could imagine telling Gareth. But when it came to my parents...

It was as though he read my mind. 'What is it about telling your parents that worries you so much?'

It was a fair question. Now, of course, I can see it was due to the layers of beliefs engrained in me as I was growing up: my inbuilt desire to meet the expectations of everyone who mattered to me. To be the good daughter my parents had brought me up to be. But back then, I didn't understand any of that. 'People matter, don't they? Especially family?' I said lamely. 'What I do impacts on other people.' I shrugged. 'It isn't just about me.'

Adam frowned. 'When it comes to getting married, I'd say it's all about you.' I was torn again. I knew he was right. But it was a step way too far out of my comfort zone – I couldn't, wouldn't, let myself see it like that. We sat there, the silence broken when Adam got up. 'This isn't fair, is it? On either of us.'

Disappointment washed over me. 'I guess not.' I stood up, looking at Adam. 'I should probably go.'

He stepped closer. 'I wish you the best, Tilly. Of everything.' Then leaning down, his lips touched mine.

For a glorious moment, I forgot everything. All that existed was the two of us. *You're marrying Gareth.* As the words came into my head, I pulled back. 'I'm sorry.' My voice was husky as I gazed at Adam. '*I'm so sorry.*' What felt like minutes passed, before I turned around. Then without looking to see if he was following, I headed for the door. I fumbled with the catch, then stepping outside, closed it behind me.

As I walked down the road, I fought the urge to look back, to turn back. But I knew deep inside, there was no point. *I'm marrying Gareth*, I kept telling myself as I forced myself to walk away. *I love Gareth. The wedding's planned, the big day I've always dreamed of, that my parents have put so much love, not to mention money, into planning... If I cancelled at this point...*

Entering the park, a feeling of relief filled me, as suddenly I felt like a fool. I'd come so close to screwing up my big day – and all for a stranger who'd made me question one or two things. I needed to forget about Adam. Focus on Gareth. Enjoy every second of the wedding; look forward to the rest of our lives together.

Back at home, I carried on sorting the things I needed for the wedding and my honeymoon, refolding clothes I'd already folded without realising I was doing it, until sitting on the bed, I sighed heavily. I needed to get real with myself. Relationships were never perfect. It wasn't reasonable to expect life to be a fairy tale.

* * *

I watch myself consumed by angst and guilt, feelings I've largely forgotten about. That's what the passing of time does; some of our memories fade. But some things stay with us, are logged in the back of our minds in a place we rarely visit. Until something happens to dislodge them.

I can remember how I felt in the run-up to my wedding. How my fears of what other people might think were only half the story. The fact was, that in agreeing to meet Adam, I was thinking only of myself. How many times did I say I loved Gareth? Words that were easy to say. And there are many kinds of love; I didn't doubt that on one level, I did love him. But back then, I was young, too self-interested. I suppose I wanted it all. But I was about to learn the hard way what marriage means.

6

The Unravelling

* * *

It's strange, really, taking a look at my life. I mean, faced with that life-changing decision just days before your wedding, would have been enough to fry anyone's mind. And we went ahead; in between the ups and downs that are part of everyone's life, Gareth and I were happy – or so I've always believed.

Or were we? When it was all I'd known, how could I tell? But *what if*, I find myself asking again. If I'd called the wedding off and embarked on a different life? Would I have been any happier? It's one of those questions I would never know the answer to.

'Tilly?'

In the hospital, the mists of unconsciousness thin as someone close by says my name. Then they say it again, before the mist thickens and I'm back in our family home, with no husband and no job. Completely alone.

* * *

I was oddly calm as I locked the door and switched my phone off. Standing there, I realised, this was it. Rock bottom. And yes, it was my choice to leave my job. I just hadn't realised how I was going to feel.

Going upstairs, I changed into my pyjamas, hurling my carefully chosen office clothes in the direction of the bin. I must have been living in a dream world to have even imagined Elizabeth offering me a pay rise. And who knew how long before I would have been next in line for redundancy? Far better, I told myself firmly, to take the initiative. To move on, on my terms. But to what?

That was the question that dogged me as, in the bathroom, I scrubbed off my carefully applied make-up and stared at my reflection in the mirror, taking in the wrinkles and circles under my eyes.

You're old, Tilly. Old and ugly. No wonder nobody wants you.

Almost immediately I was berating myself.

You're alive, Tilly. You have a roof over your head. So life hasn't worked out the way you thought it would, but get over it and stop feeling so sorry for yourself.

Which didn't exactly help as still feeling wretched, I pulled on my ugliest, saggiest jogging bottoms and a fleece that my son Alex used to wear. Shame filled me that I still hadn't told my children what was going on. The truth was, I couldn't face it. Going downstairs, I retrieved a bottle of whisky that belonged to Gareth. I never usually touched whisky, but this afternoon, I didn't care. I took it through to the sitting room and sank into one of the sofas.

As I sat there, a darkness came over me. I poured myself a glass and took a sip, which instantly triggered a horrendous coughing fit but that didn't stop me taking another sip. Then I drank the remaining contents of it down in one.

Feeling the whisky start to circulate in my veins, despite my very many sorrows, I giggled. I mean, there I was, truly a divorce cliché, a Bridget Jones surveying the wreckage of her life; the star of my own mini-tragedy. I contemplated that Gareth's decision had rendered the past twenty or so years of my life utterly meaningless. That this house and its contents, everything I'd poured heart and soul into, would simply be sold off and become irrelevant. It was shit. But there wasn't anything I could do about it.

At some point, the sound of the landline reached me. But I had no wish to talk to anyone and I ignored it, just sitting there, unmoving as the light faded.

The house had always felt like a nest I'd woven into being. A cosy sanctuary lined with softness that now felt like a cuckoo had been in and decimated it. Walls that used to echo with laughter were deathly silent; the homely atmosphere reduced to a sense of emptiness by the knowledge of Gareth's betrayal. My hand shook as I poured myself another whisky I didn't really want, my head filling with questions. *Why this? Why now? Why me?*

There really was nothing like a crisis to make you question your entire existence. Then I was thinking back to when Gareth and I met. How happy we were; how carefree. We had all these plans, a whole life to share – or so I'd believed. *What happened to your dreams?* I asked myself. *Remember? The happy-ever-after you were always so sure was out there waiting for you?*

But I suppose that was the point of dreams – to stay just as dreams. Cosy little flights of fancy designed to see you through when times got tough. They weren't real. And meanwhile, I was just Tilly, I reminded myself. I wasn't particularly special in any way. I was just a small person with an even smaller life, undeserving of anything more.

And sitting there, I knew exactly what was real. It was the husband who had left me. It was getting older, being jobless, and a hundred other things. A mother whose babies had flown the nest. Then as I thought about the boys, I felt my heart break.

Tears cascaded down my face, soaking into Alex's old fleece. For everything I didn't know, one thing I was sure of. This wasn't how my life was meant to be.

But I managed to stop wallowing in self-pity just long enough to give myself a talking-to. Summoned my inner Bridget Jones again. If she rose from the depths like a phoenix from the ashes, there was no reason why I, Tilly, couldn't do the same.

* * *

The next day followed a similar pattern. I hid away from the world, grieved, cried, ignored all calls. It was interspersed with irreverently playing loud music that Gareth hated and dancing like no one was watching, which made me think of Lizzie then want to cry again, until Robbie called my mobile.

'Mum? Are you OK?' He sounded worried. 'Dad called earlier. He told me what's happened.'

I imagined the sanitised version Gareth would have put together for his sons. *Your mother and I haven't been getting on. We've decided to separate. Of course, it's sad. But these things happen... Blah blah blah...* Skirting around the fact that he'd been shagging someone else and she happened to be pregnant.

'I'm sorry. I should have told you what's going on. But I'm fine,' I said, blinking away my tears and swallowing the lump in my throat. 'Or at least, I will be.' I made a heroic effort to pull myself together. 'You mustn't worry, Rob. It's really sad... But we'll be OK. All of us, I mean.' Trying to sound more convincing than I felt.

'That's what Dad said.' There was sadness in his voice. 'I didn't see it coming, Mum.'

'For the record, nor did I,' I said quietly. 'Robbie? You mustn't worry. Wherever I end up, you will always have a home.'

'You're selling the house?' He sounded startled.

I shouldn't have been surprised that Gareth had conveniently chosen not to allude to that part, either. And I couldn't imagine an alternative. I mean, neither of us could afford to buy the other out. For a moment, I wondered exactly what he had said. 'We haven't talked about it yet.' When it was the last thing I wanted to do, I was still hoping we wouldn't have to. 'Listen. You just focus on your course. Your father and I will sort things out.' I wondered if he knew he was going to have a tiny half-brother or sister.

It was as if he read my mind. 'Dad said – about Olivia being pregnant.'

I was not expecting that. '*Oh.*' It felt like I'd been kicked in the gut.

'It's a mess, isn't it?' He sounded so sad.

'It could be much worse,' I said more bravely than I felt. 'Things are going to be different. But in a way, they already are. You and Alex... you're at uni and you have your own lives to think about. We're all going to be OK, Rob. I promise you.'

His call was followed by a similar one from Alex.

'I can come home, Mum. The course doesn't matter.' His voice was filled with concern.

'Don't you dare say that,' I told him. 'Your course is really important.'

'I can't believe Dad could do this.' There was anger in his voice.

'I don't think any of us saw this coming,' I said quietly. 'But you're going to be fine. So is Robbie – and so am I.' I took a deep breath. 'We just have to accept things are going to change.'

Speaking to my boys triggered another encounter with Gareth's whisky bottle that sank me to my lowest level yet and led to another evening of playing all the sad songs and debating with myself what the actual point was of being alive. How all the threads I'd held together over the years were, one by one, slipping away from me: Lizzie, Gareth, the boys... Even my job. Yet paradoxically, it was as I thought of my sons, I galvanised myself into action, because I really couldn't go on like this.

So it was that the following morning, I showered and washed my hair. Feeling marginally better, I called Elena.

'Hey, El. Are you busy later?'

'Tilly... How are you? I've been trying to call you. But then I realised you'd probably switched your phone off. Have you listened to your messages? Anyway, I'm not doing anything – well, not this evening.' Obviously in a hurry, Elena didn't stop for breath. 'Come over. I'll cook some food, and I'll get some wine. Around seven? Stay over if you like.'

'Thanks. I'll bring the wine,' I said.

'That would be great. Are you OK?' She sounded anxious. Then a phone rang in the background. 'I'm so sorry, Tilly. I have to get this. Can we talk later?'

Cheered by the prospect of an evening with my friend, I put on some make-up and after checking the pitiful contents of the fridge, ventured out to the shops. Perusing the shelves of the local supermarket, I contemplated that for the first time I was shopping for one; as sadness washed over me, I banished it. I could choose whatever I wanted without worrying if Gareth would like it.

It had to be the way to go, I decided. To turn those moments of loss on their heads and look for the flip side – shopping being one of them, music another. Just like not washing my hair for days if the mood took me, or wearing my oldest, scruffiest clothes.

I pushed my trolley across the car park. Then as I reached my car, I heard a voice call out.

'Tilly?'

I turned to see Tallulah standing there. Tallulah was a therapist I'd met while I was pregnant with the twins and Gareth's unwanted impending fatherhood almost broke us up. But I was digressing. She and I became friends, but lost touch a few years back after she moved to the States. Tall, with mobile eyebrows, Tallulah was a little irreverent; friendship giving her the right to speak her mind, at times somewhat bluntly.

'You're back,' I said delightedly. 'Why haven't you told me?'

'I got back last week, and funnily enough I have called you, only for some reason you haven't been answering.' She looked at me questioningly. 'Is everything OK?'

I took in Tallulah's oversized loose-fitting jeans and emerald-green T-shirt, her long red hair messily scrunched into a topknot. 'Great, thanks.' I paused. Why was I lying to her? 'Actually...' Faced with a sympathetic face, I completely forgot about flipping the script. Taking a deep breath, there in the middle of the car park, I blurted out the whole sorry story of Gareth leaving me for Olivia who was pregnant, how useless I felt. How in a short space of time, I'd lost Lizzie and left my job, how I was most likely about to lose my home, too. How my entire life was in ruins.

'Fuck.' She looked shocked. 'I'm so sorry, Tilly. I didn't know about Lizzie. That's so sad.'

'Thanks. It was.' I swallowed the lump that was suddenly in my throat. 'Truth be told, I'm up and down. But I'm trying to pull myself together.' I squared my shoulders, channelled my inner Bridget Jones. 'Don't really have a choice, do I?'

'I can't believe this.' Tallulah genuinely looked amazed. 'The way I remember it, Gareth never wanted children.'

'I know. It's a joke, isn't it? I just want everything to go back to how it was,' I said quietly, watching one of her eyebrows tilt upwards slightly. But as I spoke I was already realising, it wasn't exactly true. 'I mean, I did to start with. But now... I'm not so sure.' I wasn't sure where the words were coming from. 'I don't think you can go back, can you? Not after something like this has happened?' I broke off, slightly astounded with myself.

'Quite likely not.' She frowned. 'There's another way to look at this. A few days ago, you didn't know your husband was cheating on you – and has been for some time, by the sounds of things.' She fiddled absent-mindedly with an escaped strand of her long hair. 'It's quite a lot to get your head around, and I imagine it's changed everything – about how you see both him and you.' She looked at me kindly. 'You need to give yourself time to process this.'

'I think you're right. That's the hardest thing, that I didn't see it coming. Gareth and I...' I broke off, not sure how to say it without sounding weak.

'Gareth and you what?' Tallulah looked at me questioningly.

I sighed. 'You must have met so many couples who have a crisis at some point. And I know not everyone stays together.' I hesitated. 'But after twenty-two years, a part of me thinks he shouldn't just have walked away – not without at least trying?'

'Are you expecting me to tell you what to do?' She raised both her eyebrows.

'You're the therapist,' I reminded her, only part jokingly.

'Tilly... You know what I'm going to say. Part of this is about finding your own answers. If Gareth really doesn't want to try and make things right between you, you can't force him. But...'

I stared at her. 'But what?'

'I don't mean to be brutal, but the question you should be asking yourself is why you would even want him back.'

It was the same word Elena had used – *brutal*. And it was easy for her to say. 'This isn't just about me, Tallulah. What about everyone else this affects? Our sons? My brother-in-law. My father, even.'

She looked at me as though I was mad. 'What about them? OK, I can understand you worrying about your sons. But if you want to know what I think, I'd say you're not seeing this clearly. And also, just to be perfectly clear, this isn't about your father or anyone else,' she said firmly. 'Firstly, it's a myth that children are better off with both parents. It really does depend on the parents. Take Gareth...' She hesitated. 'Is he a wonderful father?' Her blue eyes gazed at me. When I didn't speak, she went on. 'In any case, your sons are grown up, aren't they?'

'They're at uni. But they still need to come home for Christmases and holidays.'

'Oh Tilly. Of course they will. But it won't matter where you are. And they have their own lives now.' She shook her head. 'Remember when you were at uni? I bet the last thing you thought about was going home to see your parents. Anyway, as I just said, your marriage isn't about anyone else. It's about you and Gareth.' She paused. 'You've had your ups and downs... but have you been happy?'

'Yes.' But it was automatic. A knee-jerk reflex, rather than a conscious one.

From the look on her face, it was clear she didn't believe me.

'Remember the first time you came to see me?' she said gently.

'Yes.' My eyes were suddenly filled with tears.

'It must have been about twenty years ago.' Tallulah looked thoughtful. 'It wasn't an easy time for you.'

'It wasn't. But that's the whole point. We got over it. We were fine. You've seen us together over the years,' I added.

'I remember you saying once that you and Gareth were comfortable together. You could have been talking about a pair of old socks.' Tallulah was silent for a moment. 'Tilly? I'm really sorry you're going through this.' She paused again. 'But have you asked yourself if it's really Gareth you're upset about? Or is it more that life as you know it is going to change?'

It was a touch too close to the truth had I been honest with myself. Such was my roller coaster of emotions that I smiled through my tears at her. 'Thanks for the free therapy session.' I hugged her. 'It's good to have you home.'

'Call me,' she said. 'We'll go out. It's time you put some fun in your life.'

There was a time when I had thought about training as a counsellor; of having my own little room with shelves of plants and comfy chairs, just like Tallulah used to have. But like many things, life went on and it fell by the wayside. And given the mess I've made of my own life, I'm not sure I'd have been any good. But talking to Tallulah had been helpful. Sometimes, you had to face the most painful of facts. Hiding them under a sticking plaster, while a short-term fix, only served to leave them festering.

Back at home, I put the shopping away then sat heavily on the sofa. On the windowsills were the orchid plants I'd nurtured over the years, including several from Lizzie and, as I took in their delicate flowers, tears filled my eyes. Wiping them away, I turned to the display of family photos taken over the years – from the boys as babies, then chubby toddlers, all the way through childhood, then as teenagers. There was one of me with Gareth, taken just after we were married, and suddenly it struck me as odd that I hadn't noticed before that as the years passed, we'd never added more of us.

* * *

That evening, I drove over to Elena's. When she opened the door, my friend looked flustered. 'I've completely lost track of time.' She hugged me briefly. 'Come in. It's a mess, I'm afraid.'

'It really isn't,' I lied, following her into the kitchen that was in its usual state of chaos.

'Boys? Bath. Now,' Elena shouted. 'Come and say hello to Tilly.'

I couldn't help but smile at her mixed messages. But she was a great mum. Her boys obediently ran in and flung their arms around me, before disappearing just as quickly up the stairs.

'Thank God,' Elena said with feeling. 'No one tells you how exhausting being a mother is.'

'It's the best thing and you know it.' I held up a bottle of wine.

She passed me a corkscrew. 'Be an angel and open it.'

With the boys in bed, and after ordering in a Chinese, Elena and I put the world to rights.

'Have you talked to Gareth about the house?' she asked.

'I haven't talked to Gareth about anything,' I said feelingly. 'Don't forget. He was the one who started this.'

'I was just thinking.' Elena screwed up her face into a frown. 'Wouldn't you like to feel you had some control back? I mean, I would really hate feeling like my future lay in someone else's hands.'

'It's a shit feeling.' I felt my stomach clench. Then I looked at her. 'You know, you're right. It's exactly what I need to do. Tell him I'm putting the house on the market. Let's see how he likes that,' I said triumphantly.

Elena looked alarmed. 'I wasn't meaning selling the house, Tilly. At least, not yet. I was meaning in smaller ways – like planning your next steps.' She paused. 'I mean, you're free, aren't you? Or at least, you will be?'

Free. I played the word back in my head. 'You know, I keep getting these flashes of the old me. I'm not talking about sad, boring Tilly—'

'Stop,' Elena interrupted. 'Do not ever call yourself that ever again.' Her eyes were flashing. 'You are one of the most wonderful women I know.'

'Who, me?' I stared at her. 'You're drunk, Els.'

'I'm not fricking drunk.' She looked at me. 'You really don't see it, do you?' When I didn't respond, she went on. 'Obviously you don't. You've completely lost sight of gorgeous, funny Tilly who makes everyone laugh, who's the person everyone goes to because they love you so much. And because they feel safe with you. And because as well as funny, you have this gentle, empathic wisdom.'

It was my turn to interrupt. 'If I'm so wise, then answer me this. Why am I making such a mess of this?'

'You haven't,' Elena said gently. 'This was Gareth's doing. You're feeling your way through. But one day, my friend, you're going to be fine.'

* * *

One bottle turned into two and I lost track of what happened after that. Elena insisted I spent the night in her spare room and I crawled home the next morning with the mother of all hangovers.

Pondering what she'd said, hangover aside, I actually wasn't feeling too bad – or maybe the booze was still circulating. But when I got home and went inside, I felt my mood plummet.

I was stupid to imagine I could put a positive spin on my marriage breaking up. And it was Sod's Law, wasn't it, that when things were shitty, they generally seemed to get worse? Hunched on the sofa in my saggiest jogging bottoms, I was watching daytime TV when I heard the doorbell ring. Unable to face speaking to anyone, I ignored it. Then the next thing I heard was a key in the lock.

Imagining Gareth coming back, I quickly smoothed my hair, trying to muster an air of dignified sadness; getting the shock of my life when I heard footsteps come closer before the door opened and a stranger walked in.

A wave of fear hit me. Then I noticed he was smartly dressed in a suit and clutching a clipboard. Leaping up, I wrapped my arms around myself. 'What the fuck are you doing in my house?'

To be fair, he did look taken aback. 'Your house? I've been asked to value the property. The owner gave me a key. He said nothing about there being anyone here.'

'He's said nothing to me about this.' I stared at him, my fear replaced by anger. 'He has absolutely no bloody right. It's my bloody house, too.' Suddenly I was seething with rage, furious with Gareth. 'Get out.'

Holding up his hands defensively, the agent turned around and hurried back towards the door. I followed, watching as he let himself out. Locking the door and bolting it, I was outraged that Gareth could even think about doing this – let alone without talking to me – and knowing I was still living here.

I was still fuming five minutes later when my phone pinged with a text – from Gareth.

GARETH

> Ignoring my messages and calls isn't helpful, Tilly. I thought you'd be back at work. We need to put the house on the market. Let me know when is convenient and I'll make appointments.

He was wrong. I hadn't ignored his messages, I simply hadn't been able to bring myself to read them yet. And it was barely a week since he moved out. No time for me to even begin to come to terms with the carnage he'd created.

TILLY

> You didn't think, but you never do, do you?
> That's the whole problem. How dare you do this
> without mentioning it to me? In any case, there's
> a process. I need to speak to a lawyer.

Angry, I pressed send.

He came back a few minutes later.

GARETH

> I didn't mean to upset you. And you're right. I
> should have mentioned it. But I honestly thought
> you wouldn't be there.

As if that made it OK.

TILLY

> It's irrelevant whether I'm here or not. In case
> you've forgotten, the house belongs to both
> of us.

It was snarky; unnecessarily so. But I didn't care. And he had no right to go behind my back. Still seething, an urge to get out of the house filled me. After pulling on a jacket and boots, I headed for the only place I could think of, my phone in my pocket pinging with more messages I ignored; as I walked, trying to clear my head. But it was impossible.

The woods were misty that morning, the silver birches ethereal and ghostly, the air damp and still. As I picked my way around the muddiest parts of the path, there was another ping from my phone, I ignored. Only when I reached the platform at

Selham railway station, did I take my phone out of my pocket, then bring up Gareth's texts.

GARETH

Tilly, I'm sorry, but we do need to talk about the house. I need to buy somewhere – quickly.

The subtext didn't pass me by; that *quickly* meant before Olivia's baby arrived. I made a note to self to find out when that was – he hadn't told me. I moved on to his next message.

GARETH

I hope it doesn't inconvenience you too much. Let me know when you've found somewhere to move to.

I stared at it. *How dare he?* As far as inconvenience went, a forced move was right up there. And houses didn't sell overnight. Presumably, he'd rather it sat empty than I carried on living in it. But this wasn't solely up to him. I read the next message.

GARETH

I don't want to make this any harder than it already is. I was thinking maybe you could stay at your dad's for a while. Ease the transition, as it were. And at least you wouldn't be alone.

My blood boiled. Stay at Dad's? Where the fuck had that come from? Had he observed my relationship with my father in any detail whatsoever, or was he blind?

GARETH

Even if you don't, we need to get it valued. Then after, we can talk about when to put it on the market.

I stared across the platform at the brambles, at the sodden piles of fallen leaves, my brain seeming to freeze. Suddenly this place I loved, that felt removed from my everyday life, no longer held the same allure for me. But there wasn't anywhere I wanted to be, while the thought of doing anything even remotely related to selling the house felt as daunting as moving a mountain.

A burst of birdsong made me turn my head and I took in the blackbird watching me from a nearby tree.

'It's all right for you,' I told it. 'With your simple life and your little feathered nest, while mine happens to be empty...' A tear rolled down my face.

The bird chirruped more loudly at me. Then, squawking, flew away, leaving me sitting there, wishing I could do the same. And for the first time I was thinking I actually would fly far away from here. But the problem was, I had no wings.

* * *

When I got home, I called Elena. 'Gareth sent an estate agent around – to value the house. Without telling me. Can you believe it? I'm fuming, El. How dare he?'

'How dare he indeed. Bastard.' Elena sounded as furious as I felt.

'He says we need to sell the house quickly – presumably before Olivia has the baby,' I said bitterly.

'Then let him.' Elena paused. 'You know what? At least you won't have to handle that side of things.'

But the reality of selling was starting to hit. 'What about all our stuff?'

'You start sorting it. You don't have to panic. Take one drawer at a time – just like you're taking one day at a time. The house won't sell overnight. You have time, Tills.'

But after I ended the call, it didn't feel like that. My emotional roller coaster was taking a dive – into the abyss. And for the life of me, I couldn't see a way out of it.

* * *

The following day, I felt no better. In my ancient jogging bottoms and shapeless jumper, my hair was all over the place and for the second day running, I hadn't showered. Suddenly in need of a friendly voice, I called Elena. But it went straight to voicemail. A few seconds after hanging up, my phone pinged with a text.

> **ELENA**
>
> Hey Tills. Sorry, at a parents' thing at school. I'll call you later when I'm home.

Despair welled up inside me. That morning, my inner Bridget Jones was nowhere to be seen. I picked up my phone again and this time I called Tallulah.

'Tilly! How's it going?'

'Not great,' I said. 'Do you have a moment?'

'Of course. So what's up?'

'You can probably guess,' I said awkwardly. 'I'm sorry to call you like this.' I took a deep breath. 'I was really hoping you could give me a common sense talking-to...' I tried to inject some humour into my voice.

'Oh Tilly.' Tallulah was silent for a moment. 'What's happened?'

I tell her about Gareth sending someone to value the house.

'Shocking of him,' she agreed. 'Especially without talking to you first.' She paused. 'Have you actually spoken – since this happened?'

'No. I don't want to,' I said childishly. 'I don't want to see him, either.'

'Wouldn't it be easier? Even if only to avoid cock-ups like estate agents turning up when you're not expecting them?'

I was silent. The thought of speaking to Gareth had no appeal whatsoever.

'You could think of it as empowering,' Tallulah suggested. 'Taking the initiative, rather than doing nothing. And in a sense, you'd be facing your demons, or however you like to think of it.'

'I'm really not sure I'm ready.'

She shrugs. 'Fair enough. That's up to you.' She's silent for a moment. 'I've been thinking since I saw you in the car park – about everything that's going on in your life. Have you considered that maybe what's happening could be a sign?'

'*Sign?*' I felt myself frown. 'Excuse me?'

'Well, you know those times when everything seems to go your way? Like there's a flow to life?'

I tried to remember a time when life felt like that. 'I think so.' Though truth be known, it was a long time ago.

She went on. 'Well, right now, it's like the opposite is happening. In simple terms, you're being opposed, Tilly. It's like everywhere you look, doors are closing around you.' She paused for a moment. 'Quite a number of them, I'd say.'

'More like slamming in my face,' I said shortly. 'And thank you, but I really don't need reminding of this.'

'Don't take this personally,' she said. 'But yes. It probably does feel like they're slamming, rather than closing. The thing is...' She paused. 'Tilly, after we spoke, I got to thinking that maybe you are in the wrong place – the signs are all around you, but you're not seeing them, so they're getting bigger. I can understand why you feel that everything's against you.'

I was sure someone had said that to me before – I couldn't

remember who. But maybe she had a point, I admitted reluctantly to myself. My job was one thing – though I'd tried to love it, the truth was I felt like a fish out of water. But if she was right, it meant my broken marriage was a sign that I'd wasted the last twenty-two years of my life. 'There probably is something in what you're saying. But the problem is, this is my life we're talking about,' I said. 'It has been, for over twenty years. I don't want to feel like I've wasted it.'

'Who mentioned wasting anything? We're talking about growing. And change,' she said ever-so-slightly sarcastically.

'Yes, well, I've always believed it's about commitment,' I flashed back. 'And perseverance. My life might not be anything fancy, but at least it's mine. And I love it.'

'I'm so sorry. You're quite right.' Tallulah sounded trite. 'But we're back where we started, aren't we? Because your life is going to change. It has to.'

'Thanks, but I'm not sure this is helping.' I blinked away my tears. 'I should go. I have to start sorting through the house.'

'Oh Tilly. Please don't go – not like this. This is really tough for you – I'm under no illusions. But I'm on your side, you do know that, don't you?'

As her words sank in, I reached my lowest point yet, my world falling apart, all my flaws and mistakes brightly illuminated by a woman who epitomised the sass and irreverence I used to have – in shedloads, as opposed to the woman I'd become. A dowdy one who was losing everything important in her life.

'Tilly?' she said in a gentle voice. 'Are you still there?'

'Yes,' I muttered; the word stuck in my throat.

'Look. It's a process. It isn't easy. But you have to trust it.' She was quiet for a moment. 'And believe me when I tell you you're going to find your strength.' She paused again. 'You've got this.'

7

So, Where to Now?

I remember how I felt after that conversation with Tallulah; how the thought that all of this could be a sign made me uncomfortable. You see, when it comes to signs, historically I'm supremely brilliant at ignoring them. I've always thought of myself as a methodical, logic-based kind of girl – or woman.

And all for what?

Of course, Tallulah was right. Ending a marriage, leaving a home, then moving on, it was a process, one that back then, I was in the thick of.

* * *

After the conversation with Tallulah, over the rest of that day, it was as though her words had taken root and were firing up some hidden, inner part of me. One that had guts. _I'm not alone_, I kept telling myself. And even if I was, I wasn't letting what Gareth had done destroy me.

Thinking about him being unfaithful, suddenly, I was incensed, angry like never before, my adrenaline flowing like a river in full flood.

Filled with a need to wrestle back some semblance of control, I texted him back.

TILLY

> After tomorrow, do what the fuck you like. I won't be here.

Pressing send, I stared at the message, realising how rash it was. But there was no taking it back. It was too late.

He replied almost immediately.

GARETH

> Where will you be?

TILLY

> None of your fucking business.

GARETH

> But I might need to contact you.

TILLY

> Texts will work perfectly, Gareth. You can start with the address of where you're staying. My lawyer will be in touch. Goodbye.

Turning my phone off, I glanced at the large wall clock. Half past six, a time I would usually be cooking for me and Gareth, pouring myself a glass of wine while I waited for him to arrive back from work. A memory that belonged firmly in my old life. At least I'd never have to do that again, I told myself. I felt a brief wave of euphoria. Then burst into tears.

But if there was one thing I did know, it was that I couldn't give Gareth the satisfaction of seeing me backtrack. I had tonight and tomorrow, then come hell or high water, somehow, I was finding a way to get myself out of there.

It was only as I started opening cupboards and drawers, I realised what a ridiculous task I'd set myself. That I was in no frame of mind to make any decisions – except the problem was, I already had.

When I started to pack, nostalgic Tilly resurfaced in full force with all her reasons why I shouldn't have to be doing this. It was the photos and old letters, which would take days to sort through. Days that, due to the rashness of my decision, I didn't have.

As I started sifting through things, a peculiar melancholy filled me. It was like Lizzie's cards all over again, as moments from my childhood come flooding back. The birthdays and Christmases. Even the Sunday lunches Mum used to cook, the cosiness of my childhood bedroom. The feeling of safety I'd always had, which died when she did. Clutching them to me, there was no way I could throw them away. In the end, I texted Elena.

TILLY

If I'm stuck, could I leave a couple of boxes in your garage?

The answer pinged back minutes later.

ELENA

Of course. So you're packing?

TILLY

I need to get away, El.

I pressed send.

ELENA

Good for you.

She followed it with a heart emoji.

It took all night. But the problem was, by the time I'd finished going through the house, it was far more than a couple of boxes. When I got to Elena's the following morning, as she stared at my fully laden car, she looked horrified.

'Tilly. What is all this stuff?'

'Letters. Photos. A few books. Old cards...'

'Old cards?' She looked at me disbelievingly. 'You're not telling me you keep old birthday cards?'

'Only special ones.' My voice wobbled, because each and every one of them was important to me.

'And the other boxes?'

I shrugged. 'There's some presents Mum gave me. One of two bits of china, that sort of stuff. They have sentimental value, El. Pictures the boys drew me when they were small, things they made. I can't throw them away. There's my wedding dress, too.'

'That does it.' Elena looked ferocious. 'I understand about photos and the boys' things, but the wedding dress is the last straw. What else is in there that links you to that scumbag?'

'My wedding photos,' I said miserably. 'They're part of the story of my life, El. And so many family and friends are in them.'

'So is Gareth. We're getting rid of them.' She stood there, watching me. 'Come on. Give me the dress and the wedding photos. Then we'll find some space where you can leave the rest.'

Feeling like a traitor, I passed her the zipped-up bag that held my wedding dress – and shoes – then rummaged in one of the boxes for the album containing our wedding photos. 'I'm going to keep one or two.' My hands were shaking as I turned the pages, pulling out a photo of Lizzie and my parents together, my eyes lingering on one of me and Gareth standing outside the church.

'Hand them over,' she said firmly.

Guilt filled me as I closed the album and passed it to her. 'What will you do with them?'

'Apart from stabbing Gareth in the eyeballs, you don't need to know – in the photos, that is,' she added hastily as I gazed at her in horror. 'Is that all?'

Nodding, I started to carry what was left into her garage, stricken with guilt as I remembered buying my wedding dress. 'Mum helped me choose it.' Looking at Elena, I felt terrible.

'Tilly, your mum wouldn't have wanted you to keep it,' she said gently. 'Guaranteed. Not after what Gareth's done. Same with the photos. I promise you.'

With too much still to do, I refused Elena's offer of staying for a coffee. Back at the house, I decided my clothes were next. I took a deep breath, knowing that this time, I had to be ruthless.

Taking a fortifying glass of wine with me, upstairs I turned the radio on. As the mellow sound of Classic FM came from the speakers, emotion washed over me. Sitting on the bed, the idea of leaving was suddenly a step too far. But then I remembered what I'd said to Gareth. I wouldn't, *couldn't*, let him see me fail.

I switched the radio channels, stopping at the first that was upbeat. Then one of my favourite songs started to play, just when I needed it. I sang along. *I want to break free...* Wondering if this was another sign, a new sense of resolve came to me. The only way anything was going to happen was if I made it happen. Without further ado, I went to my wardrobe, pulled all my old work clothes off their coat hangers and piled them onto the floor; feeling lighter as I carried on, emptying drawers, chucking out anything that made me think of Gareth, keeping only the clothes I really liked.

By the time I'd finished, I looked at what was left, astonished that after all this time, how little there was. But this wasn't just about my stuff. There were the twins to think of, too. First, I went to Robbie's room, quietly pushing the door open, standing there for a moment feeling a Robbie-sized pang in my heart. It held his smell, the echo of his childhood, the things he'd collected over the years – which weren't many. Unlike me, Robbie wasn't a hoarder.

Alex, however, was. On the shelves in his bedroom were models he'd kept from his childhood, books he hadn't been able to part with. Photos of him with friends Blu-tacked onto the wall.

I felt another pang, this time Alex-sized, before sadness overwhelmed me. The boys were the most important people in the world to me. I had to talk to them again. Let them know I'd be back before the house was sold; that whatever was going on right now, one day, there would be another home, with me; a place for all the things they wanted to keep.

* * *

When I spoke to them, Robbie was pragmatic. 'I'll get my stuff sometime, Mum.'

'I've packed away a few things I thought you'd want to keep. But you should probably go through the rest.'

'It's only stuff, Mum. And I'll talk to Alex. Maybe we can come down together in the next couple of weeks.' He paused. 'Are you sure you're OK?'

'Yes.' I tried to keep my voice steady. 'Seeing as I don't have a job right now, it seems the perfect time to go away for a bit. Not sure where yet, but I'll let you know when I get there.'

'Wow.' He paused. 'Good for you, Mum. Dad's an idiot. Be careful, won't you?'

'I will.' Tears filled my eyes. 'You too.'

I gave myself a couple of minutes before I called Alex and told him what was happening.

'Fuck.' He was silent. 'This is really quick.'

'I know. But your father wants to buy a house with...' I couldn't bring myself to add *Olivia*.

'Does this mean I need to pick up my stuff?' He sounded anxious.

'It might be a good idea to go through it. But of course you don't have to take it all with you. You will always have a place to stay. We'll make sure of that. And I'm sure you can ask Dad to store it for you.' I paused. 'I'm so sorry you're having to do this, Al.'

'It isn't your fault,' he said mutinously.

'There's no point blaming anyone. It's happened.' I didn't want to make this any harder for my boys than it already was. 'Look, I will get another place – eventually. When I get back.' I hadn't overthought any of this; it was almost like someone else had decided for me, that going away was what I needed.

'Where are you going?' Alex sounded surprised.

'I'm not sure yet. But once I have another house, you can leave as much stuff as you like there.'

'It's going to be weird, Mum. You not being there.'

But it was already weird, before this happened. Life hadn't been the same since the boys left. 'I love you Al. And I'll only be a flight away. I can be back in a day if you need me.'

Steeling myself, I then called my father. 'Hi, Dad. I thought I should let you know, I'm going away for a bit.'

'Away?' He sounded bewildered. 'How long for?'

'I'm not sure.' I hesitated. 'I'm going to buy a one-way ticket. I just need a change of scene while I figure out what to do next.' I waited for him to speak. In that moment, I'd have given anything for him to sympathise; to tell me to have a big adventure. That however tough it seemed, life would be OK again.

But he was silent. 'You're not going to fix anything by running away.' There was disapproval in his voice.

'If there was anything to fix, I'd stay,' I said sadly. 'You know I suggested you find a cleaner? I think the time has come, Dad. Like I said, I'm not going to be here.'

I took a car load of stuff to a local charity shop. Then that night, Elena came over.

She looked somewhat doubtfully around the slowly emptying house. 'There's still a lot of stuff.'

'Well, bloody Gareth can pull his finger out. I'm not doing all of it. I've packed.' I nodded towards the rucksack, an old one of Alex's he never used but couldn't bring himself to throw out. 'Most of my clothes have gone to a charity shop.'

Elena looked astonished. 'I have to say I never thought you'd be able to do this.'

'The clothes were the easy bit.' Actually, none of this was easy – but it was done and I wasn't going to dwell on it. 'I just have to decide where I'm going.' I frowned, but while I'd been going through my old letters and photos, wallowing in nostalgia, a song had kept coming back to me. It was one I remembered my mum playing while she was cooking Sunday lunch, when Lizzie and I were young, as suddenly I made my most rash decision yet. 'This might sound mad, but actually, I know where I'm going. To San Jose.'

Elena looked at me in bewilderment.

'You know, El. The song – "Do You Know the Way to San Jose?" By Burt Bacharach and Hal David? Dionne Warwick used to sing it. You must know it.' I frowned at her. 'Everyone's heard of it.' Then I felt myself freeze, because I remembered it playing at Adam's, too, that afternoon I was at his.

'Not me.' She looked curious. 'Where is it?'

'Er...' Faltering, I googled it.

'You're telling me you're going somewhere because of a song from the past and you don't even know where it is? Tilly, even given your obsession with nostalgia, this is crazy.'

But I was on a roll. 'It's in California.' I did know that, by the way. 'And I happen to know British Airways fly there.'

Elena looked amazed. 'When are you coming back?'

'I haven't decided.' I was silent for a moment. 'I suppose the whole point is I need options, El. I'm buying a one-way ticket.' It only came to me as I spoke the words. I looked at my friend. 'I don't want to be tied down to anything. You see, for once, believe it or not, I know what I need to do.' I smiled at her, because at some point over the last days and hours, I'd worked it out.

If I couldn't have the old life I loved, the least I could do is try to rediscover *me* again.

* * *

So much for my best of intentions. After Elena left, I surveyed my rucksack somewhat dismally. I mean, I had no idea how long I was going to be away. There was no way I'd packed enough stuff.

I fetched one of our ancient suitcases – well, not so ancient it didn't have wheels. But it was one of the earlier versions, which meant it was rather like driving a tank without the benefit of power steering. I unpacked the rucksack and repacked the contents in the suitcase, adding more clothes, including a T-shirt of Robbie's that had a hint of his smell and an old scarf that Alex used to wear. Then I piled in some toiletries, a scented candle and my favourite pyjamas. Ridiculous, when you can buy a scented candle almost anywhere. But there was nothing like a few luxurious touches when you were far from home and it felt like the entire world was set against you.

8

There Is a Light

I feel myself pulled back to the present day; like last time, the images of the house fading, thoughts drifting from my mind like a slowly ebbing tide.

Tilly?

Through the hazy whiteness of the hospital, I hear my name.

'Tilly?'

It's as before. I try to force my eyelids open, to shape the faintest word on my lips. I'm aware of a hand taking hold of mine. But as I attempt to flex my fingers, nothing happens.

'She is still not responding.' The voice sounds distant.

As someone shines a light into one of my eyes, suddenly I'm terrified. *I'm here... My mind is working,* I want to cry out. *But I can't move... It's like I'm trapped inside myself.* But another thought comes to me that's even more terrifying. What if I never recover from the fall? If my inability to move is permanent? What if I can't tell my boys how much I love them? If I can't hug them tightly ever again? If I never get the chance to live the rest of my life?

Another voice comes to me, startling me. It's Lizzie's voice. *Hold on, Tills. Don't give up. You're going to be OK.*

9

Leaving on a Jet Plane. Almost...

Of course, when it came to the end of my marriage, there was no way anything of this magnitude was ever going to be easy, and of course, the next morning brought a reality check. One of those *oh shit, what have I done* moments. In fact, I couldn't remember doing anything this rash in the whole of my entire life and doubts were setting in.

A moment of desperation consumed me and in my panic, I called Tallulah.

'I thought I knew what I was doing and now I don't,' I told her.

'Tilly, you're not making sense. Is this going to take long? I have a hair appointment I need to get to.'

'I'm about to book a flight to San Jose,' I said anxiously. 'But I'm terrified I'm making a mistake.'

'Cool.' She sounded impressed. 'I'd love to go there.' She hesitated, then added, 'Which one, by the way?' Then before I could answer, she went on. 'Travelling is the best thing in the world. How on earth can you even imagine it's a mistake?'

'Because...' But as I racked my brains, I couldn't think of a single reason. 'I think I panicked,' I said, feeling calmer again.

'I'm sorry to rush you, but is that it?' she asked. 'Only I really should be going.'

'Of course.' I started to feel foolish. 'Sorry to have kept you.'

'No worries. I wish you were going to be around. It would have been nice to spend some time together. But good for you, doing this.' There was pride in her voice. 'I hope you find what you're looking for.' It sounded as though she was smiling.

'Thank you, Tallulah. Me too,' I said.

I ended the call and booked my flight, only after I'd done it remembering to check the cancellation policy. Just in case. After all, it was good to be sure of your facts. As I was reading it, my mobile buzzed with a text. It was from Gareth.

GARETH

> Two estate agents coming round tomorrow. Just
> checking you won't be there, we don't want a
> repeat of last time.

My calm evaporated as suddenly I was furious. How dared he be so patronising.

TILLY

> I've already told you, I'll be gone by then.

It was less than twenty-four hours away. But I pressed send regardless, before sending another brief but in the circumstances, entirely necessary and to-the-point follow-up.

TILLY

> Fuck off, Gareth.

Making a cup of coffee, it occurred to me that I needed to get rid of food. Getting a bin bag I opened the freezer and stared at it all – the expensive steaks Gareth liked, an unopened chocolate cheesecake that I should have given to someone in need – like my brother-in-law Rick, for instance. I liked to pride myself in always thinking of other people – but look where that had got me.

The thought of Rick brought me up short. I couldn't believe I hadn't told him I was leaving, but then I hadn't seen him for a few days. Aware I needed to tell him I wasn't going to be here, I had a sinking feeling. Knowing how much he'd come to rely on me, it wasn't going to be easy. I picked up my phone and sent him a text.

TILLY

How are you, Rick? Call me.

Putting down my phone, I carried on throwing the food into the bag. This wasn't about being kind to everyone else any more. In any case, the steaks had been there for months – and throwing a cheesecake away amounted to nothing of any significance. It was just a cheesecake, after all, but even so, I was astonished at how bizarrely cathartic it felt.

Presumably he read my text, but while I was still clearing out, Rick turned up. Where Rick was concerned, I'd developed a kind of radar which until recently, had been pretty well honed. I was aware that Rick tried to maintain a balance between constant, but not too constant. When he hadn't been here for several days, it was unusual to say the least.

I glimpsed him through the kitchen window as he came around to the back door, a stooped figure on whose shoulders, it appeared, the cares of the world were resting. Pushing the door open, he stood there, looking apologetic. 'Hey, Tills. Wondered if you have time for a cuppa.'

'Hi, Rick. Sure.' Filling the kettle, I switched it on.

In Rick's eyes, I was a receptacle for all his grievances against the world. It wouldn't have occurred to him to talk to the trees, or a therapist. Why would he, when he had me? I was the person to whom he could talk uncensored and uninhibitedly. As a result of which, I had become privy to the inner workings of Rick's mind. I knew how lost he felt, the unhappiness that seemed to linger long after he left here. I listened, because Rick was lonely and there were times we all needed someone. And there was a part of me that wanted to help.

On any other day, the quick cuppa would invariably have turned into a minimum of two hours of unburdening grief onto me, all without stopping to draw breath, and without so much as pausing to ask how I was. It was a process that would leave me crushed and Rick lighter, invariably and temporarily. And I let him, because I cared. But today was different.

'I'm afraid I only have twenty minutes, Rick,' I said, slightly less sympathetically than usual. After all, when it came to missing Lizzie, he didn't have the monopoly. She was my sister, after all.

I made him a cup of tea, glancing slightly guiltily at the rubbish bag of fridge contents, listening as he started talking. And I knew he was hurting, but I'd heard it all before, almost word for word. The same questions about the pointlessness of why someone as wonderful as Lizzie died so young; when so many mostly lesser mortals continued to walk this planet. About what was the point of any of it. And I agreed with a lot of what he said. But repeating the same thing, over and over, wasn't helping anyone.

His heavy sigh was followed by a five-second silence. 'Makes no sense, does it?'

Poor Rick. In three months, his mental processes had not moved on even the tiniest quantifiable amount. Nor had his need to share it with me. And I was grieving, too – in more ways than he knew. But when Gareth wouldn't have told him about the demise of our marriage, it was hardly Rick's fault he didn't know.

I interrupted him in full flow. 'Rick?' His sad eyes met mine for a moment. 'I'm not sure if you saw it, but I texted you earlier.' I paused. 'You see, there's something I have to tell you.'

As I always tried to, I put myself in Rick's shoes; explained as gently as I could, bearing in mind Rick depended on me and that he didn't have anyone else.

'I can't believe it.' He looked utterly stupefied.

'Gareth wants to sell the house,' I said. 'That's why I'm having a clear-out.' I nodded towards the plastic bags holding the contents of our freezer. 'I'm moving out.'

A look of shock washed over his face. 'You don't think it's a bit quick? I mean, you two have been together for decades. Surely it can't be over.' He looked hopeful for a moment. 'Maybe I should have a word with Gareth – man to man.'

For whose benefit? I wondered somewhat uncharitably. I shook my head. 'Thanks, but we've gone way past that. It's nice of you to offer, but there's no point.' I paused. I could see it from Rick's point of view, that when he would have done anything in the world to have Lizzie back, Gareth and I breaking up took some getting his head around. 'I suppose it's like when you meet the one,' I said sadly, remembering before I met Adam, when I used to think Gareth was the one. 'Like when you met Lizzie. Only in reverse. When you know it's over, you absolutely know, if you get my drift.'

'I'm so sorry, Tilly.' A tear rolled down his cheek. 'I can't bear to think of you being alone.' Something dimly lit up his eyes. 'If you want the spare room at our place, you're welcome, any time.'

In a million years, I couldn't imagine how that would have worked out. Besides, their gorgeous cottage echoed with too many memories of Lizzie. 'Thanks, Rick. That's really kind. But I've decided I'm going away for a bit.' I glanced at the clock on the wall. 'Tomorrow, in fact. I'm sorry, but I have quite a lot to do.'

Still looking shell-shocked, he took the hint. 'I suppose I should leave you to it.'

'Don't worry about me. I'll be fine, Rick.' I paused. 'And I know right now, it's impossible to imagine, but one day, you will be, too.'

He came over and hugged me. 'I'm going to miss you.' Pulling away, he blinked at me. 'Gareth's an...'

'Arse. Yes, I know.' I forced a smile.

Hanging his head, Rick started walking towards the door.

'Rick? Hold on a moment.' My hub-instincts came to the fore one last time as I hurried over to the bag of discarded freezer contents, unable to stop myself as I fished out the cheesecake. 'For you.' I held it out to him, noticing it was already defrosting. 'It was in the freezer. It should be fine for a day or two.'

He took it from me and I watched him walk outside. Standing there, I listened as he started his car and drove away. Rick had a nice car, but these days, even the engine managed to sound sad in some way. As the noise of it faded, I sighed. Of course I loved Rick, in a sister-in-law kind of way, and of course I was sorry for him. Lizzie was his world. But in time, he'd meet someone else. Probably sooner than he could imagine.

As I carried on sorting the house, my new reality descended over me. There were no two ways about it – as chapters go, this was a pretty shit one. But when I thought of Lizzie, I had to accept I was lucky. I was still here. However much I felt sorry for myself, I had to hope what I said was true. That however hard this *now* bit was, however long it took, I would be fine – eventually.

* * *

Later on, it all got slightly surreal as I called the boys to tell them I was leaving tomorrow.

'Way to go, Mum.' Robbie sounded impressed. 'It's really cool you're doing this.'

'Thanks.' I liked how that sounded. 'I'm a little nervous, Rob, but please don't tell your father that.'

'No chance. I'm not speaking to him.' Robbie's voice was bitter. 'I called him last night and told him what I thought of him.'

'Oh Robbie... He is your dad. He might be...'

'A dickhead?'

'Dickhead will do. But he loves you, Rob. Give it time, hey?' There was so much more I could have said about Gareth, but none of it was going to help my boys.

'Mum?' Robbie's voice was warm. 'You sound really good. Have a safe flight. Let me know when you get there, won't you?'

* * *

'Tomorrow?' Alex sounded shocked. 'How long for?'

'I haven't decided, Al.'

'Hang on. You haven't said where you're going.'

Suddenly I realised, I hadn't told Robbie. 'Well, you know that song, "Do You Know the Way to San Jose"?'

'You used to sing it all the time when we were kids!' Alex said. 'What about it?'

'That's where I'm going.' I wondered if he'd get it.

'Wow. Mum, that's awesome.'

'It's an adventure.' Suddenly it felt like a long way away. 'You know, you can still go back to the house – any time you want to.'

'Yeah. I've spoken to Rob – about picking up our stuff.' Alex was more practical than Robbie. 'We're going to come back together.'

'That's a really good idea.' I was aware how strange it would feel to them; grateful neither of them would be there alone. 'I've already packed some things and I've left them at Elena's. Important things, to do with you and Robbie growing up, mostly.' I paused, imagining Alex feeling like I was, about the family home that had always been there, that suddenly wasn't going be. I swallowed the lump in my throat. 'You do know you can come back any time,' I said again. 'Until it's sold? And I will be back. I'm just not sure when, yet.'

'Will you be OK? On your own? Only you've never...' He tailed it off.

'Never been away on my own? No,' I said gently. 'I haven't. I think maybe that's why I have to do this.'

* * *

On my way to see my dad, I gave myself a talking-to. *He won't understand. But that isn't your fault. It's the way he is; the way he always has been. He's never going to change.*

'San Jose?' He frowned. 'That's a long way.' His frown deepened. 'Does Gareth know?'

'It's in California,' I said. 'And Gareth doesn't know. It has absolutely nothing to do with him. Dad, just so you know, he and I are not on speaking terms.' When my dad didn't say anything, I went on. 'You seem to think I've done something wrong. But I haven't, and it wasn't me who wanted anything to change. It was Gareth.'

'He must have had a reason,' my father muttered.

This time, I gasped out loud; my dad's bizarre solidarity with my cheating soon-to-be ex-husband utterly flabbergasting me. 'His reason is he's got his girlfriend pregnant.' I shook my head. 'It's me you should be supporting, Dad. Not Gareth.' Then I had my most brilliant idea. 'I know since Mum died, you've come to rely on me. But I'm sure Gareth will still help you out from time to time. You have his mobile number, don't you? You two have always got on so well.' I paused. 'And there's always Rick.'

My father made a tutting sound. 'Drives me mad, Rick does. Comes here and only talks about himself.'

'He's just lost his wife,' I reminded my father. When it wasn't so long ago my mother died, his lack of empathy astonished me. 'You, of all people, should understand.'

* * *

It was unnerving how little time it took to unravel a life. Even one that had been built up over more than twenty years. By the time I went to bed that night, the fridge and freezer were clean and empty; old clothes and bedlinen had been piled into bags labelled either 'tip' or 'charity shop'. I'd also left detailed instructions for Gareth, about the boys coming to sort through their stuff; about recycling as much as he could of what was left in the house. I finished it off with, *I've taken the contents of our joint account.* It amounted to a few thousand pounds, which he wouldn't like, but along with the money my mother had left me, it would keep me going until the house was sold.

I went from room to room, lingering in the doorways, replaying scenes from the past. Ethereal, wraith-like memories of the boys as kids, of family Christmases; for a moment my doubts returning as I considered that this was all a misunderstanding. That Gareth would come back. That we could get over this.

But my heart had the answer. There was no *we*. No *us*. The house would be sold, a divorce would follow, leaving Alex and Robbie the only links that would bind us.

It hit me hardest when I opened the sitting room door. Instead of seeing an empty space, I conjured the image of a tall Christmas tree laden with decorations, a log fire burning in the fireplace, the boys' stockings hung as they had been on twenty Christmas Eves. I wiped away the tear that rolled down my face. *You're being ridiculous, Tilly,* I told myself. *A sofa is just a sofa. The dining table we've sat around for birthdays and Christmases over the years, it's just a piece of polished wood. You never even liked it that much.*

But the wrench I felt as I thought of never doing any of it again was visceral.

Later that night, I was emotionally and physically drained as I lay in the bed Gareth and I had shared; for a whole host of different reasons, unable to sleep. It seemed no time ago that my life was predictable, that I was a wife and mother, someone who had a job, who whiled away time rereading sympathy cards people sent after Lizzie died – albeit too much time, I can see that now; that since then, I'd left my job and Gareth had moved out.

I visualised the threads I'd held onto all those years, that had drifted away, one by one, until I was forced to admit that I was redundant in every sense of the word.

It wasn't a comfortable feeling; being needed had defined my life. It was who I was and how I saw myself. But slowly it came to me that there was another way of looking at this – at least, I knew that's what Tallulah would have said. And as I eventually drifted off to sleep, I realised what it meant: that for the first time in decades, I was going to be free.

10

What Should Have Been the Happiest Day of My Life

I love *Sliding Doors* – it's one of my favourite movies. The idea that one person's life could play out in two different directions has always made me wonder: *what if*. What if I'd made different choices, if I'd moved to live somewhere else; chosen to be with someone else? Armed with the hindsight that only time can bring, hasn't made me any better prepared for watching a younger version of myself. Instead, it only leaves me questioning why I couldn't understand myself better and kind of fast-tracked my life path; saved myself a whole load of pain.

But maybe I wasn't meant to. I'm starting to get a sense that the things that are playing out in my life, in whatever form that takes, are all part of me learning to find my way.

And in some way, too, maybe that includes now, in this strange place I find myself, unconscious, caught between the past and what is yet to be.

* * *

So it was that in the days leading up to my wedding, as I weighed up my relationship with Gareth, I'd told myself the initial chemistry between us was slow burning into something more lasting. There was the way we'd fitted our lives together, the way our families, our friends, had embraced us as a couple.

It was what I wanted to believe. But then I thought about Lizzie's doubts about us. How I hadn't known, suddenly wondering if my mother had doubts about us, too. Not that it should matter. Only two people mattered in this whole shebang that was unfolding around us – and they were me and Gareth.

Keeping myself busy, I stayed away from places I might bump into Adam, knowing it wouldn't have helped. Then on Thursday afternoon, I drove over to see my parents. When I got there, I found my mother in the garden.

'Tilly!' She looked pleased. 'This is a nice surprise. Just let me finish weeding this bit, and I'll put the kettle on.'

'You don't have to stop, Mum.' I sat on the grass and watched her digging up a particularly obstinate weed. The sun was warm, the garden in glorious full bloom, the results of years of my mother's hard work. 'It looks really lovely out here.' It's true – the borders were filled with lavender and other flowers I couldn't name, but which spilled into each other to give a luxuriant yet subtle mass of colour.

'I must say I am rather pleased with it this year.' Standing up, she looked at me. 'Is everything OK, Tilly?'

'Yes! Of course it is!' But I couldn't meet her eyes.

'It's rather hot for tea. Why don't you sit in the shade and I'll get us a cold drink?' She nodded across the garden towards the table and chairs that were set under the dappled shade of a silver birch tree.

I wandered across the garden, then, sitting down, turned to study the house that had been my childhood home, the peacefulness soaking into me, memories flitting through my head of me and Lizzie growing up, of the family barbecues and summer parties that had taken place here over the years.

'You're miles away.' My mother placed a tray on the table, of glasses of icy lemonade and home-made sponge cake.

'I was just thinking...' I took one of the glasses. 'Where's Dad?'

'He went out for lunch with Richard.' She rolled her eyes. 'I don't suppose I'll see him until tonight. They'll be putting the world to rights – you know what those two are like.' Richard was one of my dad's oldest friends and like Dad, a devout member of the local church. 'So, how are you feeling?'

'About Saturday? I can't wait, Mum. It's going to be an amazing day.' But even I could hear the lack of excitement in my voice.

'It is.' Sitting down, she turned to look at me. 'It's a big day – a wedding always is. Sometimes I think they get a bit out of hand. I mean, it's about you and Gareth spending the rest of your lives together, not the fancy food and wine – and all those frills, I suppose you'd call them.'

I looked at her, completely astonished. I thought she loved all that. 'You're right, Mum. You really are. You shouldn't have gone to so much trouble.'

'I wanted to.' Reaching across, she patted my hand. Then she frowned again. 'For someone whose wedding is forty-eight hours away, you don't look very excited about it.'

I sighed. This was the moment I hadn't wanted, that in another sense, I knew I needed. A moment of honesty, if only I had been brave enough. But I held back. 'I am. I suppose it's just the realisation that it's *such* a big day, and it's almost here.'

She was silent for a moment. 'Before I married your father...' She paused before adding quietly, 'Don't tell him I told you this, but I almost called it off.'

My eyes were like saucers as I looked at her. She'd never so much as hinted at anything like this before. And I'd never questioned my parents' marriage. Not ever. I'd had no reason to. 'Why?' I said, incredulous.

She shrugged. 'I suppose it was fear of getting it wrong. I mean, I knew we loved each other, but how did we both know our feelings wouldn't change? What if I met someone else – or if he did? I couldn't bear the thought of the upheaval of a divorce – it was much more frowned upon in those days.'

'Did you tell Dad all this?'

She nodded. 'Well, most of it. I left out my thoughts about divorce – we both know your father's thoughts on the subject. But we had a good chat. He was quite reasonable about it. But...' She frowned. 'I suppose it was when I realised the hold the church had over him.'

'How did that make you feel?'

She sighed. 'A little daunted, if I'm honest. He's always known it isn't as important to me. I'm sure he hoped in time I'd become as dedicated as he is.'

'But you haven't,' I said quietly.

'No. And he knows. We just don't talk about it. For the most part, I don't let it bother me. No relationship is perfect and I decided that rather than argue with him, it was better to keep the peace.'

And there it was, dragged out into daylight. The elephant in the room. My dad's dedication to the church and all it decrees, including what he considered to be the unspeakable one – divorce; the way my mother had been wary of taking him to task over it, opting instead to keep the peace. A philosophy she'd passed onto me.

I looked at her, flabbergasted. It was another of those *Sliding Doors* moments, when if my mum had made a different decision, if my parents hadn't married, neither I nor Lizzie would have been here. But more than anything, I was trying to get my head around the idea that my mother had been where I was, with the big day looming, questioning whether or not she should be going ahead with it. 'What did Dad actually say to you?'

'That none of us could see into the future, and that we could only make decisions based on what we knew today. Hopefully, we'd work out – and God would help us.'

As she mentioned God, it was on the tip of my tongue to ask what He had to do with any of this. But I didn't want to offend her.

She went on. 'After that, I decided that whatever I did there was a risk. He was right. No one truly knows what the future holds, and there wasn't anything I could do about that.' She smiled. 'I needn't have worried. We've been very happy together.'

'You've never had regrets?' I wasn't sure I wanted to hear the answer, but the words were out before I could stop them.

'No,' she said softly. 'Of course, we've had our moments. But that's to be expected. It will be the same for you and Gareth. What matters is how you deal with them.' She looked at me quizzically. 'It wouldn't be right if you weren't asking yourself some soul-searching questions. It means you're thinking about what you're committing to. And that's a good thing.'

'Is it?' I blurted out. 'I just keep thinking, what if Gareth isn't the one? I'm not sure he wants children, Mum. And I really want them.' Seeing the troubled look on her face, I instantly regretted telling her. But it was too late.

'You're both young,' she said quietly. 'My advice is to iron it out now if it's important to you. But I wouldn't worry too much – everyone wants children eventually!'

I'd taken some consolation from her words, but this close to my wedding, I knew I'd worried her. Yes, Gareth and I could live together relatively easily – we'd already proved that. I thought of my mother's comment again, about everyone wanting children. But I was slightly uneasy. I wanted to believe her – my mum was right about a lot of things, but on the subject of children, I wasn't so sure.

* * *

That evening I went for an evening walk in the park. It felt like a risk because I might bump into Adam. And I couldn't lie to myself – I wanted to see him, just as I wanted to cling onto the dream of what might have been, of a future I could imagine opening up, had a *Sliding Doors* moment actually materialised for us.

But fate had other plans that day. Just as I thought I caught a glimpse of the back of Adam's head, my mobile buzzed in my pocket.

It was Gareth. 'Hey! When will you be home? I thought we could drive out to the river and go to the pub.'

'Sounds lovely. I won't be long.' It was a long time since he'd suggested anything like this. Romantic even – though I happened to know he particularly like the beer they served there.

'Great!' He sounded pleased. 'See you in a bit, then.'

Standing there, I ended the call and put my phone in my pocket, then glanced in the direction of where I thought I'd seen Adam. But in the time I'd been speaking to Gareth, if it was him, he'd gone.

Going home, I brushed my hair and put on some lipstick, then Gareth drove us to the pub. Sitting outside, I watched the little families of waterfowl as he went to order us drinks, then came back with a menu. Passing it to me, he added slightly selfishly, 'Wouldn't mind driving, would you? It would be nice to have more than a pint.'

I could have said, *It would be nice to have more than one glass of wine*. And of course, I didn't want to spoil the mood between us – but it took the edge off what was otherwise a lovely evening, the kind of evening that once, I would have dreamed of spending with someone special, sitting in the sun overlooking the water, eating delicious food. If I was quieter than usual, Gareth didn't notice. Tucking into his steak and chips, he didn't notice either that I only ate a little of my salad. Instead, as I sat there, I was thinking about how we didn't talk. Not about anything important – other than the conversation about having children, which to my mind remained unresolved, while Gareth was acting as if we'd never had it.

It left me feeling trapped. If I brought up the subject again, I knew what Gareth's reaction would be, that he'd fling it back at me for mentioning it when I already knew how he felt. The only alternative was to say nothing – and that's what I chose. Yes, I was my mother's daughter, already walking on eggshells. The alternative, this close to our wedding, meant all hell would have broken loose.

After we'd finished eating, Gareth got up. 'How about we take a walk? It's a beautiful evening.'

I was taken by surprise. It was so unlike Gareth. Berating myself for misjudging him, I felt myself smile. 'Good idea.'

We set off along the footpath that was edged by long grasses. I felt Gareth's hand brush against mine, before he took it in his. It seems stupid to say it, but I felt fleeting, stabbing hope that despite my misgivings, we would have a long and happy future together. That in his own, unemotional way, Gareth cared.

A family of swans came into view and we stopped to watch them glide past us on water that sparkled in the evening sunlight.

'We should come here more often,' Gareth said softly. Then turning, he took my face in both his hands and kissed me. Closing my eyes, in what should have been a magical moment, I kissed him back, searching for the faintest glimmer of how I used to feel.

* * *

Wasn't it obvious enough? Weren't there enough signs? And the answer is well, yes, to all those questions. But it wasn't that simple. I knew that relationships changed. That the early, giddy days of love gave way to something more enduring. And Gareth and I had stood the test of time. That we were together after so long was proof that we had something.

I remember a conversation with my parents, just before Gareth and I moved in together. When I told them, the news had been greeted not so much with disapproval, but with my mother's sideways glance at my father; his silence. My dad didn't mention living in sin, exactly, but he may as well have. He held a view he wouldn't be challenged on, that living together wasn't morally right. It didn't matter that I had my own views. When it came to challenging my parents, the problem was two-fold: my father was intransigent, and I wasn't brave.

Don't get me wrong. They were wonderful, caring parents. I've thought so many times, Lizzie and I were lucky. But we were different people; even as a child, Lizzie had an independent streak that I for some reason lacked.

Oh my God. And I'm sorry, God, that's if you do exist and you happen to be listening to me instead of all the other billions of people. But how the heck has it taken me so long to see this?

* * *

Somehow I got through that week, mostly thanks to Lizzie keeping me sane – and busy. On Friday, we set up hundreds of jam jars of flowers on the tables in the marquee, stringing up some pink and silver bunting Lizzie had acquired at the last minute.

I dismissed Lizzie's idea that I should be getting a massage or a manicure and generally be pampering myself. I knew if I was alone in my own company for too long, there was a very real risk I'd go mad.

Then the evening before our wedding, I piled everything into my car and drove over to my parents' house. I was doing the right thing, I kept telling myself. This was my life now. Real, not some imagined set of maybes with a man I barely knew. I needed to count my blessings, to remember how lucky I was.

But as I pulled up in my parents' drive, I sat there for a moment, thinking about what I was turning my back on. In the brief time Adam and I had spent together, I'd learned how it felt to instinctively know someone. To feel seen for who I was. To not be judged. All things I could never have explained to Gareth because he wouldn't have understood.

Discomfort churned inside me. Then the front door opened, and Lizzie came running out. 'Tilly!'

In jeans and a halter-necked T-shirt, her long hair was messily tied back, her eyes anxious as she came over to me. 'Are you OK?'

Getting out, I nodded. 'I'm fine.' I forced a smile. 'I can't believe it's tomorrow.'

She held my gaze. 'You are sure, aren't you? Because if not, if you want to call it off, it isn't too late. Everyone will get over it.'

As I looked at her, I knew I wasn't sure. But just the thought of calling it off triggered a wave of nausea. Instead, I told myself yet again, that on the eve of committing the rest of their life to someone, it was natural to be having a wobble about things. 'I'm fine. I'm really looking forward to it.' Saying what anyone would expect a bride to say the day before her wedding.

Frowning slightly, Lizzie opened her mouth to speak, closing it again as our mother came walking towards us.

'Tilly.' She kissed me on the cheek. 'You're just in time to eat. Shall we take your things inside?' She went around to the back of the car, then opened it. 'It's going to be the most wonderful day tomorrow. I went to the church earlier. It looks divine! The flowers are just perfect... And the weather forecast is clear skies and sunshine... I've also checked in with the caterers, so you've no need to worry. Everything's going to be just as you wanted it,' she said happily, barely pausing for breath.

I caught Lizzie's eye briefly, before smiling at my mum. 'Thank you,' I said quietly. 'You've done so much.'

'It's your wedding day.' For a moment, she looked surprised. 'I'd do it again in a heartbeat. Now, hurry along. Your father's about to open a bottle of rather nice champagne.' She picked up one of my bags and started walking towards the house.

After grabbing another of my bags, Lizzie linked her arm through mine. 'We haven't finished talking,' she muttered under her breath.

'It can wait.' But it didn't matter what anyone said any more. I could feel time slipping through my fingers like grains of the finest sand. The decision was made. Here, in the bosom of my family, there was nothing more to talk about.

* * *

Now, it seems incredible. Every part of it, not least that I was marrying someone who was more like a best friend rather than a man who made me want to be my best self; who would inspire me to embrace every precious second of my life, to follow my dreams. Adam, Lizzie, they'd both had been right. I should have been buzzing with happiness, boring everyone half to death about Gareth's and my wedding plans.

And I wasn't. A wave of sadness washes over me for the younger me, that I felt so trapped, so obligated. So misguidedly loyal to a man who proved over time that my instincts had been right; that I'd been so unable to do what was right for me. That I couldn't see I was committing to spending my life with a man with whom I was so unaligned in almost every sense.

But I've gone through most of my life adhering to the same philosophy. What the heck's that about? Talk about Tilly-with-her-head-in-the-sand. More than twenty years on, I've been too busy being what other people expect; that hub, as I've always described it, instead of chasing my dreams. The realisation makes me really sad.

* * *

And then it was here. I remember everything about that morning, but watching it all over again, I see what I didn't the first time around. The sun streaming through the window of what had been my childhood bedroom, the beautiful dress I was wearing, which had been altered to fit me perfectly but was now loose because of the weight I'd lost in the last week; my carefully made-up face wrinkling into a frown as I'd thought about the afternoon I'd spent with Adam, the memory of his lips on mine. The realisation that I'd found someone special, the heart-breaking reality that the timing was out, that he was someone I had to let go of.

With just hours to go, I'd been trying to rationalise my feelings again; telling myself that Gareth and I were the real deal, instead of listening to my heart, paying more attention to my doubts.

I watch myself stand in front of the mirror, my eyes wandering disbelievingly over the beautiful dress again – I'd forgotten how slim I was. It was closely fitted and off-white – pure white has always made me look *translucent*, for want of a better word. My long hair was falling in loose curls, some of which were invisibly pinned up, and I was wearing the familiar white gold necklace my mum had worn on her own wedding day.

There was a light knock on the door before it was pushed open and Mum came in. In her floaty mother-of-the-bride dress in shades of green and blue, she looked so proud.

Suddenly I miss her, *so much*. I feel a rush of emotion as I watch her walk towards the old me and stand next to me, her reflection in the mirror smiling at me in one of those precious mother-daughter moments that nothing else came near.

'You look so beautiful,' she said quietly.

'Thank you, Mum.' There had been a lump in my throat. 'So do you.'

She looked surprised. 'Thank you. Lizzie helped me choose it. I'm glad you like it.' But from the way she looked at me, I knew she'd picked up on something. 'Are you feeling all right?'

I remember, as I stood there, wishing I could tell her how I was really feeling. But so late in the day, how could I? 'Just a little overwhelmed,' I said honestly. 'I just want to say...' I paused. 'I'm so grateful to you – to you and Dad.' I turned to her. 'For everything you've done to make today so special.'

'We're your parents. It's our pleasure.' As she smiled, the corners of her eyes crinkled the way I remember. 'All we've ever wanted is for you and Lizzie to be happy. Your wedding day...' She looked wistful. 'I know it's only one day, but it's one of the most memorable days of your life – at least, I hope it will be.'

'It already is, Mum.' The old me turned to her. 'How did you feel? The morning you and Dad got married?'

'So happy.' For a moment, her eyes misted over. 'Of course, I was glad I had that conversation with him. It cleared the air. By the time the big day was here, I knew that it was right.' She took one of my hands. 'What I told you about me and your father...' She hesitated. 'You do know, don't you? It has no bearing on what you and Gareth make of your life together. That's up to you and no one else. Tilly?' It was as though she wanted to say something. 'Never mind.'

Frowning, I touched her arm. 'What were you going to say, Mum?'

'Just some middle-aged musings about marriage that you really don't need to hear – I promise you!' Smiling, she glanced at her watch. 'Heavens. I need to make sure your father is ready.' She looked at me. 'I guess I'll be seeing you at the church.'

'Don't go, Mum...' I rested a hand on her arm. 'Tell me your middle-aged musings. I want to hear them.'

'Oh. They're nothing really. Just some trite nonsense about weathering life's storms, but I'm sure you don't need me to tell you that.' Her smile faded, in its place a frown wrinkling her brow. 'It's a little late to say this, but I've been worried since we talked the other day. And forgive me – I should have asked. But you are sure, aren't you?'

I stared at her, shocked. 'Of course.' Saying anything else would have been tantamount to admitting I was making a mistake. 'Why, Mum? What's brought this on?'

She sighed. 'I suppose I see a lot of me in you. You're a giver.' She smiled. 'Just make sure that lovely man of yours doesn't take you for granted.'

So my mother *did* have doubts. My heart was starting to race as I realised, that it was still possible not to go ahead. But my courage failed me. 'He does – sometimes. But no one's perfect. And we're good, Mum. Honestly we are.'

She rested a hand on my arm. 'Don't let him, Tilly. Marriage has to work for both of you. Never forget that.' She was silent for a moment. She glanced at her watch again. 'Goodness! Look at the time! I should be going.'

'You should. See you there, Mum.' I watched her walk towards the door. Then as she opened it and pulled it shut behind her, it was a defining moment, as though she was closing the door on my childhood.

Panic welled up inside me. Then the door opened again and Lizzie came in. My beautiful, vibrant sister, who had yet to meet Rick; who had no idea her life would be cut short, years, decades earlier than it should have been.

Her face lit up. 'Wow, Tills. You look stunning.'

'Thanks.' I had to admit that for once, in spite of the turmoil I was feeling, I was kind of liking how I looked. I glanced at my sister, in a dusky pink dress that showed off her tan. 'So do you.'

'When you said my dress was pink, I was horrified,' my sister said. 'But you know, I really like it.' Her eyes glanced towards the bed. 'Are those our flowers?' Going over she carefully picked up the two bouquets that had been delivered earlier, my artfully imperfectly shaped posy of pale, scented roses, her smaller one. Coming over, she passed me mine and stood next to me.

Side by side, we gazed at our reflections. 'Thanks for being my bridesmaid,' I said.

'I was hardly going to let you ask anyone else. Especially not Jasmine.'

'It had to be you,' I said honestly. 'We both know Jasmine would have loved to upstage me.'

'She would.' Lizzie was silent for a moment. 'Remember when we were little? I remember us running riot and fighting all the time. We used to drive Mum mad, didn't we?' A smile played on her lips. 'Seems such a long time ago, doesn't it?'

'It does.' Yet in the weirdest sense, our childhood felt like yesterday. A wave of nostalgia washed over me for those days. But so many years had passed, and so many more would follow, filled with things neither of us could have imagined yet.

'Tilly?' She hesitated. 'You are sure you're OK?'

I couldn't believe this. Or could Lizzie and Mum see what I was blind to? 'Mum just asked me the same.'

'She did?' Lizzie's eyes widened. 'What did you say?'

'The same as I'm saying to you. I *am* sure! I think you need to stop asking me.' Saying it as brightly as I could.

'OK, I'll stop!' There was relief in Lizzie's eyes. 'I was guessing you must be, or you wouldn't be doing this. Talking of Mum...' She glanced at the clock on the chest of drawers that I'd had since I was eight. 'I'd better go and find her. She's been going on about not being late.' She paused, smiling as she looked at me. 'You deserve the best day, Tills. And the best life. Don't forget that, will you? Not ever?'

'I won't.' I turned away to hide the tears in my eyes as, trying not to squash my dress, I hugged her.

* * *

And so I relive what really was *the* best day, one in which my mother's carefully orchestrated plans ran completely seamlessly; one in which as my father walked me down the aisle, I banished all thoughts of Adam. It was the beginning of a brand-new chapter, the most exciting one of my life so far. With the man I loved to share it with, come rain or shine, to weather the storms that would come our way – to use Mum's words, because that's just life. We loved each other – or so I was thinking, as I searched for what I'd always seen as love in Gareth's eyes.

Only this time, I notice he doesn't really *see* me, that he's distracted; that his eyes flit around our guests, rest on Lizzie just a tad too long. I feel a wave of shock. Did Gareth fancy my little sister? Is that what she'd wanted to tell me just before she died?

There's another thing about that day. You see, at that point, I didn't know. Nor did Gareth. After our glorious week in Malta, a week that was everything a honeymoon should have been, we came back sun-kissed and happy, never expecting something truly wonderous, and also a little bit scary, was waiting in the wings to rock our worlds.

11

Waiting for the Miracle

When it comes to children, there are those who want them desperately yet for some reason, are unable to have them. While others, it seems, fall pregnant at the drop of a hat. Of course, there are all kinds of scenarios in between. But for some reason, I fell into the latter category, though in many ways it might have been easier if I hadn't. But such was the way my life was destined to unfold.

* * *

'How?' Two months had passed since our wedding; in a white shirt that showed off his fading tan, Gareth looked bewildered.

'I guess the usual way.' I shrugged. 'I can't think how else it could have happened.' I was making a joke of something that was anything but humorous; that was the biggest thing to happen in my life. Thinking of the conversation we'd had not so long ago, I was also worried. But in a sense it felt like a kind of validation, that marrying Gareth had been the right thing to do, because now, we were going to be a family.

The colour bleached from his tan. 'But you can't be.'

'That last night of our honeymoon… I don't think we were as careful as we might have been.' I paused. 'And I know it's sooner than we planned. But it will be amazing,' I said gently. 'This time next year, we'll have a baby.'

Already I wanted to tell everyone, never mind that it was early days. But the joy I'd felt was marred by Gareth's silence. At the time, I'd told myself that he'd get his head around it. We were married. We'd agreed we wanted children. OK, so this was sooner than he wanted, but now that it had happened, I wanted to believe that he'd come around to the idea.

After I'd broken the news, an uneasy silence had fallen between us. Then that evening, while I was cooking, Gareth came into the kitchen.

'Tilly? Look, we really need to talk about this.' He sounded far from happy.

'Gareth, I know it's happened faster than we planned.' As I looked at him, I frowned. 'What is it?'

'I thought we'd agreed to wait,' Gareth said. 'Look at us. We live in a small flat. We both work. We're hardly ready to be parents.'

'I know. But it's a bit late to say that now,' I said.

'Tilly…' Gareth spoke in a voice I hadn't heard before. 'I'm not sure about this. Like really not sure.'

A cold feeling came over me. 'What are you saying?'

'Having a baby is going to change our lives.' He sighed. 'I thought we'd have a few years to do our own thing. I wanted to have those years.'

'We can still make plans,' I said persuasively. 'It's just that we'll have a baby with us.' I frowned at him. 'Life doesn't stop when babies come along, Gareth.'

'Babies change everything.' He folded his arms, his face was unreadable.

'In a good way,' I said quietly, sitting down next to him. 'I thought you'd be pleased. It takes two to make a baby, Gareth.'

'You think I don't fucking know that?' he said angrily. 'Did that conversation we had mean nothing?' He stood there, silent for a moment. Then he turned to look at me. 'I'm sorry, Tilly. I know you won't agree. But the way I see it, this just isn't the right time.'

I stared at him, shocked. 'What do you mean by that? I'm pregnant, Gareth. It's not like there's any going back from this.'

'There are options,' he said tightly. 'Maybe we need to seriously consider them.'

Getting up, I felt sick as I folded my arms around myself. 'You're talking about terminating the pregnancy?'

He shrugged. 'It's one option. You should think about it – after all, this isn't just about you.'

I was gobsmacked. 'This isn't just about you, either.'

Refusing to look at me, he picked up his keys. 'I need to get some air. I'm going out.'

'Where?' Suddenly, I felt powerless. 'You can't go out. I'm cooking supper – and we need to talk about this.'

'I need to clear my head.' As he went out to the hallway, I heard the sound of the door opening and closing.

Standing there, I was in shock. Then I felt a tear trickle down my cheek. There was no way I was terminating my pregnancy just to suit Gareth's lack of readiness for fatherhood. I mean, we were married. We'd talked about having children. Admittedly, it was sooner than we'd planned. But his response had shocked me.

I held my hand protectively over my belly. I couldn't believe that Gareth cared so little. If it had been Adam... Yes, I barely knew him. But I knew he wouldn't have behaved the way Gareth had just now.

The magnitude of what I'd committed to was catching up with me. Here I was, just eight weeks into our marriage, and already I had cause to seriously question it. *But I'd had doubts before*, I reminded myself. I had no one to blame for the position I found myself in. No one, that was, but me.

It was a major red flag in our relationship, one I kept to myself, pinning on a smile when we met up with Lizzie or my parents, determined that none of them would know what was going on between me and Gareth. I was also waiting to have my twelve-week scan. But after my parents had organised our magical wedding and spent a small fortune on it, I couldn't bring myself to disappoint them.

Meanwhile, behind closed doors, Gareth and I were at an impasse. To me, terminating my pregnancy just felt wrong. Meanwhile, for the first time being totally honest with me, he admitted he didn't want children – not just now, but ever. And what saddened me most was that had I known this for sure before the wedding, I knew it would have been the dealbreaker.

I held onto the hope that Gareth would get over the shock and change his mind. That we'd sit down one day and he'd apologise, tell me he'd been an arse. That of course he wanted children; that we'd get back to where we were before I was pregnant. That he'd do his best because we were a family.

Waiting in vain, I watched him go about day after day with a face like a thundercloud. Not sure I could endure much more of this, I thought about leaving him, bringing my baby up as a single mother. I had all the love in the world for this child I was carrying. It didn't need Gareth's love.

* * *

But if things were bad between us, a month later, they were about to get a whole lot worse.

'Twins?' He looked utterly stupefied. 'Are you sure?'

'Yes.' Knowing this would only multiply his misgivings, my stomach churned nervously as I watched his face. 'I had a scan this afternoon.' Not wanting his negativity to ruin the occasion, I'd gone alone. 'We're having twins.'

'Jesus.' He stared at me disbelievingly. 'Have you even thought about how we're going to afford this?'

We would manage, of that I was in no doubt. People did – and yes, the flat was small. But babies didn't need a lot of room. Not at first, at least.

With some trepidation, I broke the news to my parents, who, of course, were over the moon. Somehow they remained oblivious to Gareth's feelings. But I guess it wouldn't have occurred to them that he would be anything other than delighted.

It was Lizzie, however, who got it out of me that things were far from right. 'What do you mean, he doesn't *want* kids?' she demanded. 'Bit fricking late, wouldn't you say?'

'He didn't tell me until after I was already pregnant,' I said miserably. 'Now, he's acting like it's some kind of immaculate conception that was nothing to do with him.'

'He's a fucking arse.' Lizzie looked furious. 'He doesn't deserve you, Tills. He really doesn't.' She paused. 'You know what you should do, don't you?' Her eyes were resolute. 'Leave him and come and live with me.'

'You're the best.' There was a lump in my throat. 'But your flat is smaller than ours. And I can't divorce him – we've been married four months. It's no time.'

'The sooner the better, I say.' She looked at me. 'Have you talked to Mum about this?'

I shook my head. 'I can't, Lizzie. Can you imagine what it would do to her? No. I have to find a way through this.'

She came over and put her arms around me. 'If you change your mind, I'm here. I'll always be here.'

Until the end, Lizzie was always there for me. Since, of course, I've had to get on without her. But back then, neither of us could have imagined a time she wouldn't be here. In my mind, I'd pictured her as an adoring aunt, lavishing love on her nieces or nephews, watching them grow up. To the boys, she'd been all of those things.

Once or twice around that time, I went for a walk, half hoping I'd bump into Adam. I knew that with my pregnancy obvious, it would draw a clear line under whatever it was that existed between us. But fate clearly had its own plan and I never saw him.

* * *

I had no way of knowing that once the news of my pregnancy with the twins broke, my parents would provide a solution to our financial concerns. Unusually, my father was alone when he came around to our flat.

'I was hoping to have a word – with both of you.'

'Gareth's not back yet, Dad.' I couldn't bring myself to tell him that these days, when he wasn't working, Gareth was usually to be found in the pub.

'In that case, perhaps you'll tell him I wanted to give you this.' Reaching into his pocket, he took out something and passed it to me.

I took it from him, realising it was a cheque for a large sum of money. Large enough for a deposit on a house. I stared at it. 'You can't do this, Dad.'

'It will all be yours and Lizzie's one day. Your mother and I thought, what with you having twins, it might come in useful now. This flat is jolly nice, but you're going to need a little more space.' He stopped. 'Hey, there's no need to cry.' He frowned. 'Is everything OK?'

I couldn't stop the tears pouring down my cheeks. There was no way Gareth deserved my parents' generosity, but I couldn't tell my dad that. Instead, I was thinking of the difference this would make, not just to us, but to the twins. 'It's just pregnancy hormones.' Wiping my face, I looked at him. 'Thank you, Dad. This is so generous of you both. You're right about this flat – it's way too small. I can't tell you what a difference this will make.'

'It was always going to be your money,' he said. 'Your mother and I thought it made sense for you to have it now.'

'Thank you.' I hugged him.

I was conflicted; didn't want money to be the sole reason for Gareth to stop acting like an arse. When I showed him the cheque, he was silent. He knew he'd upset me. He muttered a few words of gratitude, but even knowing we could now afford a family-sized house, he couldn't bring himself to apologise.

It should have been the time of our lives – searching for our dream home, knowing that the arrival of the twins in a few months would make our family complete. But after an initial truce, Gareth continued to act like a sulky child. Meanwhile, wanting our children to grow up with both their parents, I was the classic enabler, continuing to make allowances for him.

Now, it seems insane. But if I could go back... Was it worth it? If I'd known how the future would work out, would I have stayed? *Sliding Doors* had never felt so relevant as I pictured the choices I had back then: staying with Gareth, or life without him.

Determined we'd stay together, I continued to look for houses – with my dad's generous cheque and our combined salaries, we could afford a home with enough space for our family to grow into. I eventually found the perfect place, Gareth reluctantly agreeing that it ticked all the boxes. But even after our offer was accepted, he remained distant.

And so we moved into what was to become our family home, the house the boys grew up in. The one that much later on, I didn't know that Gareth would want to take over with the woman he left me for.

With a couple of months before the babies were due, I threw myself into decorating, helped by Lizzie who made it very clear what she thought about Gareth.

'He fricking doesn't deserve this,' she said, sanding a door even more ferociously.

'I'm trying not to think of it like that,' I said. 'I'm thinking of the twins.'

She stopped sanding, then turned to look at me. 'It's so exciting.' Her eyes were bright as they wandered to the expanse of my belly. 'You have two babies in there,' she said with wonder, as if she'd only just found out. 'That husband of yours better come to his senses, or he'll have me to answer to.'

In my bubble of impending motherhood, I didn't stop to consider that maybe Gareth felt trapped. That he, too, felt our marriage had been a mistake. That his carefree life as a young man had transited overnight into responsible adulthood, and albeit for different reasons, he was struggling every bit as much as I was.

Oh, to see ourselves as others see us. But isn't everything easier retrospectively? As I observe the single-mindedness of our younger selves, I glimpse our inability to see things from each other's point of view. The quickly formed opinions we chose not to question: mine that Gareth was shallow; Gareth's, that I was selfish for wanting what he didn't.

* * *

As my pregnancy went on, I told myself that once the twins were born, Gareth wouldn't be able to resist them. He'd wonder what he'd made such a fuss about. And now and then, usually after a few beers, he'd apologise, explaining he was scared about what parenthood would do to our lives. I tried to persuade him he'd feel differently when the babies were born. But if anything, the distance between us was growing wider.

One night when he came in late, I was sitting in the kitchen crocheting a baby's blanket. The dark look that crossed his face sent shivers down my spine.

'We need to talk, Gareth,' I said quietly. 'I can't go on like this.'

'Not now,' he said shortly, turning his back on me. 'I've had a long day.'

'So have I.' I paused. He seemed to forget that as well as working, I was growing our babies. 'Gareth? Do you want a divorce?'

He froze in the doorway. Then he turned to look at me. 'Is that what you want?'

'Can't you answer my question?' I put down my crochet. 'It's obvious you don't want to be with me.'

'I'm in a situation I never wanted.' He couldn't meet my eyes.

'You've made that all too clear. But it doesn't change the fact that we're going to be parents.' I got up and fetched a glass of water. 'You should have told me how you really felt before the wedding.'

'I did,' he said heatedly.

'You didn't.' I tried not to sound angry. 'What you said was you didn't want children straight away. That it would be better if we waited a few years. You said we needed a bigger house, which thanks to my parents, we now have.' It was all true. 'But it was never about the house, was it?'

'What would you have done if I had told you before the wedding?' he said coldly. 'Cancelled it?'

I was silent for a moment. 'Maybe I would have,' I said quietly. 'But there's no point going over it again. You've made it abundantly clear how you feel about becoming a father, even though you are going to be one and there's nothing you can do about it. I suppose what it comes down to is, I've had enough of being treated like this.'

'You've had enough?' He stared at me. 'You have a nerve, Tilly. You're absolutely right – there is nothing I can do about this. But it was you who presented me with this... this... *situation*, and just expected me to be happy about it.'

'This situation is not entirely of my doing.' I was starting to get upset. 'My eggs, your sperm, in case you've forgotten...'

'Of course I haven't fucking forgotten.'

'Then stop acting as though I've done something wrong.' My voice was shaking. 'In a couple of months' time, the twins will be here.'

Gareth folded his arms. 'I don't need reminding.'

I fought back the urge to slap him. 'This is crazy.' I stared at him, wondering how I ever thought him good-looking. 'We shouldn't have got married, should we? It was a mistake.'

As we both stood there, his silence told me everything I needed to know.

'I'm moving out.' There was a lump in my throat. 'I'll go and stay with my parents. We can figure out what to do with the house after the babies are born.' I held my hands protectively over my belly. 'It's hard enough that my body is supporting three of us at the moment. But we're better off apart than living together like this.'

I remember Gareth saying nothing; that I would have given anything for him to have a change of heart. In the silence between us, that was what I was hoping for. But now, I know how his mind works, that he wasn't conjuring a heartfelt apology; he was doing the maths. Working out how much money he had to lose.

'You don't have to,' he said reluctantly.

I stared at him. 'You're going to have to do better than that.' As I watched him, a defeated look came over him.

Coming over, he sighed. Looking up, he met my eyes. 'I don't want you to go, OK?'

'Why is that, Gareth? Because you don't want my parents to know how unsupportive you're being – when they've bankrolled the deposit for the house we've just bought? Or because it shows you up as the weak, self-centred person you really are?'

Hurt flickered in his eyes. 'Is that how you see me?'

'Yes.' I wasn't going to lie. 'It is. I didn't used to. But now... Things have been said. Things we can't undo.' By *we* I meant *him*. 'If we're going to stay together, our best hope is to try and put the past behind us. We're about to be parents. I want to give our children everything they need. Security. Comfort. Love. Hopefully, once they're here, you'll want that, too.'

'So do I.' But he didn't sound convincing. It was clearly only the maths working in favour of me staying. 'Look. I know I've let you down. I just wasn't expecting to feel like this.'

It was the closest he'd come to an apology, but there was no sincerity, no emotion in his words. 'We're running out of time before the babies are born. We need to make a decision.' My voice shook. 'We stay here and do this together. Or we sell the house and I do it without you.'

I waited for him to respond, the length of silence telling me everything I needed to know. I was still convinced it was better to do this with Gareth. But even so, I'd reached my limit. 'I love you, but I don't need you, Gareth.'

Watching myself, I can't believe that after everything he'd said, I was talking about love. But I can remember at the time, how desperate I felt.

It seemed to shock him out of his lethargy. 'Are you saying *you* want a divorce?'

I shook my head. 'No. I'd prefer us to be a team and do this together – for the sake of the twins. But if you can't...' I shrugged. 'Then I guess it's inevitable that's what comes next.'

* * *

There are many kinds of love. But oh, how foolish I was, for mistaking this as one of them; for not seeing that what he wanted most was a claim on the house. Now, it's obvious. But what staggers me most about that time, is that when all this was going on, we'd been married less than a year. If only we could have been honest with each other; both of us must have known that as long ago as back then, there wasn't enough between us.

12

A man is a poor creature compared to a woman.

— HONORÉ DE BALZAC

Don't get me wrong. I'm actually not having a dig at Gareth, this time. And I'm all too aware that I'm far from perfect, too. But when the twins made their entrance into the world, at least I was devoted, putting my babies first, something Gareth would forever have been incapable of. From those first moments of mother-hood, those boys became my everything; compensated for what was lacking between me and Gareth. And once they were here, I couldn't think about anything else.

* * *

'Look at their tiny hands.' Lizzie's voice was filled with wonder. 'And their tiny noses. And teeny little toes.'

'I know.' I couldn't keep the pride out of my voice.

'Don't look much like Gareth, do they? Thank God,' Lizzie

added with feeling. 'Oh, Tilly. They are the most adorable little creatures I've ever seen.'

Those first months of motherhood were both lacking in sleep and full of wonder. They were also taken up with washing. They were exhausting and they pushed our marriage to new limits, yet they were probably also the reason Gareth and I stayed together. Having two tiny humans entirely dependent on us meant there was little time to think about ourselves.

There were the most heart-warming moments – when a tiny Robbie gazed at Gareth and gave him a gummy smile that his father didn't appreciate; when Alex first uttered the word, *mum-mum*.

'He's teething,' Gareth said dismissively, as Alex thrust one of his tiny fists into his mouth.

'That was definitely *mum*,' I said indignantly.

The presence of the twins in our lives had papered over the rift between us. There was no way of knowing how long it would last – whether the paper would thicken over time; if we would endure. Or whether the next row would gouge another split and be the end of us.

In other words, we were fragile. It broke my heart. I mean, we had these adorable babies. It didn't get better than that, did it? But after Gareth's self-confessed ambivalence towards parenthood, I felt a claim over the twins, as though my feelings about motherhood had decreed me a right that he had yet to earn.

I was grateful he supported us, that he slept through the nights meaning I had the dark hours with my babies all to myself. *Why did I stay?* I asked myself many times while the boys were growing up, only to push the question from my mind. But this wasn't just about me; having children complicated everything a thousandfold.

Meanwhile, Adam was no more than a distant memory, ever

since I'd discovered he'd moved away. It's true about the lies we tells ourselves, our tangled webs that catch us out. I never told anyone at the time, but when I was twelve weeks pregnant, the morning of my scan, I went back to Adam's house. I know how bad it sounds. I mean, what kind of pregnant woman does such a thing? My only defence being, and it wasn't strong, that I wasn't a happy one.

Apart from the time I glimpsed the back of his head, I hadn't seen Adam since the days before my wedding. That day, I figured it was in the lap of the gods as to whether he would be at home or not. As fate would have it, when I knocked on the door, it was opened by a stranger.

'Hi.' I tried not to notice my heart plummeting. 'Is Adam home?'

The guy frowned. 'Adam? I think you've got the wrong place.'

He went to shut the door but I pushed a hand against it. 'But he lived here – about three months ago.' I was about to go on, to tell him about the windowsill of miniature cactus plants, about Adam's beautiful eyes. But I stopped myself.

The guy gave me a strange look. 'You mean that journalist guy? He left a couple of months back. I can't tell you where he went, I'm afraid. He didn't leave a forwarding address.' He paused, as if he was going to say something else, then thought better of it. 'Would you excuse me?'

I stood there as he closed the door, a feeling of powerlessness descending over me. Quite what I'd been hoping for by going there, I couldn't put into words. All I did know, with certainty, was I hadn't found it.

On the way back to the flat, I stopped in the park and sat on a bench under a tree. Around me, the dark greens of late summer had turned to shades of gold, a scattering of leaves on the grass. I felt the coolness of a breeze that heralded the change of the season, as in the strangest way, it was as though I could sense it. *Adam had gone.* I didn't know when or where. And I knew I shouldn't have cared. But all I could feel was this well of emptiness.

It's one of the saddest things in life to never have tried; to not know how things might have turned out, had the timing been different, had they been given a chance. I told myself that Adam and I were simply not meant to be, and this time I had to believe it. I allowed myself to wallow in the sadness I felt, completely forgetting that had I been open to a future with him, Adam most likely would have been there for me. But as I made it very clear at the time, I hadn't been.

Anyway, it was just as well. I was pregnant, wasn't I? My future lay with Gareth, I reminded myself as I walked away, back to the flat. We were going to be a family.

* * *

Immersed in those early years of motherhood, I never imagined them ending. That my chubby, tousled-haired little warriors would go to school, make friends, join football teams. Grow into teenagers, battle an adolescent self-consciousness neither of them had had before. Learn to drive; go to uni.

But we don't, do we? I mean, motherhood is a whirlwind there's no stepping out of. And why would I have? Being a mother was the best thing that ever happened to me.

In all this, it's fair to say that Gareth's part was, well, just that. A part. A smallish one, which extended to kicking a ball around the garden when he was in the mood. He wasn't a bad father. He just wasn't a particularly engaged one, his strengths peaking as the boys got older, amounting to helping Robbie put up shelves in his bedroom or showing Alex how to fix a puncture.

In short, Gareth's emotional disconnect extended to his children. Never was it more apparent than during one of the few parent–teacher evenings at school he came with me to.

'Why is Alex studying art?' He seemed mystified.

'Alex is creative,' I said as though explaining to a stupid person. 'He loves it and he's really good at it.'

'Waste of time,' Gareth said dismissively. 'I'm going to have a word with him about it.'

'Please don't.' I stared at my husband. 'It's important to him. In any case, you have no idea what Alex is interested in.'

'Rubbish. He's my son. Of course I do.' He frowned. 'You can't stop me, Tilly. I'm his father, and this is important.'

'I know it is,' I said wearily. 'But Alex is fifteen. It's his life.' I wanted to explain to him that he couldn't maintain the distance he kept and expect the boys to suddenly take notice of him. But I gave up. The more I battled Gareth, the harder he fought back – and in this case, I knew it would be Alex who got the brunt of that.

There were other, similar episodes with the boys when Gareth was compelled to express his opinions. Opinions that were uninformed, because most of the time, he took no interest in them.

* * *

It was in the midst of the boys' teenage years that I reached another crisis point. Not because anything major had happened. It hadn't. It was more the weight of the years passing, the loneliness I felt in my marriage.

I remember talking to Elena about it, trying to describe the emptiness I was feeling. My dilemma, that the boys needed both their parents. It wasn't as though anything had changed. It was more like my soul was deeply weary. And that was when the Universe stepped in.

I'd gone into town to pick up something for one of the boys when totally unexpectedly and out of the blue, I bumped into Adam – coincidentally not far from the bar where I had my hen night.

'Oh.' My heart missed a beat. As I stared into his eyes, I couldn't look away. I couldn't believe it was him. 'Hi.'

'Tilly.' He gazed at me. 'What a surprise.' His face crinkled as he smiled. 'You look great. I mean, it's great to see you. How are you?'

'It's great to see you too.' I felt warm, deep inside. Alive, too, in a way I wasn't used to. 'I'm good. How are you?'

'Good.' Still smiling, he was as gorgeous as ever. 'How's Gareth?'

I was taken aback; astonished that after all these years, he'd remembered Gareth's name. 'He's OK.' My warmth dimmed, but then it was back. 'We have two sons. Twins. They're fifteen – swotting for exams and growing up.'

'So he got over it,' Adam said quietly. 'The children thing.'

I nodded. 'Kind of.' It was easier than saying, *not really*; that we almost broke up over it. Instead, I changed the subject. 'How about you? What brings you back here?'

'I had to check up on one or two things.' He didn't elaborate. 'I'm glad you're OK,' he said. 'I've often wondered how things worked out for you.'

My heart skipped another beat. There was so much I wanted to say to him. That I went to see him, but he'd moved away. That barely a week passed when I hadn't thought about him. But then he looked past me as a woman joined him. 'Tilly, this is Louise. My wife.'

I was stunned for a moment, which was ridiculous when I

thought about it after. It wasn't like I'd imagined Adam would stay single. It was just that face to face with the reality of his real-life actual wife felt very odd to say the least.

She held out a hand. 'Hi. Nice to meet you.' Louise was, well, actually, a bit like me. A similar height, similar build, similar clothes even. Hair a similar shade of brown. But what she had that I didn't have was this sense of peace that seemed to radiate from her. She also had Adam.

'It's nice to meet you too.' Shaking her hand, I held her gaze for a moment; wondered if Adam had ever mentioned me, before deciding it would be better if he hadn't. 'Well, I should be getting on. You know, things to do before I pick the boys up, and all that.' I beamed at both of them.

* * *

It should have been the closure I needed, even after all these years. Should have made me appreciate what I had. My boys, my lovely home, my friends. In many ways, I knew I was lucky.

But seeing Adam had brought back memories. Memories that until now, I'd buried. And the thing was, pulled out into sunlight, they were beautiful.

13

A journey of a thousand miles begins with a single step.

— LAO TZU

That day I met Adam, I spectacularly misread the signs. Instead of it reminding me of how it was possible to feel, I saw it as proof that Adam and I would never be together; ignored the truth that there wasn't enough between Gareth and I. Time would tell, leaving me two decades later, alone; about to embark on an adventure that should have felt like the trip of a lifetime, but instead felt like the biggest wrench from everything I'd always known.

The day of my departure arrived and after a night of fragmented sleep, I was awake long before my alarm went off. There were two hours to spare before my taxi arrived – I'd turned down Elena's offer to drive me to Heathrow. It felt important to me to do this alone.

I got up, trying not to think too much as I dressed, then packed up the last of my things. But I was aware of a change in the house, almost as though overnight it had emptied itself of us. After dragging my case downstairs, I made myself a cup of coffee, my eyes filling with tears as I wondered when I'd be coming back; or whether the house would be snapped up. Unhelpful thoughts that were interrupted – thankfully – when the taxi turned up.

Now that I was actually doing it, there was a significance I hadn't anticipated to be closing the door for the last time – and doing it without anyone there to shore me up. Mistake number one, as it happened, because in the event, it didn't quite go like that.

'Blimey. How long are you going for?' As the taxi driver heaved my suitcase into the back of the taxi, I was already wishing I'd stuck to the rucksack.

'I don't know.' The words stuck in my throat.

He looked at me anxiously. 'Are you sure you're OK?'

'Yes... No... Yes...' I howled into a handful of already sodden tissues, dragging my eyes away from the pale pink New Dawn rose growing up the front of the house, a present from my parents when we'd first moved here. 'There's just so many memories in that house... It's really difficult...'

'Here.' He handed me a dry tissue, as though he'd seen it all before. 'You can't go off on a trip in a state like this. Sort yourself out. There's plenty of time.'

Mistake number two was believing him. By the time I'd redone my minimal-for-travelling make-up and we'd actually set off, the finest layer of mist was settling in the air. Sitting back, I watched it thicken to form fog, the landscape suddenly eerily monochromatic, as a shocking thought struck me. What if the fog was really bad and the airport closed?

'Jolly good thing aircraft can auto-land these days.' The taxi driver read my mind. 'Back in the day, you wouldn't have been going anywhere.'

'Lucky for me.' But as I looked outside, barely able to see the other cars, I was apprehensive. 'Are we nearly there?'

'Six miles to go,' the driver said cheerfully. 'Told you we had plenty of time.'

I sat back, fantasising briefly about the duty-free shopping I'd built in time for and the bottle of perfume I'd planned to treat myself to; relaxing for all of a few seconds until we left the motorway and on the slip road, the traffic ground to a halt.

'Probably been an accident,' the driver said, fiddling with his radio.

But as nothing moved, I was starting to panic. Then suddenly I was wondering if maybe this was a sign – that I shouldn't have been going; that Rick was right about things happening too quickly. That if I stayed, Gareth would leave Olivia, our lives would go back to how they used to be. 'Seriously, if we don't get there soon, I'm going to miss my flight.'

'You won't be the only one,' he said unhelpfully. 'Why don't you look on your phone? Heathrow departures? Check if it's still leaving on time – if you're worried?'

I couldn't believe I hadn't I thought of that. Fumbling, I brought up the British Airways flight status page, my heart jumping for joy as my flight came up. 'It's delayed! Yay! Looks like there's plenty of time! I'm going to make it!'

The traffic eventually started crawling, the final mile seeming to take longer than the rest of the entire journey. But no matter. We reached the terminal building. Getting out, relief filled me that I was there. And so, by the looks of it, were thousands of other people, all milling around on their phones or looking at their watches.

While the taxi driver lifted out my suitcase, my relief vanished and a sinking feeling took me over as I realised, it looked like none of us were going anywhere.

'Good luck,' the taxi driver said. Frowning, he glanced around, scratching his head. 'Though I must say I've never seen it quite like this before.'

Which didn't exactly make me feel any better as I dragged my case through the crowd and found a check-in desk, where I joined the queue of outraged people behaving as though the airline itself was responsible for the weather. I was still trying to stay hopeful – that the weather would change; that when it came to fog, British Airways planes had super powers. Then I reached the front and it was my turn.

The check-in person looked apologetic. 'I'm afraid your flight's been cancelled.'

My heart felt like a plummeting rock. 'It can't be. Don't you have auto-land, or something? It's only a bit of fog.'

He frowned. 'The problem is the aircraft operating your flight has been diverted to Paris. The whole of the UK is fogged out. The only flights getting in are those that can auto-land, as you said.' He gave me a look. 'I'm very sorry but yours isn't one of them.'

So much for super powers. I stared at him stupidly. 'So what do I do now?'

He shrugged. 'Go home and come back tomorrow. There's another flight at the same time, and another to San Francisco a little later. Hopefully, the weather will have cleared by then. We'll try to get you on one of them.'

Suddenly I felt helpless. 'What if you don't? Get me on it, I mean?'

'You can apply for a refund. I'm sorry, madam, there isn't anything else I can do right now...'

I couldn't believe this was happening. Not now – to me. Not given everything else that was going on in my life. 'You don't understand,' I said quietly. 'My husband has left me, I don't have my job… This was supposed to be an adventure. The biggest adventure of my life.' Words were bursting out of me. 'And your stupid, horrible airline, not to mention the stupid, selfish fog, have completely ruined everything…' I broke off, knowing I was being unreasonable; my voice wavering.

'I really am very sorry, madam,' he said in a way that made it clear he wasn't remotely interested in my life. Then he passed me a leaflet. 'This tells you everything you need to know about claiming a refund. Have a really nice day.'

Not sure if he was being sarcastic, I crumpled up the leaflet and shoved it into one of my pockets. I briefly thought about going home, then of the empty fridge, before remembering the estate agent was due there this afternoon. Then I thought of my boys, waiting to hear where their mother had made it to and I felt a new surge of resolve. I wasn't going to let them down. I wasn't going to let me down, either. If planes were out of the question, I was getting a train!

Where to? The question stopped me in my tracks. There was rather a large body of water between here and San Jose. But it didn't matter. I could go anywhere, as long as it was away from this grim, fogbound little country; from Gareth and his floozy. After all, I wanted an adventure. No way was some minor trifle like the weather going to stop me.

Anyone who knows me would say, I am not known for being impulsive. This new, spontaneous Tilly was someone I was unfamiliar with. But I had to say I was getting to like her.

For the second time, I was cursing myself for not sticking to my guns and travelling light as I made my way through the airport to the Underground. While the train sped towards London, I googled routes to Paris and booked a seat on the Eurostar from St Pancras station, then sat back and tried to decide what next.

With San Jose out of the picture, at least for now, I contemplated heading for the Côte d'Azur, Barcelona, Italy, even Greece,
a surreal feeling taking me over knowing I could pick any one of
them and in a matter of hours, a day or two tops, actually be
there.

The closer to London I got, the more crowded the train
became. But then the chances were I wasn't the only one who'd
been forced to change their plans. After arriving at St Pancras
and checking in for the Eurostar, I found my seat and it wasn't
long before the train set off.

As the Eurostar headed south towards the coast, for the first
part of the journey the landscape was blanketed in fog, but just a
short way into France on the other side of the English Channel, I
took it as a sign that I was on the right track when it rapidly
cleared. Gazing out of the window, I watched the fields and little
French towns flash past, aware of the miles falling behind me, the
two hours it took passing rapidly before the train slowed down as
we arrived in Paris.

Another time, I would have thought about spending a day or
two here, but today, after British Airways almost managing to
scupper my escape plan, it was about putting maximum distance
between me and Gareth. Finding a taxi, I headed for Gare de
Lyon, where I bought another ticket – another impulse purchase
– this time to Barcelona. Then with remarkable ease, I found the
platform and waited for the train.

But as I stood there, I realised it wasn't such an impulse
purchase and that the seed of a memory had dislodged itself from
a far-flung corner of my brain. Because Adam had talked about
Barcelona – he'd been there several times in his capacity as a
travel writer.

Suddenly I knew it was where I was meant to go. Maybe the

Universe was weaving its unpredictable magic around us again; maybe Adam was, at this moment, headed there, too.

The next part of my journey was effortless. Far from the crammed carriages I'd been expecting, they were half empty and I found my allocated seat next to a window. As the train got going, I WhatsApped the boys.

TILLY

> Hey guys, I thought I'd update you. My flight was cancelled – heavy fog. So I'm on a train to Barcelona. Enjoying it! Should be there early evening. Hope you've both had a good day. Love you loads and loads xxxx

As the steward passed with his trolley, I bought an overpriced baguette and a quarter-bottle of wine. Sitting back, I drank a toast, to this new chapter, to adventures, thinking, *Screw you, British Airways*, as my phone buzzed.

It was Alex.

ALEX

> Keep us posted Mum! Enjoy! xx

Followed shortly by Robbie.

ROBBIE

> Oh wow! Safe travels. Hope the weather's better there than here xx

I was suddenly mindful of what Tallulah had said, about the difference it makes when there's a flow to life. And that, it seemed, was what was happening now. All the delays and obstacles meaning I was on a train heading somewhere I hadn't planned to be, but that wasn't the point. I was having an adventure in every sense.

But as I sat back and watched the houses whizz past,

suddenly this crazy day, the weeks, months, even the last two years since Lizzie was diagnosed, all of it seemed to catch up with me. My new-found bubble of euphoria collapsed, as one thought loomed above the others and lodged in my brain.

What the hell am I doing here?

It was one thing planning to get a flight and find a hotel in California where my song came from. There was a *point* – at least, to me there was. But beyond the most tenuous link to Adam, there was nothing about Barcelona that beyond a couple of days of sightseeing particularly drew me.

Was that how my life was going to be now? A sequence of random decisions in the name of the passing of time? Losing the plot entirely at this stage, I stifled the sob that stuck in my throat, grateful there was no one sitting opposite to hide my distress from. I got out my phone again and, with shaking hands, I texted Elena.

TILLY

Flight didn't leave because of fog, so I've made a mad decision and am on a train to Barcelona. I don't know who I am any more, Els. What have I done?

A feeling of panic had me in its grip. I was so far out of my comfort zone, I may as well have been on the moon. Googling a map of France on my phone, I frantically scrutinised the names of places between here and Barcelona. But, of course, I recognised none of them; my sense of panic growing just as my phone buzzed.

ELENA

What have you done? Made a *brilliant* decision,
I reckon! Barcelona is cool, Tilly! Bars,
restaurants, beaches – need I go on? Sagrada
Familia, La Rambla… Jealous! Btw, Gareth
turned up. He said you weren't answering your
phone and he assumed you were staying with
me, so I told him you were on a flight to the USA.
You should have seen his face! I don't think he
imagined you were going very far. He's a dick,
Tilly. Don't think too much. Just have a ball.

Good friends were really the best. It was exactly what I
needed to hear as suddenly I was furious again. Bloody Gareth
being bloody patronising, thinking he knew me better than I
knew myself; not thinking I was capable of going anywhere on
my own. Any doubts I had vanished as I picked up my phone
again and finishing my wine, I started googling Barcelona.

There was a fire inside me – probably for all the wrong
reasons as it briefly crossed my mind that I should have felt sad –
or at least, sadder than I did. But instead, as I pictured Gareth's
face, all I was thinking was, *I'll show him.*

Harnessing my fury with Gareth, I gazed out of the window
watching the landscape change, the colours of northern France
turning to paler, more sun-bleached shades the further south we
travelled. As daylight faded, I glimpsed a distant sea, a coast
bedecked in twinkling lights.

It was dark by the time I arrived in Barcelona. Dragging my
case, I found a hotel not far from the station, up a quiet back-
street. My room wasn't fancy but it was clean and quiet. And
small – too small for both me and my anger with Gareth. After
depositing my suitcase, I went back out, determined to forget
about Gareth, reminding myself instead there was much to be
grateful for. And not just the obvious, like trains not being subject

to the same disruptions as aeroplanes. As I was discovering, there was a long list of things the UK didn't do very well. Train snacks were better here. Wine was cheaper; so were hotels. Also, by the way, so was the weather, which brought me full circle back to the whole reason I'd ended up here.

I stopped briefly to call Tallulah, partly to tell her where I'd gone, and mostly so that she knew that I'd picked myself up and was getting on with my life. The call went straight to her voicemail.

Hi. I'm calling to say goodbye. I'm in Barcelona. Tomorrow, I'm going to... Actually I'm not sure where I'm going yet. But I'm OK with that. I just wanted you to know. And also to thank you for listening to me.

Then switching off my phone, I focused on what Elena had said. *Don't think too much.* They were wise words, and as it turned out, it was a lovely evening in Barcelona. Absolutely zero fog, for starters. I walked along streets buzzing with life, marvelling at the architecture as I discovered Elena was right. Barcelona really was the perfect place to break my journey, as uncertainty tripped me up again. *Journey to where, exactly?*

But somewhere along the course of today, my mind had distilled what the purpose of this trip was. And it was less about reaching San Jose and more about pushing myself to go somewhere new, that I was unfamiliar with. It didn't matter that right now I didn't have a plan. In fact, I needed to get more used to not having plans; to being more spontaneous. In any case, it was a decision that could wait until tomorrow, as I found a bar and ordered a glass of wine.

Now, as recently as a month ago, if anyone had told me I'd be sitting alone in a country I'd never been to before, I would have laughed at them. *Me, Tilly, being brave enough to go away on her own? I'm sorry, but you've got the wrong person.*

As I sat at a table waiting for my drink to arrive and watching the world go by, I was finding unexpected pleasure in my anonymity. I had only one brief moment of maudlin reflection. It was somewhat telling that it wasn't for the house I'd left. It was for the trip to San Jose I'd been forced to abandon. But as I'd already worked out, that wasn't important.

I had never ventured so far out of my comfort zone before and I could easily have started to panic again. But for some reason, I didn't. If I really couldn't do this, there was nothing to stop me going home – except perhaps for one, very small problem. Right now, I had no idea where home was.

You can always stay with Elena, I told myself, taking a sip of my wine as I started to panic again. Or as a last resort, for a little longer at least, I could have gone back to the house. But after a hell of a day, it wasn't the time to be thinking about any of this. I needed to adjust to life being different; give myself a night, I told myself. A few hours' sleep in a comfy hotel bed. Everything would look different in the morning.

I took another, larger sip of my wine – a luscious Rioja – then as I got out my phone and brought up a map of Europe, I looked up to see a woman sit down a couple of tables away. She was obviously younger than me. Her hair was a mass of long, unruly curls, and she was wearing jeans and a multicoloured jumper shaped like a poncho. But, what struck me most was how comfortable in her own skin she seemed, as she sat there alone and ordered a drink.

As I watched her, suddenly I realised it was more than that. It was the light in her eyes, her air of confidence that dimly reminded me of how I used to be.

Out of the corner of my eye, I noticed someone. Gazing past the woman, I felt the blood drain from my face. I stared in shock at the figure of a man. *It couldn't be.*

As I watched him, it was as though I'd seen a ghost. Then as he turned, and I saw his face.

He wasn't a ghost. This was the reason the Universe had conspired to bring me here. It really was him. A little older, as we all are, but definitely Adam Cameron. After half expecting to see him here, I wasn't sure why I was so surprised. Adam had always had a knack of turning up when I reached a major milestone in my life.

As he started to walk, I forgot my drink. I got up and hurried after him, keeping him in sight until he disappeared into a small crowd and I lost him.

As I walked back to the hotel, I continued to scan the streets for him. I'd seen him only a few times over the years, since that first time, days before I married Gareth. I saw him when I'd been at a low point, when the twins were teenagers; again when Lizzie was diagnosed. It means I shouldn't have been surprised I was seeing him now, when my entire life had fallen apart around me.

That night, in the safety of my hotel room, as I thought about the house, it already felt less important. That all that really mattered was the people we loved, suddenly thinking of the boys, then Elena, my dad and Rick, realising how grateful I was to have them all.

As for those who didn't love us back, they weren't worth losing sleep over. I imagined it wouldn't be long before Olivia was as irritated as I was by Gareth's snoring and bed-hogging, just as I was hoping he would wake up one day, and take a good, long look at himself. After all, it was about fricking time. But already I knew I wouldn't be there for him; that it was too late for us.

It was the best night's sleep I'd had in ages. More than that, over the course of the night, things seemed to slot into place, the way they often did during our sleeping hours and I awoke early the following morning with a clear head and a new-found sense of purpose.

After pushing open the shutters, I lay in bed listening to the noises from the streets and brought up a map of Greece on my phone. Studying it, I suddenly decided I didn't need a plan. That I could do what I did yesterday – take another train to another city; go with the flow, see where it was going to take me.

On impulse, I booked another train ticket, to Cannes, then I got up and showered before packing my suitcase. After checking out, I dragged it along behind me as I found somewhere to have breakfast. As I walked, I cast my eyes around for Adam. It was, after all, the strangest of coincidences that he was here the same time that I was. But that morning, wherever I looked, there was no sign of him.

After a coffee and a croissant in the autumn sun, I found the station. The views from the train were breathtaking, of pale stone houses, wooded hills, the clear blue Mediterranean Sea. I fell in love with Cannes and its out-of-season lethargy. Then after a couple of days there, I went to Genoa, and from there, to Rome.

For reasons I couldn't explain, I found myself drawn further south as I studied the map again. For no reason in particular, I settled on Crete. If I hadn't, it would have changed the course of the rest of my life. But at the time, I had no way of knowing that.

14

The Writing on the Wall

After the time I saw Adam with his wife, it felt as though a shadow hung over me. For a couple of weeks, more than ever before, I distracted myself by throwing myself into family life, until I was going through the washing, and it was shattered.

It was a cliché, wasn't it? Finding a receipt in your husband's trouser pocket? 'The Ivy?' I laid the receipt on the kitchen table in front of him while the boys were watching TV in the sitting room.

'I've no idea how that got there.' Gareth didn't meet my eyes.

'Then let me refresh your memory.' I sat down opposite him. 'According to the receipt, you were there on the tenth – so two weeks ago. Just in case you're wondering, I called The Ivy – to see if they'd found the pen you lost. They confirmed you were there.'

Gareth looked confused. 'I haven't lost a pen.' Then a shadow crossed his face. 'You shouldn't have done that.'

'What – called a restaurant where you took another woman?' I said lightly. 'Why not, Gareth?'

He got up. 'It isn't what you think.' Going over to the window, he stood with his back towards me.

'So what is it?' Somehow I stayed calm. 'Am I not enough for you?'

'It isn't that.' His shoulders were tight as he stood there. Then he turned around. Looking at me, he sighed. 'Don't you ever wonder about us?'

I gasped. Of course I had wondered, many more times than Gareth had any idea about. 'Yes.' I paused. 'It's not like we got off to the best start. But we're married. We have a family. The way I see it, we made a commitment. We vowed to weather our storms, Gareth,' I added more quietly, thinking of my mother's words on the morning of our wedding. 'Or at least, I thought we did.'

'Storms?' He frowned.

I watched him closely. 'How long has this been going on? And please, just tell me the truth.'

He hesitated. Then he came back to the table and sat down. 'Three months.'

My eyes widened. How hadn't I known? But our sex life was non-existent. Had been for years. And this emotional disconnect was nothing new between us. Even so, it was hard to imagine Gareth emotionally connected to anyone. 'Is it serious?'

He rolled his eyes heavenwards. 'I have no idea.'

'OK. So let me rephrase that. Do you want it to be serious?'

'Tilly—' he started.

'Don't just say *Tilly* like that and stop,' I said. 'What were you going to say?'

'I do love you. And I love the boys. It's just that sometimes I think... I want more.' His eyes briefly met mine.

I was speechless, but not for long. 'Don't you think that depends on your definition of love?' I said heatedly, not at all sure why I didn't chuck him out and tell him to never come back.

'From where I am, if you loved me, you wouldn't have done this.' I sighed. 'You can't expect it to always be a bed of roses. Love is different things at different times in life. Lust doesn't last.' He needed to be reminded of these things, particularly at this point.

'Don't start on about storms again.' A look of guilt crossed his face. Yes, actual guilt, which for Gareth was a first.

I was in the grip of an odd sense of calm. 'So what do we do now?'

He sighed. 'I really don't know.'

'In that case, I'll make it easy for you.' I was remarkably civil. 'Either you stop seeing her, or you move out. You can't have both of us.'

'What about the boys?'

Right on cue, the kitchen door was flung open and Robbie came in. 'Mum? Is there any cake?'

'Sure, darling. In the tin. I made one earlier.'

As if Robbie needed instructions when he could sniff out a cake from a mile away. Boys were like that – born with a kind of food-radar. 'Cool.' Looking pleased, he was already snuffling it out like a truffle pig. After opening the tin and cutting two wedges, he took them back to Alex.

Left alone, Gareth glanced at me. 'I suppose I should move out.'

My stomach turned over. 'If that's what you want.' My husband was leaving me and all I could do was agree with him – it was hardly the response of someone who loved him with all her heart.

'It's that simple?'

I shrugged. 'Apart from the boys.' As I thought about our boys, a rush of emotion hit me. 'It isn't me I'm worried about,' I said. 'It's them. How do we tell them?'

'Jesus.' Gareth rested his head in his hands.

* * *

Of course, it was left to me. And of course, in order to protect the boys, I found myself lying by omission, protecting Gareth, knowing it would be easier to break the news once they'd got used to him being gone.

'Your dad's been offered a promotion. It means taking a job in another department. He's going to be away for a bit.'

'Wow. That's amazing.' Robbie looked in awe.

'It'll be odd without him here. But we'll be fine, Mum,' Alex said a little anxiously.

Did I say we wouldn't? 'Of course we'll be fine.' Hating that I was lying to them, I filled the kettle and switched it on. 'Who's for a cup of tea?'

I know what most people would say. *Why not just tell the boys the truth about their arsehole of a father? Surely you won't consider him coming back – not after this?*

* * *

Elena was uncompromising. 'This has to be it, Tilly. You really don't deserve this.'

'The trouble is...' But I couldn't find the words. In the end, I sighed. 'You know what? You're right. I've had enough, El.'

'Thank God,' she said quietly. 'You need to find yourself a good divorce lawyer.'

'What about the house? It's the boys' home.' My voice wobbled.

'That's why you need to find a lawyer. You should stay in that house, and bloody Gareth should pay for it. That's my opinion, anyway.'

I wasn't sure it worked like that, but I needed to find out. That afternoon, I managed to find a lawyer who had a last-minute appointment available. It wasn't pleasant, unpicking the threads of a marriage, however rotten it was.

After, I didn't want to go home. The boys were at a friend's house – in any case, I needed time to think. Stopping at a café, I sat at an outside table and ordered a glass of wine, my mind all over the place as I waited.

'Tilly?'

My heart leapt as looking up, I saw Adam standing there. I did a double take. I couldn't believe I was seeing him again so soon after the last time.

'Are you OK?' he asked.

Where the heck did I start? 'Yes – and not really,' I said.

'Like some company?'

It was like my heart breathed out, a breath that carried with it my frustrations, my sadness, my weariness. 'I'd love some.'

The waiter brought my glass of wine. 'Could I have the same?' Adam said. Then he looked at me. 'You look like you're carrying the cares of the world.'

'Really?' Tears pricked my eyes.

'What's wrong?' he said gently.

I sighed. 'I've spent the last hour dissecting the nuts and bolts of my marriage. I've just been to see a divorce lawyer,' I explained.

He looked startled. 'You've really reached that point?'

I nodded. 'Gareth's been having an affair. He's moved out. I haven't told the boys yet.' I had a lump in my throat just thinking about it. 'How do I do that? Tell them their parents are breaking up?'

'I can't imagine.' Adam looked sympathetic. 'But shouldn't you do it together?'

I shrugged. 'I don't know. I don't know anything right now.' I tried to make a joke of it. 'I'm sorry. But you did ask!' I changed the subject. 'So what brings you back here – again?'

He hesitated. 'Louise asked me to pick something up – and I suppose I was hoping I might bump into you again. Not that I was wishing anything like this on you,' he added quickly.

I was silent for a moment. I wanted to see him too, but I couldn't tell him that. Not when right now, life was already far too complicated. 'Are you happy?' I asked. 'You and Louise?'

I knew in the silence that followed that there wasn't a simple answer. But maybe there never was; maybe all of us had something going on.

'We're OK,' he said at last. He picked up his glass and sipped some of his wine. Then he got up and left some money on the table. 'What would you say if I suggested that we get out of here?'

It was like time had rolled back; like it was days before my wedding again. Except years later, Gareth had met someone; I was starting divorce proceedings. I was free to do whatever I wanted. I got up, then Adam and I started walking towards the park where we'd walked all those summers ago. At some point, Adam's hand found mine, then tightened around it.

I didn't know where we were going, just that my heart was racing; sparks flying between us, sparks that were such it seemed that people were turning to watch us. Until I stopped. I knew how it felt to be betrayed.

'Adam? What about Louise?'

The light left his eyes, leaving in its place angst. 'Of course. Louise.' He let go of my hand. 'Tilly? Louise and I...' he started to say.

I placed a finger to his lips. 'Don't say anything,' I whispered. 'There's already so much going on right now.' I shook my head, suddenly overcome with sadness as reaching up, I kissed his cheek.

* * *

I remember how I felt back then. How, in spite of everything, I tried to keep us together while Gareth was intent on walking away. Maybe that was the time I should have accepted we were over. When I look back, it seems like the Universe was on our case again. Seeing Adam twice like that when my life was falling apart... The signs were loud and clear, but yet again, I ignored them. Instead, I'd put divorce proceedings on hold, wanting to talk to Gareth about it before it went any further. But in the event, he and his woman lasted a month. I never found out her name. I didn't want to know. I'd had a hunch it would only be a matter of time before he'd come grovelling back. Sure enough, I was right.

* * *

'I made a terrible mistake, Tilly.' Gareth looked miserable. 'I never realised how much I'd miss you and the boys. I love you. I should tell you more often. And I'm sorry. Please... Can we give us another chance?'

Whatever I'd imagined happening, I hadn't been prepared for this, for Gareth's remorse and regret, his declarations of love. Knowing I wouldn't have to tell the boys we were breaking up, relief washed over me.

'We need to talk about this,' I said. 'Things have to change. You left me, Gareth. You can't just come back and expect everything to go back to how it used to be.'

'I know.' He looked wretched. 'We will talk – I promise.' Coming closer, he took my hands. 'I just want us to be a family again.'

* * *

'I can't believe you're thinking about letting him move back in.' Lizzie was incensed. 'He's a scumbag. He'll never change.'

'Don't say that about him. He's my husband. And if they found out what had happened, the boys would be devastated.' I poured her another glass of wine. 'I can't do that to them.'

Lizzie shook her head. 'I honestly think if they knew the truth, the boys would understand. Anyway, what's to stop him doing it again?'

'I don't think he will. And Lizzie, please don't tell Mum and Dad,' I said. 'I'm fine – I really am. And I know it sounds like I'm making it easy for Gareth, but the only reason I'm doing it is for the boys.'

'I won't tell them – not this time. Only because I'm thinking of them,' she said furiously. 'It would really upset them to know what that bastard has put you through.'

I changed the subject. 'How's Rick?' Rick was Lizzie's boyfriend, the latest in a long line of them, none of whom had lasted.

'Fine,' she snapped. 'Don't change the subject. Tilly, you need to tell Gareth he's on his last warning.'

'I'll talk to him,' I promised.

But as things often do, something else came along, seemingly out of the blue – almost.

It hadn't escaped me that my parents had been unusually absent of late. But they had other things on their minds.

For a while, Mum hadn't been well. Nothing she could put her finger on.

'I'm getting old,' she said, smiling, when I questioned her. 'Everyone gets little niggles. Our bodies don't go on forever.'

'You're not that old, Mum. You're only sixty-two.' More weeks had passed, more appointments leading to more tests, revealing that these were not just niggles. My lovely mum had bowel cancer.

While I was still dealing with the aftermath of what Gareth had done, it felt like a bomb had exploded in my world. But as the pieces of it settled never to be the same again, this one focused my mind with razor sharpness. First up, I compiled a list of what was important. Up at the top with supporting Mum were the boys, my family. Lizzie. It should have spoken volumes that Gareth only figured somewhere below midway, sliding towards close to the bottom.

Timing really was everything. There was no longer any question that Gareth wouldn't move back in. When the boys were worried enough about their grandmother being ill, it was important they had consistency in their lives. Gareth moving back was easier than breaking up with him. And to my surprise, Gareth came into his own.

'I can hold the fort here – if you need to be with your mum.'

I accepted – gratefully. Besides, right now, our differences seemed less important. And so we fell back into the familiarity of our time-old routines. As I'd said to Gareth before, we'd vowed to weather storms and I for one was prepared to honour that. But any peace was short-lived. In the thick of my mother's illness, I could sense storm clouds gathering.

'It's like life is transitioning,' I tried to explain to Lizzie. 'One minute the boys were, well, boys. Now, all of a sudden, they're talking about uni courses, – and at the same time, Mum and Dad are getting older, and Mum's sick.' I stared at her. 'Do you think life goes like this for everyone?'

'I'm guessing shades of. But isn't it just part of getting older?' she said quietly. 'Tills. I've been dying to tell you something.' She held out the hand I hadn't noticed she was hiding behind her back. On her ring finger was a large, glittering diamond.

'Oh my God.' I did a double take. 'Rick proposed?'

Nodding, her face lit up. 'It was so romantic. He brought me roses and took me out for dinner. Honestly, I'm so happy.' Her grin was infectious as she hugged me.

But I already knew how happy Rick made her. From the start, it seemed like they were meant for each other. 'I'm so happy for you.' All these emotions were welling up inside me, my happiness for my sister poignant, bittersweet, because of what our mum was going through. 'More than anything else, I'm so happy you're happy.' I looked at her. 'Do Mum and Dad know?'

Her eyes were shining as she shook her head. 'We're going to see them this evening.'

'Mum will be beside herself.' My smile dropped as I thought of her. I knew how she'd want to plan a big wedding for Lizzie just as she had for me. But we both knew it would be too much for her.

'I can't wait to tell her. But it's going to be a small wedding, Tills – Rick and I have talked about it.' She paused. 'I have a favour to ask… Will you be my matron of honour? I swear no pink dresses…'

I grinned at her. 'Try stopping me! And I really don't care what I wear!' Then tears filled my eyes. I blinked them away. 'Sorry! I'm so happy for you… You know I am.'

'Don't be sorry,' Lizzie said gently. 'It's an emotional roller coaster, isn't it?' Her eyes were bright as she hugged me again.

Lizzie's and Rick's happiness was like a ray of sunlight on us all at a time our family most needed it. It also illuminated the shortcomings of my own marriage far too brightly. Lizzie and Rick were a team in a sense that Gareth and I had never been. He had her back; would have done anything in the world for her.

Under no illusions that Gareth and I had a way to go, I was discovering there was no quick fix, that the scars of infidelity are lasting. But life was moving on in leaps and bounds, the way that it does sometimes. Very soon, while Lizzie and Rick were making wedding plans, our household was obsessed with A-level grades and degree course requirements. My tour of the UK began for uni open days and interviews, one Gareth opted out of. It was a part of the boys' lives I wanted to be there for, to hold their hands through, knowing before long, they'd be flying the nest; I'd be alone.

Alone. That word again. I never paused to think that given Gareth lived in the same house, it was a strange choice of word. I wasn't alone – not physically. But emotionally, spiritually, despite our best efforts, it was like we lived on different planets. He contributed to our mortgage, but his investment ended there. Everything else was down to me.

But thus had it always been and I took it all on, not even once stopping to question it.

* * *

The same way my mum had, too, suddenly I'm realising, as I find another missing piece of the jigsaw of my life. *It's come from her*. It explains why my dad was so lost without her.

Now, it's obvious my mum had an impact on my life. Our mothers are our constants through our most formative years. Our emotional support as years go by – if you're lucky, that is. And Lizzie and I struck gold, I've always thought. But we're all human; even mothers have their baggage. Added to that, they can pass it on. And in my case, I've taken on the way my mum always had, of giving, to the extent it was at a cost to herself. Of not living true to herself, but to my father's ways. I've known this for a long time. I just haven't appreciated the impact it's had. And that's it, in a nutshell, one that as I crack it, a veritable kaleidoscope of realisations explode out. You see, obvious though it is, I am not my mum. I do not have to always please everyone else. They are their own people; they are more than able to look out for themselves.

The boys are different; we never stop being parents. Nor do I want to. But even with them, it's high time Tilly the hub let go of the strings. Let everyone fly away. Started thinking about what's right for myself.

But, back then, when my mum was ill, I hadn't realised any of that.

As the days and weeks passed, I watched my mum battle her illness – bravely, with her trademark brightness, as not once did she let her mask slip.

'It's a little bit uncomfortable,' she said now and then. 'But all in all, I'm very lucky.'

That's how I choose to remember that time. One when our family became more closely knit than ever; one where I'd never been more aware of life's bittersweetness, the joy of my little sister getting married, contrasting with the reality of my mum's illness.

* * *

While my mum said little, I had my suspicions about where this was going. But it wasn't until shortly before Lizzie's wedding that they were confirmed when she shared her prognosis with me, that at worst she had weeks, at best a few months.

'I'm so sorry, Mum.' Tears poured down my face. 'This is crap.'

'It is.' Mum's voice wobbled. 'But I've been so lucky. I've had a wonderful life – and it's not over yet.'

I took one of my mum's hands. 'We should tell Lizzie.'

She shook her head. 'Please, Tilly. Not yet. I'll talk to her after her wedding.'

'She'd want to know, Mum,' I said gently.

'I know. And she will. Just let her have this time.' My mum smiled too brightly.

If Lizzie had guessed, she didn't say. Despite the obvious sadness I felt, it wasn't lost on me that given how sick our mum was, we were lucky she was still with us. We made the most of those days, aware that time was no longer open ended.

The boys' final term of college came to an end and the celebrations started. Then a week later, we all gathered for Lizzie and Rick's wedding in the breathtaking gardens of a barn that had been converted into a wedding venue. It was a lot less grand than where Gareth and I held our reception, but from start to finish, it was a beautiful day in every respect. The sun shone, the bride looked stunning, while Rick just walked around looking dazed, presumably because he couldn't believe Lizzie had agreed to be his wife.

It was bittersweet, yet still the happiest day. It was also one that affirmed what family was really about. What love was about, too. A day during which Gareth was oddly silent.

Having returned to the fold, the boys had remained unaware of the real reason for his absence, a fact that I was oddly proud of, despite the emotional turmoil I'd been through. I should also point out that my parents also were unaware of the whole shebang, completely buying my explanation that Gareth's absence had been work related. For Christ's sake, they even congratulated him. Yes, so ridiculous, you couldn't make it up. And with my mum so ill, it was hardly the time to enlighten them.

Anyway, back to the wedding and Gareth looking somewhat perplexed. 'They really love each other, don't they?' His eyes rested on Lizzie and Rick.

I shrugged. 'That's generally the case when people get married.' I didn't want him reflecting on us, putting a downer on today. 'Not all marriages are the same, Gareth.' I paused. Then I couldn't stop myself. 'Honestly, when you think back, we probably shouldn't have gone through with it.'

He looked at me, startled. 'Why are you saying that now?'

'Because we're talking about it now,' I said. 'It's no secret you didn't want children – and if we'd talked about it honestly, it would have been a dealbreaker,' I said quickly as he opened his mouth to interrupt. 'I'm not blaming you. I knew you were reluctant. I just didn't realise the extent of your reluctance.' But more to the point, I hadn't wanted to. 'I still don't know why we were so afraid to be honest with each other.'

'You really think it was a mistake?' He looked gobsmacked.

'In some ways.' I shrugged. 'I think you do, too. What else was your affair about? We don't have sex. We don't talk about anything important.'

He set his jaw. 'We're talking now.'

I nodded sadly. 'But only about what's gone wrong between us.' I added more kindly. I changed the subject. 'Look at the boys. Wonderful, aren't they?' I watched them – tall and handsome, sun kissed, and more than any of those things, so filled with kindness that I could feel my heart bursting with pride. 'I'd say, on balance, we've done OK.'

For a moment, Gareth didn't say anything. He poured himself another glass of champagne, then looked at me. 'Do you want a divorce?'

I studied the face I knew so well, realising that after all these years we'd spent together, I barely knew the man behind it. 'I don't think that's a conversation for today.' I swallowed the lump in my throat. Even now, I struggled with the thought of divorcing him.

I'll never know if Mum overheard us talking. Or whether her

mother's radar kicked in one last time. But the day after Lizzie's wedding, I had a call from my dad.

'It's your mother, Tilly. She wants to see you.'

There was a gravity in the way he spoke and a sense of alarm filled me. Why hadn't she called me herself? 'Is she OK? I'll come over now.' As I spoke, I was already picking up my bag, then searching for my car keys.

'No rush,' he said. 'But I think it would be good if it was today.'

His words sent a chill through me. I ended the call and scribbled a note to the still-sleeping boys. Then closing the back door, went out to my car. It was another scorcher of a summer's day, the trees clad in the deep, dark green of summer leaves, the roadsides dusty. Things I barely noticed as I drove. I knew Mum was sick. That she was dying. But I wasn't ready.

But is anyone ever ready to lose a loved one? I turned into my parents' drive, my heart in my mouth as I went inside, already expecting the worst, to my surprise finding my mum sitting in a chair in the kitchen.

'Tilly.' She smiled. 'Thank you for coming.'

'I was coming over anyway.' I went over and leant down to kiss her cheek, then pulled up a chair next to her. 'How are you, Mum?'

'I'm OK.' Her eyes were distant. 'But I don't want to talk about me.' She paused. 'It's you I'm worried about.'

'There's no need.' I gazed through the sliding doors that were open onto the garden. 'I'm fine.'

'Oh Tilly...' She sounded wistful. 'I wasn't going to say anything, but I know if I don't, I'll regret it. Apparently, it's best not to die with regrets, or so I'm told.' For a moment, she sounded more like my old mum, before she was sick. 'It isn't anything new.

I've been noticing for some time. And forgive me, for not saying anything before, but...'

Going on, she told me how she'd noticed the distance between me and Gareth. How he seemed to be emotionally switched off; how she'd always had the feeling something was missing between us.

I listened. I thought about lying. Then I thought how the knowledge that her life was coming to an end had only served to sharpen her focus. So, in the end, I did what felt right. I was honest with her. 'You're right. About everything, Mum.' I felt a weight come off me. Then I told her about meeting Adam – OK, so leaving out the part about the afternoon we'd spent together.

She was silent for a moment. 'I wasn't expecting that.'

'You mustn't worry,' I said hastily. 'It was a long time ago and I'm fine with it all. Really.'

Shock washed across her face. 'I remember him. He was the man who sent a bottle of champagne to our table – on your hen night.'

I nodded. 'That was him. That was the first time I met him. Do you remember what you said?' I watched her face.

A look of realisation dawned in her eyes. 'It was about weddings bringing out the best in people, wasn't it?'

I nodded. 'Mum? Can you keep this just between us?'

'If you mean "can I not tell your father?", of course I won't.' She frowned. 'Does Lizzie know?'

'Yes.' I sighed. 'She's never liked Gareth – did you know that?'

My mum's eyes widened. 'I had no idea. I have to ask, though. What made you go ahead with the wedding?'

'I thought about calling it off,' I said slowly. 'But in the end, I suppose it felt like the right thing. I thought Gareth and I would be good together.'

My mum made a *harumph* kind of sound.

'Anyway,' I went on. 'Who leaves their fiancé for a man they've known less than a week?'

'I suppose that would depend on the man.' She looked at me sadly. 'So many secrets, Tilly... I've always liked to think that we could be open with each other.'

'Sorry, Mum.' Guilt flooded over me. 'But I was struggling, to be honest. At the time, it was easier not to talk about it.'

'Well, I'm jolly glad you have told me. Just imagine, me going to my grave not knowing *that*.'

I looked at her, startled. 'You're not going anywhere just yet, Mum.'

She sighed. 'I don't think it will be long.' She was silent for a moment. 'Tilly?' Her eyes gazed into mine. 'You deserve happiness as much as any of us. You do know that, don't you? If you're not happy with Gareth, why don't you leave him?'

I stared at her, shocked. 'The trouble is, I don't know how to. And there's the boys...'

'The boys are going away before too long.' She was silent again. 'Life is short, Tilly. Happiness doesn't come our way all that often. But if it does, promise me. This time, you'll grab it with both hands.'

'OK,' I said shakily, wiping away a tear. 'Thanks, Mum.' My emotions were all over the place. 'You're the best.'

'I'm not, am I? Or I would have said something a long time ago.' She was on a roll. 'If at any point your father starts up about the evils of divorce, don't listen to him.' She sounded determined. 'Far better to cut your losses than waste the rest of your life with a man who doesn't – who's never – deserved you.'

It was the last conversation we had, just the two of us, as too soon, it was followed by the saddest day. After rallying to see Lizzie married, my mum waited until she and Rick were back from their honeymoon, before passing away peacefully in her sleep.

We'd known it was on the cards, but it made no difference. Coming sooner than any of us were prepared for, our entire family was devastated. I knew from that point onward, life was never going to be the same. There were the inevitable calls to people to whom my mum had been important, her funeral to plan; her loss weaving a thread of sadness into all our lives.

Meanwhile, Lizzie had the bright idea of giving my dad a cat. She also had an answer to my objections, that our dad was struggling to look after himself, let alone anything else.

'It's company, Tills. Another heartbeat in the house – don't you see?'

The cat proved a distraction, if nothing else, as our lives slowly morphed to fit this strange world we found ourselves in. After worrying about my mum, now I was worrying about my father. When it came to the practicalities, my mum had always done everything. See the recurring theme? It meant that without her, I had no idea how he was going to cope, which meant someone had to help him. With Lizzie newly married, and hard at work on her interior design business, it was the unspoken yet nevertheless obvious solution that that person was going to be me.

With hindsight – that word again – my mum's death should have galvanised me into taking a good hard look at my own life. Into seizing each day; to make the most of the rest of my life, as she'd urged me. But instead, the disconnect between me and Gareth seemed less important than it ever had. Our marriage was reduced to coexisting in the same house, as I busied myself looking after everyone else.

Then in what seemed like no time, the boys left for uni and I found myself a part-time job as everything changed yet again.

15

Do not spoil what you have by desiring what you have not.

— EPICURUS

Lying unconscious in the hospital, whiteness surrounds my unresponsive body, the only sounds the electronic noises of the machines that are keeping me alive, buying me more time, as I become aware of people moving around me; faint voices speaking accented English.

'We have traced her family. A friend is contacting them. It will be good for them to come here.'

Euphoria fills me at the thought of seeing the boys. But then panic wells up inside me. The boys will be so worried. I don't want them to see me like this. But suddenly the realisation dawns on me that maybe my time is running out.

I have another sudden wake-up call. It's seismic; the magnitude of when I met Adam. You see, it's never been more obvious to me that what's important is what you see in other people. How you go about your days. What's in your heart. Time takes on new significance as I lie here, fighting off fear, while sadness overwhelms me. Regret, that I haven't done half of what I wanted with this precious life of mine. That maybe I never will, as I consider.

Maybe I'm not coming out of this.

16

Nothing endures but change.

— HERACLITUS

So here I am. Back on the last leg of the journey that's brought me to Crete. At the time, I remember feeling a little proud of myself. After all, as one forty-something soon to be ex-wife who'd never been anywhere alone, I was moving swiftly and impressively on to the next chapter of my life. And coping pretty bloody admirably, I couldn't help thinking – albeit still with the hindrance of my rather large suitcase.

I remember it briefly crossing my mind that pride comes before a fall. But only briefly. But given what I was coming through, I was doing OK – with one caveat – as long as I didn't stop and think too much. To be honest, *not thinking* is probably what kept me going.

* * *

Meanwhile, there were plenty of other things to occupy my mind, such as the views from the train and exploring new cities, before I found myself at the airport in Rome, where, after leaving my suitcase in the bag drop, I was busying myself trying to find the right departure gate.

As I walked, I was marvelling how everyone around me seemed to know where they were going – and not just at that. They had a distinctly European look in a kind of effortlessly stylish way, while I looked very English – and not in a good way. *But you are English*, I reminded myself. I also looked more than a bit frumpy, as it occurred to me it really was time I did something about that.

Imagining getting a very European haircut and a snazzy new pair of jeans, I wondered what the shops in Crete would be like. Lingering in duty free, I picked up the bottle of perfume I'd planned to buy at Heathrow, fantasising briefly about spending some of Gareth's money on presents for the boys and expensive make-up I'd probably never wear – it was just as well I wasn't travelling light. But this morning, there wasn't the time. There were more urgent things to attend to – like making sure I caught my flight. Having found the gate, while I waited to board, for no reason, my brain slipped sideways as I had a sudden pang of longing for the familiarity of home, for my empty old house, even Rick's sorrowful presence.

But then I shook myself. If melancholy had become my comfort zone, I needed to work on that. Pushing all thoughts of home aside, I looked out of the window where aircraft were taxying. I was in Rome, for goodness' sake, about to board a flight to Athens, where I was going to take a ferry to Crete. It wasn't the time for feeling maudlin. This was the stuff dreams are made of.

As boarding commenced, I joined the slow-moving queue, where I had a sudden out-of-body moment that planted me firmly back in England, getting out of bed when Gareth did, cleaning our already clean house, then if I wasn't working, which I hadn't been for some while now, going for a walk to Selham railway station. If not every day, most days – and mostly because hardly anyone else ever went there and I liked to be alone.

Except that's not quite true, is it? Tallulah's voice popped into my head.

'Oh, be quiet,' I said out loud, suddenly self-conscious as a number of faces turned to look at me.

I smiled at the woman just behind me. 'Lovely day, isn't it?' I said overly brightly, realising too late, she probably didn't understand a word of English, added to which she was probably thinking I was losing it, which, quite possibly, I actually was. Head down, I stayed silent as I shuffled along with the queue until we reached the plane.

After shoving my jacket into an overhead locker, I squeezed myself into the seat I'd been allocated. The middle seat, rather than the aisle or window, which to my mind was the least desirable seat. But on a full flight, I supposed someone had to sit there.

In any case, it wasn't a long flight. Less than two hours, which would have been fine if it wasn't for the relentless rap from the earphones to my right, or the loud snores from the man to my left. But these were small annoyances in the grand scheme of things. Sitting back, I pictured the increasing miles between myself and Gareth, a smile spreading slowly across my face.

I was fast getting used to travelling. I mean, even peering past someone else, there was an incredible view from the window. And it was eye-opening. And multicultural: the cities I'd seen, the people and different cultures; languages, too. It was too easy to forget there was a whole big world beyond tiny, sodden little England.

But Lizzie never forgot that. Lizzie's eye had been firmly on the bigger picture long before cancer came along.

Our lives are so insular, Tilly. Tiny little bubbles we never step outside of. When you look at the rest of the world you wonder, why don't you?

At the time, I didn't know what she meant. But then I was one of Lizzie's insular people, living in my little bubble. More to the point, I was perfectly happy that way until my world fell apart. Happy in a blinkered kind of way... Except, was I really happy? And it's slightly disconcerting to think of the scale of what had to happen for me to even begin to prise my eyes open.

But it was too much to figure out that morning. After landing in Athens and disembarking, I reclaimed my suitcase and made my way through the busy airport, somehow finding my way outside and onto a train that took me to the port, and another terminal where I waited to board the ferry.

Standing there in the sunshine, I took in the boats and ferries coming and going; the sound of the water. Airports and ferry terminals were prime places for people watching I was discovering, and I studied the other passengers waiting with me, amongst them several young backpackers, which made me think of my boys. A Greek family with three small, excited children. An old man with a white beard and a walking stick. A girl with long brown hair and sad eyes. I found myself wondering what their stories were.

I watched the ferry arrive and dock, then, half an hour later, we were called to start boarding. There was a surge of people as out of the corner of my eye, I noticed the old man struggle to his feet then attempt to pick up his bag. I hesitated then started walking over to help him – old habits die hard. In any case, it was part of my make-up that I couldn't abide seeing anyone in difficulty. But one of the young backpackers beat me to it, taking the old man's bag, then his arm before helping him slowly towards the ferry.

See? You're not the only person who likes helping people, I reminded myself. And it was good to see a nice young man doing something like that. Then I stopped myself. Was it really so unusual? Or was it more about the way I'd chosen to look at the world?

On board, I stood outside on the deck as the ferry pulled away, watching the port fading into the mist behind us, liking that just for a few hours, I was uncontactable. I suddenly realised that the last few days had gone in a blur and that the house would have been valued by now. Just the thought made my heart beat faster. But there was nothing more I could do. While I was away from England that was in Gareth's hands.

Thinking of Gareth... I got out my phone and reread the text he sent a few days ago.

GARETH

> If you've gone away, there's no point in waiting. We may as well put the house on the market. Let me know if you have any objections. By the way, you might have left it tidy. The estate agent said there were bags all over the place.

Not once had he mentioned the boys, but it clearly hadn't occurred to him to think of them. And up till now, I hadn't responded. Quietly seething, I typed my reply.

TILLY

> It was you who was in such a hurry to get things moving. Honestly, what do you expect? If you bother to go around there, Gareth, you'll see I've left you a note about what to do with everything. You also need to speak to the boys about this. And yes, there are a few bags, but nothing you can't cope with.

I stopped myself from adding, *maybe Olivia would like to help you, seeing as she's had a hand in this.* And it took iron will, but I managed not to. After all, the sun was shining and I was on my way to Crete. Poor Gareth was stuck in gloomy old England, I thought sarcastically, about to become a father again when he still hadn't got his head around the first time it happened.

And the boys were fine, I reminded myself. As long as that remained the case, I had nothing to worry about.

It wasn't the shortest of ferry crossings – seven and a half hours to be precise, which was quite a long time to be sitting doing nothing, an experience that was completely alien to me. But having failed to bring a book with me, I gazed through the windows and studied the islands we were passing, taking in the white sand of the beaches dotted with bars and tavernas, the many fishing boats moored a little way out to sea.

As more time passed, I settled in for some serious people watching. There were the seasoned travellers lounging at tables, totally at ease, as if they did this every day. Greek people of various ages, a family speaking what to my untuned ear sounded vaguely like French. Not a single other Brit, I noticed with amusement that was followed by relief that there was no one I felt the need to have the most superficial conversation with, let alone explain myself to. Though it would have been nice to have Elena here, I couldn't help thinking.

But it meant, in short, I was free to be myself. Which was a whole other thing, because if I wasn't Tilly the hub any more, who the heck was I?

I was still me, I reminded myself. So Gareth and I were no more; the house would soon be on the market. But honestly, so what? People were funny creatures, I was realising. We took ourselves so seriously – and I should know. After all, I was as guilty as anyone else, constantly worrying about what everyone else thought, weighing myself down with unnecessary stuff. Take the contents of our house that I'd been agonising over. My emotional connection to flipping sofas and a table, for frick's sake, not to mention the routines and obligations that had come to dominate my life.

It was something of a revelation to realise that far from feeling pointless without them, I was finding their absence positively liberating. But this whole journey had already been filled with revelations, of which my ridiculously oversized suitcase was oddly symbolic; the way I'd lugged it on and off far too many trains. I made a note to self to dramatically reduce the contents once I got to Crete, if not throw it away altogether. You see, it didn't need to be like this, did it? Being loaded down with clutter I didn't need. I had a choice.

Talking of obligations, I wondered how my dad was doing. It made me sad, thinking about my dad. I mean, he had so much to be grateful for. But he was intent on living such a small, lonely life, his glass forever half empty. It didn't occur to him that it could be any different. It was the religion in him, I couldn't help thinking. That melting pot of guilt and suffering he subscribed to. I couldn't imagine him embarking on a journey such as I was on.

But we are all different; not everyone wants to leave their life, step into the unknown with the contents of a rather battered and oversized suitcase. The comfort of home is a lot to give up. And I probably wouldn't have been on that ferry had my marriage not come to an end. Lizzie, I know would have loved my adventure. As would my mum. But what they most would have loved was that I was doing it for me.

That day, as the ferry rumbled on, needing a caffeine hit, I got up and went to buy a coffee. It was amazing how tiring doing nothing could be. But maybe it depended on your definition of doing nothing. If you thought about it, the last few days had been the biggest transition I'd ever embarked on, away from my old life to exactly what, I still wasn't sure.

OK. So, I did now have a plan, and that was to stay in Crete a while, however long that turned out to be. Beyond that... I didn't know. But now wasn't the time to think about that, I told myself firmly. Sipping my coffee, I got out my phone and texted Elena.

TILLY

> I'm on the ferry, El, to Crete. It's...

I broke off, not sure how to describe it, before carrying on:

TILLY

> It's the best thing I could have done. Everything to do with Gareth seems so far away. To be honest, all I want is to keep it like that. xxx

About ten minutes later, Elena replied.

ELENA

> So glad you're doing this, Tills. Miss you. But so so proud of you.

She followed it with a heart emoji.

Sitting there, I started googling Crete, realising how many jaw-dropping sights there were to see, pleased to know there was plenty to do there.

It also looked like the perfect place to pick up a few little things for Robbie and Alex. One or two mementos of this trip – for the new home I'd eventually be moving into, further down the line.

But I was getting ahead of myself. One thing I was learning on my venture into the unknown was to take each day, each step, one at a time. The first was to find myself a place to stay. I imagined a tiny studio, tucked away up a narrow street, a short walk from the harbour at Chania; with blue shutters like you saw in travel photos, framing a window from which I could lean out and watch the world go by, catch a not-so-distant glimmer of the sea.

Sitting back, my mind flitted back and forth. Then it catapulted me back in time to the early days of my marriage. Gareth and I were so young – no older than our boys are. But now, I can't help wondering were we too young? If we'd waited, would we have stayed together?

In my pocket, my phone buzzed. Taking it out, I read the text message, from Gareth.

GARETH

> Call me, Tilly. We need to talk about the house.
> There's been an offer.

Staring at the screen, I felt sick all of a sudden. Despite my brave words, underneath I was still coming to terms with the end of our marriage; had thought going away would buy me time to get my head around it. I'd envisaged months passing before anyone made an offer near the asking price, and while we were on the subject, the asking price was something Gareth had yet to enlighten me about.

TILLY

> Thanks a whole bloody lot, Gareth. I thought you
> said we'd discuss when to market the house.
> You haven't even told me what it's been
> valued at.

I hesitated. There was so much more I wanted to say. Like how selfish he was, and that was just for starters. But I was questioning the point. This wasn't anything new. The writing had been on the wall almost since day one. What was staggering was how I'd managed not to see it.

How the actual fuck did that happen? But you knew, didn't you? I reminded myself, as, far away from home, I confronted the reality of that time. *Think about those days before your wedding, Tilly. Remember how you weren't sure you could go through with it? You knew, as long ago as then, that Gareth wasn't right for you.*

It was as though the sunlight had dimmed. It was a very long time, if ever, since I'd admitted the truth to anyone – let alone myself. But back then, nothing seemed easy. It was one thing to have doubts. But I'd made a commitment to Gareth. And I'd gone through with it; then unlike Gareth, I'd given our relationship my all.

Anyway, it was a bit late for recriminations. Twenty-two years too late, to be precise. Sending Gareth the message, I started googling property websites to see if our house had been listed, as almost straight away, Gareth replied.

GARETH

It isn't on the market yet. The agent knows someone.

Did he indeed? Suspicious, I had the feeling there was something he wasn't saying, that Gareth's impatience to sell could end up costing both of us.

TILLY

Before I agree to anything, I'd like to know the valuation and the offer, Gareth. Send them through and we can talk about it. After all, there's no rush.

I switched my phone off and put it away. Yes, I was upset. It was impossible not to be. But sitting on this ferry, gazing out across the sea, as I watched the sun sink lower, I wasn't upset in the same way I was before I left the UK. In the strangest way, I even felt a flicker of sympathy for Gareth. I mean, he didn't want children when I got pregnant all those years ago and there he was, about to do it all over again.

I winced, imagining Tallulah's voice ringing in my ears – wearing her friend hat rather than a therapist one. *How dare you waste your time feeling sorry for that despicable man, Tilly. You'd think by now he'd know how babies are made.* And the fact of the matter was I didn't want to dwell on Gareth. The next chapter was already there, waiting for me.

Through the darkness, I made out the lights twinkling as the port of Chania came into view and this time nothing could stop the thrill of excitement I felt as we drew closer, before the ferry slowed down, then came to a stop.

As from the deck I watched the activity as the ferry was secured, my trepidation made a brief reappearance. Of course, there were practicalities to observe. I was, after all, a lone middle-aged woman disembarking from a ferry in a place she'd never been to before and where she hadn't even booked a hotel room – and where she didn't speak so much as a single word of the language.

Note to self. Download an English–Greek translation app.

And there was no going back – at least, not tonight. I followed the line of people as they made their way off the ferry. Standing on firm ground, I looked around, catching sight of the old man I saw in Athens slowly shuffling along with the help of the same young backpacker as before. Clearly I wasn't needed here and so, flagging down a taxi, I headed for Chania Old Town.

The road was quiet as we drove, the darkness broken by lights in some of the windows of houses we passed. A short while later, we reached the harbour. After paying the driver and getting out, I just stood there for a moment. The metallic clinking from the boats reached my ears as I took in the twinkling lights, the feeling of peacefulness. Starting to drag my case along, my arm was hurting and I resolved to exchange it for a rucksack as soon as possible.

It didn't mean I couldn't shop, I told myself, completely forgetting my earlier musings about living a less material life. I mean, I could have everything sent back – and I'd been fantasising about creating a Mediterranean-themed kitchen in the home I'd eventually have. After all, there couldn't be many better places to pick up some design tips.

Passing a few bars and tavernas, I was surprised how many were closed. But it was October, I reminded myself. Stopping at one of the smaller ones, I manoeuvred my case off the street and took a seat at a table outside. I took out my phone, switched it on and saw the rows of missed calls from Gareth.

This offer must have been good – he was obviously desperate to get hold of me. But as a waiter came up, I put down my phone. Gareth could wait. I picked up the menu and pointed to the wine list. 'Good evening. One glass,' I said, holding up one finger to make sure he understood.

'You like Greek wine?' he asked in heavily accented English.

I breathed a sigh of relief that I didn't have to attempt to speak Greek. 'I don't know. But I'd like to try it.'

'OK.' He wrote on his notepad. 'Would you like to order some food?'

'I would. I'm just not sure what.' Looking at the menu again, I frowned, considering. 'Do you have something small? Hot – maybe with fries?'

'If you like, I choose? And, of course, with fries?' he added.

'Thank you. That's really kind,' I said. Then I remembered something I'd read about the Greeks eating goat. 'Not goat, though. No offence,' I added hastily. 'It's just that I've never eaten goat before.'

'No problem.' He bowed his head. 'Leave it with me.'

Minutes later he came back with a glass of red wine. I sipped it slowly, savouring the rich feel of it on my palate. Then I put my glass down and breathed in air that was fragrant with the smell of freshly cooked food, turning my gaze upwards to take in a night sky that was clear and sparkling with stars. Sitting back, I looked towards the harbour. Soaking up the moment, after everything that had brought me here, it was as though I was in a dream.

The thought startled me. Maybe that was what all of this was. A dream. I pinched myself, to make sure it wasn't, just as the waiter came back with a large plate of food and a basket of bread.

I stared at it. 'This is so much food.'

He shrugged. 'I know you said small. But you eat. When you have had enough, you stop.' He put down a bottle. 'Olive oil. It is from this island. It is good.'

Feeling my stomach rumble, I couldn't help but smile at him. 'Thank you.'

He bowed his head. 'You are most welcome. Enjoy.'

As he walked away, I realised how hungry I was. I tentatively cut into the crisp calamari, which tasted like nothing I'd ever eaten before, then started on the tomato butter beans, drizzling them with the olive oil and mopping up the sauce with some of the bread, before turning to the frites. By the time the waiter came back, my plate was empty.

'It was not so big, then,' he said.

'It was so good,' I told him. 'Not like I usually eat.'

'That's because it is grown and harvested on this island,' he said. 'It is food for the soul.'

The way he said it resonated with me. You see, I'd never thought of food that way before, but maybe it was another change I needed to make. To see it as more than nourishing the body. 'Do you mind me asking you something?' I frowned slightly. 'Only I don't have anywhere to stay. Do you know of somewhere?'

'Perhaps. You want for how long?' he asked. 'My brother has a place. It is not far.'

A feeling of relief filled me again. 'I'm not sure. A week, maybe. But it could be longer.'

'I will call him.' He took his phone out of his pocket and made a call, murmuring in Greek before he stopped for a moment. 'He says you can have a room.'

'Can you tell him thank you? And can you ask how much?' I said anxiously.

He murmured in Greek again, then turned to me, mentioning a price that seemed overly cheap.

I blinked at him. 'Is that all? I mean, is he sure?'

'Of course. Or he would not say. Winter is coming. His place is not busy.' He shrugged. 'You want it?'

'Definitely,' I said hastily.

'My brother asks, what is your name?' he said.

'Tilly.' I watched him tell his brother, before ending the call.

'It is organised,' he said. 'I am Nicos. My brother is Andreas.' He started to clear the table. 'I will get your bill, Tilly. Then I will call you a taxi.'

As he walked off, I sat there, marvelling at how what had seemed like a problem had been taken somewhat effortlessly out of my hands. Maybe it was the benefit of the wine, but already, it was the complete opposite of how life felt before I left England, when one problem after another had kept hitting me head-on, seemingly relentlessly.

But maybe it was as Tallulah had said. I had been in the wrong place. It kind of followed, I couldn't help thinking, that given the ease with which events were unfolding around me, that at long last I was on my way to where I was meant to be.

17

Anyone who has never made a mistake has never tried anything new.

— ALBERT EINSTEIN

I used to live such a safe life – until the winds of change blasted through it. Then, it would have freaked me out. I mean, just the thought of arriving somewhere without a room booked. But that's what I did. And of course, it all worked out.

Life was supposed to be an adventure – wasn't it? Only I'd forgotten the inner recklessness I used to have. I used to covet that feeling – it came to the fore after meeting Adam, before responsibility filtered in like a fine cloud of mist that thickened over time. By that time, I was well on the way to becoming middle-aged Tilly who couldn't see beyond the world outside her window – until Gareth left me.

Something Adam said to me comes back. It was just before my wedding, about how if we ignored the signs the Universe sent us, they'd keep coming until we took notice of them, which is a bit of a shocker. I haven't thought about it like this before, but as if Gareth's first infidelity wasn't a huge great red flag, the second time was the biggest kick up the butt yet. And the fact remains that if he hadn't moved in with Olivia, chances are I'd still be in England, still living with him; most likely applying for another uninspiring part-time job, then being rejected because it was better suited to the younger, more glamorous and tech-savvy applicants. Rick would be calling in, telling me the same old stories he's told me so many times before that I know his spiel almost off pat. My dad would be summoning me to run the most trivial of errands for him. My only escape would be those solitary, nostalgic mornings on Selham railway station, where I'd sit, alone in the rain, lost in the past.

In short, my life would have stayed exactly the same, whereas now, at least I can say I made it to Crete. There's comfort to be taken from that single fact. If it all ends here in this hospital bed, at least I've been somewhere.

As I lie here, I think of my dad again. He hasn't been the same since my mum died. OK, so he's hidden his grief in a way I can only describe as stoic, storing it inside. It's brought out a side of him I hadn't seen before – or maybe it was one my mother used to mollify. You see, I've started to see a darker side to my father. A tendency to withdraw that seems at odds with his outspokenness.

I know that grief can cloud the everyday. That he is lost without my mum's light. But if you bury emotions, they fester inside you, so much so I think they damage our bodies. All that unexpressed sadness and guilt... Not healthy, is it? I picture it as black and noxious, seeping into your cells, slowly spreading, taking your body over, pushing out all the nice things like joy, happiness. Even love.

Since Lizzie died and the boys moved out, I'm the only person in our family who talks about love. I used to tell the boys I loved them with almost every goodbye. Lizzie, too. Not so much Gareth, for obvious reasons. And I still say it to the boys, but it would be so nice if there was someone else to say *I love you* to.

Thinking of Lizzie again, my mind winds back to a rainy spring morning about six months after Mum died. I was in the kitchen, mulling things. I was doing that more and more, still avoiding the bleeding obvious that if only I was brave enough to cut ties with Gareth, my life would have changed for the better, overnight.

But being the Tilly I was then, I couldn't. Instead, just back from work, I was wallowing. *Dear God. Since when had wallowing become my comfort zone?*

* * *

That morning, hearing a car pull up outside, I'd glanced through the window just as Lizzie got out. My heart lifted. There was nothing quite like a couple of hours with my sister to make my soul sing.

She came in, her fair hair long and wavy, smiling the way she always did. But as she hugged me, I could feel it before she spoke. Something was wrong. Holding her at arm's length, I frowned. 'What is it?'

For a moment, she didn't speak. Then her eyes filled with tears. 'Tilly, I found a lump.'

Lizzie's entire life – or at least, all those parts I knew of it – were literally flashing before my eyes as I reeled in shock. From the baby sister I remembered, to the gangly child who morphed into a beautiful teenager; who was my best friend in the entire world. 'You need to see someone.' My hands were shaking as I searched around for my phone. This couldn't be happening now, so soon after losing Mum. 'I'll call the medical practice for you.' Seeing my phone, I picked it up. We were both registered with the same doctor and scrolling through, tears filled my eyes as I found the number. Then I felt her hand on my arm.

'Tilly, they already know. I've had a biopsy, and a scan.'

As I looked into her eyes, I saw both her calmness and the depths of her despair there. I tried to take in what she was saying, to pull myself together, but sitting down, it didn't feel real as she told me about the form of cancer she'd been diagnosed with; her prognosis – it wasn't good. Listening in shock, I had no words. 'There has to be something they can do,' I said at last.

'Surgery. Then chemo.' Lizzie's voice was small.

'You should have told me.' I hated the thought of her carrying this alone – forgetting that she wasn't alone. She had Rick.

'I couldn't. Not until I was sure.'

It turned out Lizzie had only found out this morning. And though two cases of cancer in our family in less than a year went way beyond the odds, as I was finding out, it happened. My mum and Lizzie were proof of that.

Coming so soon after mum's illness, it put a whole new complexion on everything. Any concerns going on in my own life were sidelined, if not parked. I had more important things to worry about. Lizzie needed me and that took priority over everything.

I'd been worried how my dad would take the news, but after the initial shock sank in, to my surprise, he rallied. I'd go round to Lizzie's to find a vase of tulips or freesias. 'Rick?' Invariably she'd shake her head. They were always from our father.

He'd clearly remembered how much they'd cheered our mum when she was ill. 'If there's anything I can do...' I lost count of how many times I heard him say that. But there wasn't anything any of us could do. All we could do was just be there, over the weeks and months that followed, knowing the treatment wasn't working and Lizzie's cancer was spreading.

One morning it was just the two of us – time I treasured, which was slipping through my fingers like grains of sand. At least, that was how I felt. When I got there, in her living room, Lizzie was lying on the sofa, a pastel-coloured blanket over her legs.

As I went over to her, she held out one of her hands. Taking it, I leant down and kissed her cheek. 'How's it going?'

'On a scale of shitness…' Her eyes glistened. 'I'd say about a nine.'

My stomach tightened. Most of the way through, Lizzie had done her best to stay resolutely bright. But it was like it was in our mum's last weeks. That instinctive sense that time was running out. 'Can I get you anything?'

'More days?' Her eyes filled with tears. 'Sorry. I'm not having the best morning. Do you have time to just sit here for a while?'

'Of course I do.'

Lizzie was silent as I pulled an armchair closer. Then once I was sitting, she went on. 'Can I ask you something?'

'Ask me anything.'

'It's a big ask.' Her eyes seemed larger, her skin paler. 'It's about Rick. You see…' She hesitated. 'I really don't think he's going to cope too well – you know, when I…'

Die, she was going to say. But I couldn't bear to hear her say it any more than she could form the word. 'You don't know that's going to happen. Not yet. You could get a phone call about the latest wonder drug – any time.'

Her lips held the ghost of a smile. 'Tilly, it's too late for that.' Her voice was weak, but there was that Lizzie strength in her words. 'I know it's difficult, but please… Can we just talk about if the worst happens?'

As our eyes met, so much remained unspoken between us. But there were times words weren't needed – especially between me and Lizzie. 'You don't have to worry about Rick. I'll look after him.' It was the least I could do. And as I spoke, I could see the relief in her eyes.

'Thank you,' she whispered.

But there was something else on Lizzie's mind. 'Tilly? Can we talk about you?' Her face was anxious.

'Must we?' I attempted to say it humorously.

'Yes.' Her hand reached for mine again.

Getting up, I went and sat on the floor beside the sofa. Taking both her hands this time, I gazed up at the face that was so familiar to me.

'You are so many things to different people. You can't deny it – I've watched you. You're selfless, Tilly. You always put everyone else's needs first. I almost didn't ask you to look after Rick, but there isn't anyone else.' Her eyes didn't leave mine. 'I've never forgotten that day you met Adam. You were different.'

Tears were suddenly in my eyes as she went on.

'He lit a spark in you. Oh Tilly... You looked so alive. I've often wondered what would have happened – if you'd called off the wedding. If you and Adam could have had a chance.'

I blinked away a tear. 'Bit late, isn't it?'

She looked anxious. 'Have you ever thought about him?'

I sighed. 'If this is a truth session...' Looking at her face, I rephrased it. 'OK. Between you and me, yes. Of course I have. So many times...' My voice petered out. Once, Lizzie had got it out of me about Gareth's infidelity, but only after I made her swear never to talk about it. I forced a smile. 'But I have also thought that if I hadn't married Gareth, I wouldn't have the boys.'

'Or maybe you would have,' Lizzie persisted. 'Only instead of looking like Gareth, they'd have looked like Adam.'

'Oh, Lizzie... That doesn't help,' I said sadly. I'd never know what would have happened. 'In any case, there's no point talking about it now. I made the decision that felt right at the time. It's in the past.'

'What about the future?' Lizzie wasn't giving up. 'Is what you have with Gareth enough? I mean, he had an affair. I don't think I could ever have got over that.'

I rearranged the pillows behind her. 'We just got on with life. You were planning your wedding and Mum wasn't well.' I shrugged. 'After Mum was diagnosed, I was busy looking after her. Any problems Gareth and I had didn't seem important.'

Lizzie looked troubled. 'Don't you think it was a sign, Tills? That neither of you have been happy? And I know Gareth's incapable of articulating anything related to his emotions, but not you. You're not like that.'

When it came to signs, it would hardly have been the first. It was no wonder I was confused. I mean, my entire life was littered with signposts which I'd ignored at every junction, instead leaving them uprooted, scattered in my wake. 'Actually,' I said slowly. 'He did. Just once. At your wedding. He was watching you and Rick together. He commented on how happy you looked. I think he was envious. It was like as though he'd realised he and I had never felt like that.'

She looked uncertain. 'He was probably just looking at my tits.' She glanced down at her chest. 'I still had them back then, didn't I?' Her voice wavered.

'He probably was,' I said gently, remembering the way his eyes had lingered on her. 'But I'd say your first assessment was more accurate. As you said, when it comes to emotions, Gareth is somewhat limited.'

'Which brings me back to what I was saying.' Lizzie looked earnest. 'Why are you sacrificing your happiness for him?'

I was used to Lizzie being direct. But... 'Sacrificing?' I frowned.

'Why do you stay together?' She stared at me. 'Just imagine for a moment, if you were free, Tilly. What would you do with the rest of your life?'

Free... I closed my eyes, felt a smile on my lips, for a moment tasting how freedom used to feel. But it vanished just as quickly. My carefree, teenaged years were long gone. Real, adult life had obligations, commitments – didn't it? Opening my eyes, I looked at Lizzie. 'In answer to your question...' I faltered. But it was one of those defining moments. When Lizzie's days were running out, the thought of simply going through the motions for the rest of my days, felt terribly wrong. 'Can I get back to you on that?'

Suddenly needing air, I got up and went over to the window. Pushing it open, I gazed out onto the pretty cottage garden Lizzie and Rick had planted. A garden that the way things were going, would long outlive her.

'Tilly.' There was impatience in my sister's voice.

I turned to look at her. 'Yes?'

'You're lucky. You still have time.' She paused. 'Please... make sure you don't waste it.'

'Staying with Gareth, you mean?' I went back over and sat on the floor again.

'It isn't for me to tell you whether to stay with him or not. You're the only one who knows what matters most to you.'

I sighed. It was a sigh of frustration, of feeling stuck. Of having too many thoughts in my head, not least about Lizzie. 'I will work it out. I promise you.'

'You'd better.' She sounded less anxious. 'Otherwise, you know what will happen, don't you?'

I looked at her warily. 'I'm not sure what you mean.'

She rolled her eyes. 'If you're not meant to be with Gareth – and believe me, you're not. Damn it... I promised myself I wouldn't say that. But I have. Anyway, what I was going to say is as far back as when you first met Adam, like I said, I think he was a sign. You weren't meant to ignore it, but you did. It's only a matter of time before there's another plot twist.'

'On the subject of plot twists, I saw him again,' I said quietly.

'Adam?' She stared at me. 'You haven't told me that, either.' She looked indignant. 'Anything else I ought to know?'

I hedged. There probably were one or two small things but they could wait. 'Actually, I've seen him a couple of times. The first time, he was with his wife.'

Lizzie's eyes were like saucers. 'What was she like?'

'Believe it or not, she was a bit like me.' I shook my head. 'She even had the same colour hair. I bet she's a hub, too.' I hadn't meant to say the last bit out loud.

Lizzie gave me an odd look. 'A hub?'

I shrugged. 'A hub is someone who's at the centre of other people's lives. I always picture them as the person holding the strings of all these brightly coloured balloons floating around them.' As she looked at me blankly, I went on. 'The balloons are everybody else's lives.'

'You're talking about you, aren't you?'

I shrugged. 'It's a good analogy, don't you think?'

A smile twitched on Lizzie's lips. 'So what colour's the hub?'

'Beige,' I said immediately. 'Not cool neutral beige. We're talking murky dingy beige – kind of unwashed looking.'

Lizzie was silent, then her shoulders started to shake – I assumed with laughter, until I saw she was crying.

'Don't cry, Lizzie.' Shuffling closer from where I was still sitting on the floor, I reached up and put my arms around her.

Lizzie wiped her tears away. 'You have no idea, do you?'

'No.' I was genuinely perplexed.

'Dearest Tilly, you are not beige.' Her eyes gazed into mine.

'You are the loveliest, most rainbow-coloured person in the world.'

Overwhelmed, I wasn't aware of the tears streaming down my face. Was that how Lizzie saw me? As heart-warming moments go, it was a stonker. One that shattered my heart into thousands of pieces. But as Lizzie held me in her arms and my body shook with sobs, I could already feel them start knitting themselves back together again, as I realised that this was a gift – in more ways than I knew. Glued together with Lizzie's love, my heart was stronger.

It was just as well. Within just two weeks, Lizzie was growing weaker. Knowing time was running out, I went to see my dad.

'I don't think Lizzie has long,' I said gently. 'A few days maybe.'

He stared out through the window. 'Has someone told you that?'

'Dad...' I went over and stood beside him. 'They don't need to. She's really weak.'

'I'm praying,' he said quietly. 'That our Lord will let her live. If she doesn't, then we just have to accept that this is His will.'

Standing there, my head filled with all these things I wanted to say to him. *Lizzie isn't religious... God wasn't a lot of help when Mum died... He has no right to decide if Lizzie does...* I bit them back; my father's faith was absolute. 'I just thought you'd want to see her.'

He went that afternoon. They spent quiet hours together and I'll never know what was said. But I was grateful at least that Lizzie found a tentative sense of peace with the ending of her life. Then by late July, my sister, soulmate, my heart, my rock, had gone, leaving this world a colder, darker place without her.

18

A good traveller has no fixed plans, and is not intent on arriving.

— LAO TZU

The thing about travelling is when you start out, it's all about the journey: the booking of tickets, the gathering of what you need to take with you, then showing up at the right time. The boarding of trains and flights – fog permitting, that is – as you navigate your way to your destination.

So far, that's what I'd been doing. My mind had been preoccupied with the getting here – but now that I was here, however, it was a whole other matter. What did I do with my days? I mean, Chania was lovely and Andreas and his wife were charming. Nothing was too much trouble for them. But I wasn't used to all this uncluttered time; all those empty hours when it was just me and my thoughts. Troublesome, uncomfortable ones I'd rather not have to think about.

'Perhaps you need a purpose, Tilly,' Nicos said one night over a cup of coffee at his restaurant as dusk was falling.

Which wasn't entirely helpful. 'I'm trying to teach myself the opposite.' I tried to explain. 'You see, I used to have many purposes,' I told him. 'In fact, you wouldn't believe how many.' I started telling him my life story – or at least, a selectively edited version of it. You know, the devastating part about Lizzie dying; the sad bits about Gareth and Olivia, then Gareth selling the house. The thought brought me up short. 'He isn't going to be happy with me,' I said to Nico. 'He wanted me to call him. He wants to talk about an offer we've had.'

'Do not feel guilty,' Nicos said solemnly. 'He cheated on you. He deserves nothing.'

It was all very well Nicos saying that. And in a sense, he was right. But the house was always going to tie me to the past. 'We have to sell it sometime. And he wants his share of the money so that he can buy another house.'

Nicos frowned. 'Where is he living now?'

I shrugged. 'At his girlfriend's, I guess. I don't know where that is.'

'So he is not homeless.' Nicos sat back. 'This man is trying to make you do something you are not ready for. Do not let him bully you.'

I stared at him, slightly shocked. 'Do you know what, Nicos? You're right.' If not exactly bullying, Gareth was definitely putting the pressure on. A sigh came from me. Why had it taken someone else to point that out to me? 'What do you think I should do?'

'I think you should not hurry, Tilly. If it is this year or next year, it isn't important. Not really.'

I stared at him. Then the cogs of my brain started turning as something fell into place. 'It isn't, is it?' Again, I couldn't believe I hadn't seen it, but it was only Gareth who was driving this. In the context of life-or-death terms, there really was no hurry for any of it.

Later that evening, however, when I did call him to tell him what I thought, Gareth had his own, very strong and uncompromising reasons on why we needed to sell the house, not just soon but immediately. 'It means we'll both know where we stand, financially. We can draw a line.' He paused. 'I think you need closure, Tilly.'

I felt myself bristle. Since when had he cared so much about what I needed? And after shacking up with Olivia, Gareth had well and truly relinquished the right to have an opinion about my life. 'I do not *need closure* as you put it,' I said furiously. 'For your information, I'm having a great time, Gareth. Our marriage is over, I realise that. And I've never been happier. But I see no reason to accept the first offer that comes along, especially when the house hasn't even been marketed properly.'

He was silent for a moment. 'It isn't that simple,' he muttered.

My ears pricked up. 'What do you mean?'

'Never mind.' He sounded like a sulky little boy.

'Look, I suggest you ask the agent to put the house on the market. Let's see what happens. If no one's interested, then we can consider this offer again.' But the thing was, I knew Gareth. I'd known him for far too long. My suspicions were growing that there was something he wasn't saying – to the point I would have bet money on it. Frowning, I felt the cogs in my mind whirring again. 'Did you say it was a friend of the agent who wants to buy our house?'

'Not exactly.' He sounded uncomfortable.

I started to get irritated. 'Why can't you just be straight with me?'

'Maybe because I know you won't like it,' he said.

Done with walking on eggshells, I cut to the chase. 'What's going on, Gareth?'

He was silent for a moment. 'OK. So it's me who wants to buy the house. Well, me and...'

Before he could say Olivia, I exploded. 'You actually thought you could cheat me out of the full value of the house, to buy it at a bargain price so that you can move in there with *her*?' Angry didn't begin to describe how I was feeling. I was incandescent. 'Even putting the money part of this aside, what about the boys? Have you even begun to think how weird it would be for them to have their father living in the family home, the house they grew up in – *with someone else*?'

'It was Olivia's idea,' he said. 'And there's no need to throw your toys out of the pram. It's a practical solution that works for all of us.'

'Except me,' I flashed. *Toys out of the pram* indeed. He really was unbelievable. I thought of all the names under the sun I wanted to call him, just about managing to hold them inside. 'About the boys... Why don't you ask them their opinion on the fact that by buying the house at a bargain price, you're doing their mother out of... what are we talking about... several tens of thousands?'

'I'd make it up to you,' he said miserably.

'When would you plan to do that?' I asked. 'After the baby arrives, with all the extra expenses that come with that? Or after Olivia's had a new kitchen put in – which believe me, she will want to, even though ours is new, just as she'll want to rip the bathrooms out.'

'Olivia's an interior designer,' he said. 'We'll get the work done at a fraction of the usual cost. In fact, we should make a—' He stopped suddenly.

But he'd given himself away. Several steps ahead of me, he'd already thought it all through. I felt my blood chill. 'Do go on,' I said icily.

'That was it. There isn't anything else to say.'

But he was lying. I could tell. 'I think I know what you were about to say, Gareth. You were going to tell me that you and Olivia should make a killing – on selling our family home once you've done it up. Of course, you didn't want me to know you're planning to screw me over – for the second time.' I paused, gathering myself. 'There's one thing I would like to say. And that is, I never want to speak to you, *ever again*. Do I make myself clear?'

Without waiting for a reply, I ended the call and switched my phone off, still fuming. Then I opened the door onto my own little balcony and stepped outside.

The air was cool and as I gulped deep breaths of it, I felt my heart rate start to slow. Then I chastised myself. It wasn't so long ago I was feeling sorry for Gareth. When he clearly cared so little for me, how ridiculous was that? And what about Olivia? If I were in her shoes, I wouldn't want to move into my lover's family home. Maybe I should call Gareth back. Tell him it's a good idea, after all. Let her find out the hard way; surround herself with memories of our family that will be like ghosts. To listen to Rick banging on when he calls in for tea and sympathy. To explain to the boys why this is *such* a good idea, even though it may not seem like that.

But I already knew that women like Olivia didn't care about any of those things. As for Gareth... The further away I got, the more I realised my husband wasn't the man I wanted to believe he was. Or maybe he never was. In my desire for us to be a happy family, I'd gone through most of our marriage with my eyes closed.

Soothed by the quiet, I was calmer as I heard the back door of the guesthouse open and close. Then Andreas's voice came through the darkness.

'Tilly? Are you all right?' he called up. 'I thought I heard voices.'

'I'm fine, Andreas. I was talking to my ex-husband. But it's over now. We're done.'

'I am sorry,' he said in a sad voice.

'Don't be.' I paused. 'He isn't a nice man. And I'm fine. In fact, I'm better than fine. Goodnight, Andreas. I'm sorry if I disturbed you.'

'Goodnight, Tilly.'

I listen to the door close again. Then, leaning against the balcony, I close my eyes. The end of a marriage was always sad. But so was someone who'd lost herself, in the passing of time. And I was not going to be that person – not any more, at least. As I stood on that balcony in that beautiful place, suddenly I was done with feeling sorry for myself. From now on, I was taking control of my life. Elena, Tallulah, Mum, Lizzie, all of them were right. This was *my* life.

I frown for a moment. When I looked back, there had been so many signs over the years. Gareth's reluctance to become a father; his refusal to accept my pregnancy; his inability to even deal with my morning sickness – Gareth's never been good with vomit. Not mine, not even the boys. His answer to such things was to make himself scarce, which in those days meant going to the pub.

But there's no point in dwelling on those days any more. Much though I wish things could have been different, they've gone.

I imagine them carried out to sea in one of the little boats in the harbour, leaving them where they're meant to be, where they can no longer hurt me.

In the past.

* * *

The following morning, planning to go exploring, I picked up a coffee and flatbread on my way to the bus stop. The sky was silvery where the sun was rising, the breeze cooler than yesterday and as I walked, I had a spring in my step. The still night hours had provided the perfect resolution to the Gareth-and-the-house dilemma. I had no obligation to dance to his tune. It was as Nicos said. It could wait.

Sitting on the bus, I took in the other passengers. Greeks of all ages, a mother and two young children; then I gazed out of the window. It was funny, but already, I was adjusting. And OK, it still felt a little odd, but no longer was I starting each day with a long list of chores. Washing sofa cushions that were still clean from last time, scrubbing the spare bathroom that never got used. Blitzing an already spotless house before dutifully calling my father – that's if Rick hadn't made an appearance. Here, I had none of that.

Thinking of my dad, I sighed. There was no way he would ever understand what I was doing here in Crete. As far as I knew, he still believed it was my fault that Gareth decided to leave me. And I hoped my dad was OK. But, at least for now, he wasn't my responsibility.

If that made me selfish, so be it. There was nothing wrong in clawing back a little time for myself. There couldn't be many better ways to spend it, either, than discovering a new and beautiful corner of this world. I took in the little villages we passed, the herds of goats, and rocky hills; the views of the shimmering sea. Then before I knew it, we reached the village of Platanias.

Getting off the bus, I found myself in a quiet street. The bus stop wasn't far from the sea. But today, I had something else in mind. Getting out my map, I put my trust in my map-reading skills and started walking.

It wasn't long before I reached my destination. And yes, maybe it was one of the nostalgic attacks that used to drive Gareth up the wall. But as it came into view, I just stared at it, in wonder. I mean, even in Greece, there was nothing quite like a deserted railway station.

* * *

'An old railway station always makes me think about what life must have been like. When it was still running,' I said to Nicos that evening.

He looked bemused. 'I think back then, you would find that life was hard. But if you like history, you must go to Knossos – and Rethymno. You will find a feast for your eyes there.'

'Sure,' I said, mentally making a note. 'But I suppose the thing about railway stations is that they're in the recent past. I mean, they're not that old, are they? I always think getting on a train is like embarking on an adventure. All those sights you never get to see from anywhere else.'

'We have not had trains in a long time.' Nicos gave me a strange look. 'We walk, and we have cars and buses. It is an island, Tilly.' He frowned. 'I do not understand.'

I sighed. 'I suffer from nostalgia, Nicos. I like things that remind me of the past – mostly *my* past. I also happen to like railway stations.'

'Then I am pleased for you. But the past...' He hesitated. 'It is gone. Now, things are different. In many ways, this is good. You must excuse me. I have to work.'

'I know.' Knowing he didn't get it, I watched him go inside the bar, then turned my attention to the harbour just as an old man shuffled into view. He looked unsteady as he made his way along the harbour front. Then just metres away from me, he stumbled and fell.

I got up and rushed over, realising he was the old man I'd noticed on the ferry on my way here. 'Are you OK?' Completely forgetting he probably didn't speak English.

Grimacing, he tried to sit up, then slumped back.

'Stay there.' I held his arm, looking around for help just as Nicos came out of the bar. 'Nicos?' I called out. 'I need your help. Quickly.'

Looking towards me, he came hurrying over. Crouching down, he spoke in Greek to the old man, before turning to me. 'I know him. His name is Michail...' He frowned. 'Did you see what happened?'

'One minute he was just walking along. Then he seemed to collapse.'

Nicos spoke in Greek to the man again, before looking at me. 'We will try to get him on his feet.'

We each took one of his arms and tried to help Michail up. But it soon became apparent, he was in too much pain.

Nicos looked worried. 'Can you stay with him? I will call the ambulance.'

I took off my jacket, folded it and put it under the man's head. 'You'll be OK,' I said – in English, obviously. But a reassuring voice, even one you couldn't understand, I figured had to be better than nothing. 'Nicos is getting help. Someone will be here soon.'

Nicos was soon back, carrying a blanket which he draped over the man. 'That is good,' he said, nodding towards my jacket-pillow. 'They should not be long.'

Michail's eyes fluttered open briefly and he said something in Greek, wincing as he tried to reach something in one of his pockets. After taking out a key, his hand was weak as he pushed it towards Nicos. Then closing his eyes, he was still.

Noticing the colour of his skin, alarm bells were going off. 'Something's wrong, Nicos. Where's the ambulance?'

Nico felt his wrist. 'His pulse is very weak.' He shook his head. 'They will be here as soon as they can.'

The longest five minutes passed – and that's really all it was. Five minutes, before the ambulance arrived. Filled with relief, I stood back and watched the paramedics check him over, before expertly moving him onto a stretcher.

Nicos picked up my folded-up jacket and passed it to me, as one of the paramedics spoke to him. Then we stood there watching as they drove away.

'Poor Michail,' Nicos said. 'He lives alone – on the edge of Chania. I must call his daughter. She lives in Heraklion.' He frowned. 'For a long time now, his legs have not been good. I have no idea what he was thinking, coming all this way.' Then he glanced at a bag Michail must have dropped. Picking it up, he looked inside. 'This is why,' he said, showing it to me. 'He came to buy fish. I will put it in his freezer – he has given me his key. He has a cat, and a few chickens. He wants me to ask his neighbour if they'll feed them.'

'I could do it.' The words were out before I could stop them. But when it came to helping others, there was no stopping me. 'Until he's out of hospital – if you show me where he lives?'

'You would do that for a stranger?' Nicos looked surprised.

I didn't know Michail. But wasn't it how the world worked, people rallying round at times like this? 'Nicos. Look at me. I'm not busy. And I'm good at helping people,' I added.

'Maybe you are a little Greek,' he said. 'We help each other – families, friends.'

'Maybe I am.' Liking how that sounded, I smiled at him.

But there was no time to stand still. 'We will go in my car,' Nicos said.

'But Nicos,' I said, 'don't you have to work?'

He shrugged. 'The restaurant is not busy. It is October, Tilly.' He said it as if I was a particularly stupid person. 'You are ready?'

* * *

Michail's house was a five or six minute drive away, and I tried to memorise the route as Nicos turned up a narrow, uneven street of terraced houses, then pulled over and parked at the side.

'It is this one.'

I took in the peeling blue paint as he nodded towards a front door. Then I followed him as he unlocked it and went inside. The house was in darkness and after finding a switch, the single bulb dimly lit what appeared to be a small living room.

'Come.' Nicos walked through a doorway into a bigger, untidy kitchen with a door that opened onto a surprisingly large garden. He switched on an outside light. 'Here comes the cat.'

A large black and white cat trotted across the garden, followed by a couple of others, one ginger and one black.

'In Greece, there is never just one cat,' Nicos said ruefully.

After opening a few cupboards and finding the cat food, he put it down then went outside, where a handful of scrawny chickens appeared out of the shadows. 'Michail keeps them in there.' Nicos nodded towards a flimsy chicken run. 'If we feed them, hopefully they will follow us.'

I watched as he successfully herded the chickens into the run and closed the door, then after checking inside the chicken house, came back holding three eggs.

'You should take these,' he said.

I shook my head. 'Thank you, Nicos. But you are forgetting. I don't have any way of cooking right now.'

'Of course.' He was silent for a moment. 'But who knows. It is possible this will change.'

I stared at him. 'What do you mean?'

'Today, things are like this. But you do not know what tomorrow will bring.' He locked the back door and I noticed the cat flap. 'None of us know,' he said cryptically. 'We are done here.'

I followed him out to the car where he handed over the key to Michail's house. 'If you are sure you can do this, I know Michail will thank you.'

'It's fine.' My heart was already warming at the thought of being able to do something to help. I mean, it was true what I said to Nicos – it wasn't like I was exactly busy. And it was a basic human need, wasn't it? To have a purpose? Anyway, it wouldn't be for long. Just a day or so, until Michail was home. Then I frowned. 'What did you mean back there? About things changing?'

'I was thinking if you like it here, you might stay.' He started the car. 'Who knows? But it is one of life's greatest certainties, Tilly. Surely you must know. That things always change.'

19

Motherhood: All love begins and ends there.

— ROBERT BROWNING

This recent chapter of the past fades like a dream, then merges with the whiteness around me, as I remind myself where I am. *In the hospital; in Crete. I need to wake up and open my eyes.*

I will my eyelids to move, my lips to form a word. A sense of panic returning. It's as if I've become removed from myself. My body is inert; however hard I try, nothing happens.

I'm not sure how much time passes, but in this strange in-between place in which I find myself, I become aware of the boys around me. Then their voices reach me. Robbie's, trying not to sound anxious; Alex, obviously concerned, love swelling in my heart as I realise this isn't a dream. That they *are* here.

'We love you, Mum,' I think I hear one of them say.

'You're going to be OK.'

Warmth wells up inside me. But it's followed by fear, too, a tumbling ocean of it. What if I'm not OK? I can't bear that when they should be living their carefree lives at uni, they have to see me like this.

I desperately try again to form the words.

I love you both, so much. To the ends of the earth. Further...

But as before, nothing happens.

The boys know I love them, though. Being a mother has been my proudest achievement. OK, so I didn't do so well on the marriage front. But where the twins are concerned, I can honestly say I've done my best to give them a sense of being firmly rooted while letting their wings unfurl. I've loved them in bucket loads. Fed them plenty of home-cooked food, too. And I mean plenty of it. I must have cooked thousands of cakes over the years, millions of roast potatoes, not to mention snacks – if you've had a teenaged son, you know how hungry they get, how much shopping is required to keep the hangry gremlins at bay.

Still so much lies ahead... I've imagined their graduations, my pride knowing no bounds. Seeing them travelling the world, watching where life takes them; in the future, with bright-eyed, adoring girlfriends. Eventually maybe weddings, grandchildren. I still haven't warned them about the wedding part of things – that if they have doubts, to listen to them; to not do what I did. But if I hadn't, I wouldn't have them in my life.

This life. The one where I'm unconscious, unable to move; my future unknown.

Not once have I imagined anything like this.

20

Nothing has more strength than dire necessity.

— EURIPIDES

It's an interesting subject, strength. Human beings possess it in immeasurable quantities. But as we all discover at some point, life is also fragile and finely balanced; can be cut off in its prime by something as everyday as a few rogue cancer cells or a wrong step on a flooded Cretan street.

Michail's house comes into my head, the chickens in his garden and the cats that were the only reason I'd gone there, as I realise that was most probably the biggest sign of them all. It hadn't been my responsibility, but Tilly the hub had taken it on – another responsibility that wasn't hers. And, quite literally, bringing me down was the only way the Universe could stop me.

And this is the thing. What happens if I'm not this hub? This person who comes to the rescue of others, who is always there in a crisis, who am I? But in the midst of this place I find myself, the answers floating around me are elusive; I can't reach them.

Sometime later, the scent of lemons reaches me. Fresh, sun drenched; evocative of a hundred summers. Alex's voice is like a dream.

She's always loved the smell of lemons. One time, we were in Italy... She made Dad stop just so that she could photograph the trees.

The memory flashes into my mind, vivid as if it happened yesterday; my heart twisting. It's of the four of us in a hire car, of Gareth's impatience to reach the hotel where we were staying, but stopping anyway so that I could stand in the shade of the lemon trees, inhaling the sweet scent of their tiny white flowers. Ten years old, the boys had been filled with excitement, joyful.

What happened to that woman? The thought dimly occurs to me. But all I want to do is take away the worry in Alex's voice. I concentrate all my effort into trying to move my hand. A hand that remains leaden.

Another thought suddenly occurs to me. I hope Gareth isn't with them. Or Rick. Even my dad. You see, in their eyes, I'm still the hub. They don't know how to see me as anyone else, least of all unresponsive in a hospital bed.

'*She fell in the street.*'

But it isn't any of them. It's a stranger's voice. Obviously, the stranger who saw me fall. I listen as he goes on.

'*There was a freak downpour. The road was like a river...*'

The voice is warm, concerned, the words connecting with something in my head, triggering the whisper of a memory as my heart misses a beat. You see, somewhere from my past, I know this voice.

'*I'm sure you'd like some time alone with your mum. If there's anything I can do, you know where to find me.*'

Two voices, in unison this time. My boys' voices. '*Thanks.*'

Suddenly I recognise the voice; my mind is in overdrive. *Is it Adam? Could he really be here?* It's too much to take in. After the chain of events that unfolded to bring me to Greece in the first place, how I ended up in Chania, how I came to be out in the torrential rain when I fell; out of all the people who could have been there when it happened, how come it was Adam who came to rescue me?

21

Never lose hope, my dear heart. Miracles dwell in the invisible.

— RUMI

Dreams can come true. And miracles come when they're least expected.

'Mum?'

Robbie's voice filters into my consciousness; I feel my hand move as his takes it.

'*Try and squeeze my fingers.*'

Doing as he says, for the first time, I feel a different sensation. It's intangible, more akin to the sense of skin against mine. But elation floods through me. It's a first since I've been lying here; there's absolutely no doubt in my mind that it's real.

'*Keep trying, Mum.*'

Has Robbie felt it too? I try again. Disappointment filling me when there's nothing. But it's enough to keep me going; to stop me giving up.

'*We'll keep trying, Mum. I'm not giving up.*'

As Robbie's words echo mine, emotion wells up inside me. I'm aware of his lips brushing against my cheek, of his familiar scent as he whispers, '*I love you, Mum. It's like Auntie Lizzie said. You're a rainbow. You're going to get through this.*'

I'm a rainbow. Am I? Is that what Lizzie told them? Is it really how my boys see me? Emotion overwhelms me. And because more than anything, I want to hang on, I choose to believe him. After all, there's nothing as powerful as a mother's love. So I start to make a plan. *When my eyes open, when my lips can form the words, when I hold my boys in my arms* – and all of these are going to happen, I tell myself. When the day comes that I can walk out of here, I'm not going to waste any more time. I'm going to live every beautiful second of the rest of my beautiful life.

For a moment, I think of the little bars along the harbour in Chania. Then I picture us sitting at a table at Nicos's restaurant – me with Alex and Robbie. We'll eat big plates of food, drink the finest Greek wine. Celebrate this life. As we watch the sun sink behind the horizon, I will listen to each and every word my boys have to say. Laugh about the past. Cry about Lizzie. Then we'll listen to the rattling of the boats moored, throw scraps of food to the stray cats. And we'll talk about the future.

With my boys beside me, there's nothing more I could ask for. Thinking of them, warmth wells up inside me. I sigh silently. Feel my lips twitch into the faintest trace whisper of a smile. Hear the whisper of a voice beside me.

'*Quickly. You have to see. Tilly is moving.*'

It seems to trigger a flurry of activity around me. As for me, I'm filled with a sense of wonder I wish I could share, because what none of them know is that it's love that's done this.

Love for my boys is bringing me back.

The signs are good, or so I glean from the voices around me. But to my frustration, it isn't immediate. Instead, another indeterminate period of time passes; but I have lost the ability to measure the days. It's time during which I'm aware of the haze around me starting to thin out now and then. But only to a point, which leaves me wondering.

If you believe in signs, am I being held where I am for a reason?

I send my plea out to the Universe.

Show me the way. Please.

Then as I lie there, my head starts to spin. Fear fills me. *This isn't supposed to be happening. I'm supposed to be getting better – they said I was.* But the haze is thickening again, the hospital fading out. And when the mist clears, I know instantly where I am.

You see, there's something I never told Lizzie or anyone else, instead choosing to block it out. It's about that afternoon a few days before my wedding; the afternoon I spent with Adam. That moment I've already told you about, when I got up to leave, when he stepped closer. *I wish you the best, Tilly. Of everything.* His lips touching mine.

I'd been about to walk away, to go back to my flat. But in that glorious moment, I'd forgotten everything else. It was as though we were the only people in the world. Feeling his lips on mine, I'd stood there. Then I was kissing him back, a kiss that became more passionate. Putting my arms around his neck, my fingers felt the softness of his skin, entwined themselves in his hair. Intoxicated, every cell in my body craving to be closer to him.

I remember his hesitation. *Was I sure?*

But the pull to Adam was too strong; even if I'd wanted to stop it, I couldn't have. In that moment, I'd never been more sure of anything in my life, as he took my hand and led me upstairs.

Realisations had come at me that afternoon. I'd known I was on the edge of something magical with Adam; that if I chose it, what lay ahead was beyond my wildest dreams. The connection between us only affirming that soulmates weren't a myth; they were real.

I wanted to find my courage. To call off the wedding. To explain to Gareth how I felt – for all I knew, he would have been relieved. But the hold of my programming was too powerful; I held myself back. And Adam knew.

'Maybe we should look at it this way.' As we lay on his bed gazing at each other, there was a lifetime together reflected in his eyes. 'Maybe we just have to say goodbye. And trust that there's divine plan or something. One thing I do know...' He stroked a lock of my hair off my face. 'However long it takes, I believe in us. I also believe there's a reason this is happening to us.'

'It's hard to see that,' I'd said tearfully.

'I know it is.' He paused. 'But perhaps we have to accept that, the way things are right now, it isn't our time.'

The saddest words – and in the years that have followed, I've reminded myself of them, over and over. *It wasn't our time.* I've kept what happened to myself, let Lizzie believe I'd walked away.

And in the years since, my boys have always been everything to me. Added to that, they've had to witness the end of a marriage. If only I could have been honest with Gareth, with myself back then, I would have called off the wedding, saved us all the pain.

A feeling of panic wells up inside me. You see, it's obvious, isn't it? I made a mistake. One that altered the course of my life. But here lies the paradox, because if I hadn't gone ahead with the wedding, I'd have saved myself from having to endure Gareth's infidelities.

But... I wouldn't have my boys.

The realisation hits me that out of all the probabilities that exist, however hard you search, there is no perfect answer. Maybe this is more about accepting the imperfectness of life, of the people around us. The way that people change, that life rarely works out the way we think it will. The reality that no matter the best of intentions, none of us know what the future holds. That only one thing truly matters through it all, and it isn't the nuts and bolts, the frivolous trimmings I've allowed myself to obsess over. Quite simply, it's love.

My psyche seems to sigh at this point, as though I'm letting out a breath I've been holding in my entire life. And that's when things start to go a bit haywire. One of the bleeping sounds grows louder, more urgent. Then becomes constant. There's a flurry of activity around me, of voices. Then it feels like my bed is moving, the haze darkening, before everything goes blank.

A single thought consumes me.

Is this what dying is like?

A feeling of anguish comes over me. If it is, I'm not ready.

By way of an answer, Lizzie's face appears in front of me. I feel myself smile. *It's so good to see you again. I've missed you.*

Her hand reaches for mine. *I've missed you too, Tills. But you're not supposed to be here. It isn't your time.*

What do you mean? It's not like I have a lot of choice. The fight seems to have gone out of me; my sense of anguish has disappeared. Instead, I seem to be floating on a wave of peacefulness, of bliss. *It's been a long haul, but I'm getting better. The boys have been to see me.*

Tilly. Listen. This isn't you getting better. This is dying.

Shock hits me. But it doesn't last. I've been so busy fighting this, I haven't realised how tired I am, achingly so, deep inside, in my soul. *I can't go on battling Gareth. Never getting anything right. I'm tired, Lizzie.*

She shakes her head. *No. Think of the boys, Tills. Think of all the life you have to live.*

As her words sink in, suddenly I realise Lizzie's right. It isn't my time. So exhausted as I am, I think of the boys, imagine a silver thread connecting us; with the remaining strength I have, I reach out and grasp it.

* * *

The haze has gone. In its place, there is pain. Pain I would tolerate magnified a hundredfold, because I can actually feel. More than that, I can open my eyes.

The blur in front of me clears to form a face. 'You've had us worried,' the nurse says in accented English. For the first time, I can see her dark eyes, her hair tied back, her royal blue uniform. 'You must rest, Tilly. You are doing OK.'

But I don't want to close my eyes; it feels like too much of a risk. Instead, I lie there, taking in the hairline crack in the white-painted ceiling, the muted sound of voices around me. Turning my head, I register the drip I'm attached to, a screen that's monitoring what I guess is my heart rate.

It's like I'm living out an episode of *Casualty*, in the starring role, no less. But my delusions of grandeur are forgotten as a familiar figure hurries towards my bed, behind him, another.

My heart. My everything. My boys are here.

22

On Not Counting Chickens

As things begin to get better, I think a lot, a little self-indulgently perhaps, about who I am and everything that's brought me here. But then I have spent many hours in this hospital bed.

And you see, in this crazily muddled mind of mine, I'm starting to work out how it all fits together. First up, there's our genes – and there isn't a lot we can do about those. There are our formative years, and by that, I mean our nearest and dearest. The parents we are born to, the friends we make, the social circle we hang out with. Even my old best friend, Jasmine, bless her, who left me with the sense that I was inadequate.

Then it all gets more complicated. I mean, throughout our lives we are *bombarded* with expectations and obligations. With rules about what's acceptable, which are basically about conforming to other people's ideas of what right is. There are our dads. And there are our mothers. Their joys, their trauma, their suffering that are a part of us, too; that if we allow them to, go on to shape our own lives.

In all this, what about what I think? How am I even supposed to know how I think? Is it even possible to isolate that from the tangle of other people's thoughts in my head? It's probably why I became a hub. It was the only way I could fulfil the sense of duty that had been instilled in me.

I think back to a couple of weeks ago, when Gareth told me about Olivia. I remember how upset I was. Actually, I was more than upset. Coming so soon after losing Lizzie, I was devastated. I couldn't bear the thought of selling the house. But it was never about losing Gareth. It was about losing control of my life. That flipping programming again – that the family home was where I'd live forever, would be a place for the boys to always come back to, in time with their own children. That marriages just somehow *worked out*.

But the reality is, life isn't like that. People are human. We make mistakes – people like me and Gareth. And meanwhile, things happen along the way. We make choices too, and ours drove us further apart from each other. There were disagreements, infidelities. In short, whatever love there was, it wasn't enough, while the house was a symbol, but no more than that. Home is wherever we are, with the people who love us.

'*Mum?*'

In my sleep, I smile a little.

'*Mum?*'

'Mum? Wake up.'

My eyelashes flutter, then I find myself looking at Alex, his lovely eyes filled with worry. It's going to take time for us to get over this. But we will get over this.

'Hey,' I say drowsily. 'Don't you have somewhere more interesting to be?'

'Not really.' He glanced behind him. 'There's someone to see you.'

This is where it gets weird, again, because as another figure comes into focus, I see it's Adam.

'Hello,' he says gently. 'How are you doing?'

For a moment, it's enough to just gaze into his beautiful eyes. I open my mouth and close it again. 'I'm OK,' I say, a little wondrously. 'You were there, weren't you? That day, in the rain?' There's more I want to say, like *What were you doing there? Why are you in Crete?* But at this point, there are just too many words.

'Don't try to talk, Mum.' Alex glances at Adam.

Which is all very well, but I have these questions. 'No,' I say quietly. 'Please stay.'

'We're under strict orders,' Adam says gently. 'You need to take things really easy.'

'We'll come back later,' Alex adds. 'Robbie sends his love. He had to go back to uni.'

Suddenly I feel terrible. It's where Alex should be, too.

He seems to know what I'm thinking. 'It's OK, Mum. I've brought work with me. Now try and get some rest.'

My eyes are already closing as they get up and turn to walk away. But fate hasn't finished with me yet and as the haze thickens and darkness swims into focus, I find myself pulled back to the place I've become so overly, ridiculously attached to. Our lovely family house.

Sitting at our kitchen table, I was going through the sympathy cards that had kept arriving since Lizzie died. I knew that at some point, life had to go on. But the fact was, I was stuck.

I didn't know how to be anyone other than Tilly the hub, at the centre of everyone else's universes. And one by one, the strings of the balloons I was holding were pulling free of my fingers and floating away.

However much I liked it or not, whatever he'd done, Gareth was an integral part of my life. It's just that even now, looking

back, the way it ended felt so *brutal*. Telling me he'd met someone, followed by the news that she was pregnant – the blow
multiplied because of how he'd behaved when I was pregnant
with the twins. As I say, positively brutal. But given our history,
given my ability to hang doggedly on no matter what was thrown
at me, maybe there was no other way.

In many ways, feeling as I did, it's remarkable that I got as far
as I did, sorting through my clothes and throwing so much away;
that only my most treasured things are stored in Elena's garage.
That I bought my ticket to San Jose, before fate redirected me and
in the strangest course of events, I ended up here.

I mean, honestly, if I hadn't offered to feed Michail's chickens
and cats, I'd never have got caught in the rain, or fallen. Or found
Adam again. But I did – and here I am. And so is Adam. Talking
of which...

'Tilly?'

This time, it isn't Alex's voice. Blinking my eyes open, I see
Adam standing there.

'Are you up for a visitor?' His voice is gentle.

'I think so.' As he sits down, I try to ease myself up in the bed,
which has the result of setting off all these bleeping sounds.

'Are you OK?'

'Fine,' I say as breezily as I can, given I've been unconscious
for... 'Do you know how long I've been here?' I ask him.

'Five days,' he says.

I exhale slowly. No wonder I feel exhausted. In five days, I've
relived most of my entire life. 'I didn't know.'

'I guess you wouldn't have.' There's an odd expression on his
face as he seems to study me.

'You found me, didn't you?' I ask.

He nods. 'Long story. I'll fill you in sometime, but...'

'Can you tell me now? If you're not in a hurry, that is?' I need to know, to start filling in the blanks. But more than anything I want to know what's brought him here.

'Well...' His eyes are warm as he gazes at me. 'I'm not sure where to start, really.'

'How about with the last time we saw each other?'

'That was years ago.' He frowns slightly.

'You were with your wife,' I say helpfully. But where is she now? And actually, we saw each other again, shortly after.

'That's right. Your boys were teenagers. They're great, by the way. You must be very proud of them.'

'*So* proud,' I say softly.

'About a year later, Louise and I separated.' He fidgeted with his hands.

I'm flabbergasted. They'd seemed so easy together. 'Why?'

'We came to the conclusion we'd grown apart.' He looks rueful. 'It was all very amicable, and we're still friends. We had a really nice life together. Both of us were happy. But I think getting older focuses the mind.' Looking thoughtful, he smiles. 'I suppose both of us knew we were missing something.' He hesitates. 'Remember we saw each other again – after you'd been to see a divorce lawyer?'

I nodded.

'I came back to look for you. It was the same when you saw me with Louise. I persuaded her to let me show her the town where I used to live. But I was looking for you that time, too.'

I find myself holding my breath. 'You should have told me.'

'It wasn't the time, was it?' There's warmth in his eyes as he looks at me.

'What about now?' I have to ask. 'Is there someone else?'

A smile plays on his lips. 'There's so much to talk about,' he says softly. 'I know you're here on your own – the boys told me.

But...' He holds my gaze. 'You and Gareth were together for such a long time. What happened between you?'

I frowned. 'You know we really are getting divorced?'

'Your boys told me. I asked if Gareth was here – that was the only reason.'

'Oh.' I'm silent for a moment. 'It's been quite shit, actually.' I sigh. 'When he told me he'd met someone else, my whole life seemed to fall apart. She's pregnant, by the way.'

For a moment, he doesn't say anything. 'It can't have been easy.'

'It wasn't.' I leave out the part about my meltdowns and drinking Gareth's whisky; how my friend Elena had to virtually wrestle my wedding photos away from me. 'When I found out, I decided to go away. I didn't know what I was doing, to be honest. So I bought a one-way ticket to San Jose.'

'Wow.' But instead of looking impressed as I'd hoped he would, Adam looks taken aback. 'You won't believe this, but I was living in San Jose until a few weeks ago. I was working out there.' He stares at me. 'How weird is that?'

I stare back at him. 'Do you know what's weirder still? It's that you were there and now you're here.' My head is starting to spin again.

Adam frowns. 'So if you were going to San Jose, how come you ended up here?'

'My flight was cancelled – the whole country was fogged out that day. I couldn't bear to stay in England, so I got on a train to Paris. Then from there, I went to Barcelona. Oh my God...'

'What is it?' Adam looks concerned.

'I thought I saw you while I was there. In Barcelona. You were there too.' I stare at him in disbelief.

He shakes his head. 'That wasn't me you saw. But actually, my brother lives there. Maybe it was him?'

'Your brother?' I look at him, firstly incredulous, then secondly relieved that I didn't make a complete and utter fool of myself.

'Then you came here.' Adam looks uncertain. 'Just randomly?'

'Completely. Well, I stopped at a few places along the way.' I gaze into his eyes. 'What brought you here?'

'I bought an apartment several years ago – not far from the harbour. I come here when I want to escape.' He pauses. 'But actually, I have a confession to make. It wasn't entirely an accident that I found you in the rain. I'd gone to look for you.'

'For me?' I screw up my face; this is getting weirder by the minute. 'But how did you know I was here?'

'I saw you with the old man when he collapsed. You know – the night the ambulance came out. You were with a Greek guy though, so I kind of thought I'd leave you alone – you seemed really friendly with him.'

'But that would just have been Nicos,' I say, aghast. 'He owns the bar.'

'I know who he is now.' Adam is smiling. 'I just didn't want to get in the way of true love – again.'

'Love?' Staring at him, I feel my heart start to race. 'You have to be kidding. You've got this all wrong. You see...' I tail off as beside me, one of the machines starts to bleep. Instantly, one of the nurses comes over.

'Your heart is beating too fast,' she says crossly. 'You must be calm, Tilly. This...' She points to the machine. 'This is not good. And you...' She points at Adam. 'You must leave. Now, please.'

'No,' I say hastily. 'I don't want him to go just yet.'

'I am afraid he has to,' she says firmly. 'I am in charge here. If you want to get well, you must do as I say.'

'Is everything OK?' Getting up, Adam sounds worried.

'Tilly will be fine. Please.' She tries to usher him towards the door.

He meets my eyes briefly. 'I'd better do as I'm told. You had, too.' He pauses. 'I'll come back tomorrow – if that's OK?'

'Yes.' But as he heads for the door, I'm realising just how much I want him to stay.

'It is important you rest,' the nurse scolds. 'These affairs of the heart, they are not good for you.'

'Tell me about it,' I say heavily. 'They have always been seriously, and I mean *seriously*, bad for me.'

'Then this must change,' she says quietly. 'That man...' She nods after Adam's retreating back. 'He is a good one. I can tell. No more bad men, Tilly.'

I gaze at her, slightly shocked at how she's summed it up; that she has the measure of Adam. But she's right. He is a good man.

Satisfied my bleeping has settled down again, she leaves me to rest. Lying there, I listen to her footsteps as she marches away. But as I think about life choices, it's true that not everything presents itself when you need it. Or maybe it does and you just don't see it at the time. But also, there's the question of how you look at it. There's the possibility also that sometimes there's some shit to wade through first.

A sigh comes from me. Am I on my way to the good part? One of these days, am I going to leap out of bed, newly invigorated, a new Tilly, ready to embrace the rest of my life?

Because right now, what's going on feels like an accelerated processing of everything that's happened to me. A kind of growing up that should have happened over the twenty-two years since marrying Gareth, years during which I've been going around with my eyes closed, that's instead been condensed into a few days of wake-up calls.

Closing my eyes, I try to calm my breathing. Then I'm

thinking of Adam, a sigh coming from me. Is it possible that even now, there's still a chance for us?

Stupid Tilly, I berate myself. He saw you fall – he simply did what any decent person would have done. *But you haven't heard the rest of his story*, I remind myself. Suddenly I can't wait to hear the rest of it – when – *if* – he does come back.

* * *

It's astonishing how much I'm sleeping at the moment. But sleep's when the body repairs itself. The mind, too – and I've a lot that needs repairing right now. Not just physically. There are all these realisations I'm processing, those spidery little neurons regrowing, so that hopefully, in some way, I learn from this.

When I next wake up, it's dark. Gazing towards the window, I can just about make out the stars twinkling; feeling a sudden pang. *Oh, I've missed the stars.*

Almost immediately, my eyes close and I drift off to sleep again, waking when a nurse comes back.

'Tilly?' she says quietly. 'The doctor is here. He wishes to talk to you.'

I know from her face something's wrong. 'Why?' My heart beats faster, the dratted bleeping machine trying to keep up.

'He will tell you.' She hesitates. 'I will ask him to come to see you now.'

It isn't a comfortable feeling at the best of times, lying in a hospital bed, reliant on other people. Especially when they know more than they're letting on. A very long ten minutes passes before the nurse comes back with a man.

'This is Doctor Elias, Tilly.' She glances at him. 'I will stay.'

His face is unreadable as he looks at me. 'I have been looking at your scan results.'

I frown. 'What scan?'

'While you were unconscious, we carried out a scan of your brain. There was some indication of bleeding.'

I gasp out loud. 'Bleeding? Why hasn't anyone mentioned it before?'

'Sometimes these things disappear untreated. But...' He glances at the nurse. 'In your case, we have concerns that it has not.'

I stare at them both. 'Why?'

'For one thing, your speech has become slurred,' he says quietly. 'We would not usually expect that – at this stage. Also, there is weakness in your left hand.'

There's nothing wrong with my speech. Ask Alex, or Adam. 'There is not,' I say hastily. 'I'll show you.' I raise my right hand with relative ease. But when it comes to my left, it takes super-human effort to move my fingers.

'This is why,' the doctor says gravely, 'we must carry out another scan. Just to be sure.'

I try to take in what he's saying. 'When?' My words sound fine to me. My tongue feels thick, but after what I've been through, that's to be expected. Isn't it?

'As soon as we can find someone to move you. You are lucky. It shouldn't be too long.'

As I stare at him, suddenly there's two of him. Then everything blurs, and I can feel fear like never before, the worst fear since all this started. A huge wave of it gathering momentum before rearing up and crashing over me.

'Tilly? Can you open your eyes?' The voice is distorted.

I try to open my eyes, to cry out, *What's happening to me?* But my body won't respond.

It's like I'm taking a step back from my life as I consider that I really haven't learned anything, have I? That's what this is about.

It's another sign. I might be saying I'm not Tilly the hub, but underneath, I still am, still thinking about everyone else. Worrying about everyone else. Dwelling on the past, on my losses, mistakes, regrets, none of which I can change. Forgetting that in all this, there's only one thing I have control over. And that's myself.

All of this whizzes through my mind at warp speed – which means there can't be too much wrong – as in that moment, I send a plea out to the Universe. Not God – like I've already said, I'm not religious.

I'll stop worrying about other people – about my dad, about Rick, Gareth, my marriage... I'll do anything. I have so much life left to live. Just please... show me how to get over this...

This time, the haziness is worse. No longer a place of in-between, it's where fear resides, a dark, overpowering presence, as I realise there are no guarantees, no reasons why the Universe should listen to me. There's no dressing it up. No spin to put on it. The truth is brutal; this last realisation one my entire life has been designed to avoid.

In essence, I am alone.

23

There is hope after despair and many suns after darkness.

— RUMI

This is where the weirdness steps up a little. This time, there isn't a haze around me, so much as a light, which scares me. I mean, you hear about people seeing a light as they're dying.

I'm not dying, I tell myself. Lizzie said it isn't my time yet, and she should know. Not that Lizzie's here. If I *was* dying, I'm sure she would be.

Instead, my mind focuses on that last bit I mentioned, about being alone. Because what I haven't realised until now, is that there's a simplicity to it. And in truth, I always was alone, emotionally at least. Buzzing around, ticking off my list of everything I had to do for everyone else. In other words, distracting myself.

Out of everyone I've ever known, Lizzie came closest to knowing how I felt. But most of us don't stop and wonder what's really going on in someone else's world. Not beyond the most surface level stuff. We don't know the dark thoughts each other harbours; share our worries, our fears, our mistakes.

We see what we see – my lonely, unhappy dad, as an example. I can empathise, but I will never know how it feels being him; after all those years with my mum, being alone. And take Rick. Of course, he's grieving – I completely get that. But I've no idea how he feels, either, deep inside; or whether the moment he stops, he feels guilty that he's here and Lizzie isn't. He's probably doing the only thing he can to keep his guilt at bay. He keeps grieving.

As for Gareth... Well, the truth is, I realise Gareth was as unhappy and lonely as I was. I shouldn't blame him for having the balls to leave. What was uncomfortable was the reminder that I didn't have them. And if I'm honest, it needed to happen. All those tears I shed with Elena and Tallulah... They were tears from a place of uncertainty. Of hurt pride; fear – of feeling the last twenty years had been wasted; of being alone.

Which takes me back to the start. I am alone. But apart from the little pieces of us we chose to share, we are all alone.

This morning, though, not for long. 'Tilly?' A hand touches my shoulder, the haze starting to lift to more of a January kind of twilight.

I move my head slightly, my eyelids opening just enough to see the same nurse as earlier.

'Hello,' she says kindly. 'It's all over.'

Shit. Is she talking about my life? Is it over?

She goes on. 'The surgery was straightforward. You must take it very easy.' There's a hint of a warning tone in her voice. 'But you should very soon start to feel much better.'

Surgery? I thought I was going for a scan? But whatever it is, it's over. Even better, I'm still here.

'Thank you,' I whisper. '*Thank you*,' I'm murmuring again as I feel my eyes close.

24

First say to yourself what you would be; and then do what you have to do.

— EPICTETUS

There's another way of looking at this. Isn't there always another way? That once upon a time, Gareth and I worked OK together. We bought a beautiful home, had our wonderful twins. Over the years, we chiselled and shaped each other into the people we are now. In a nutshell, Gareth and I were meant to be. Just not forever.

But that's probably true of many of us. In my biggest revelation yet, I realise that not all relationships we attach such permanence to are meant to last.

Others, however...

'Morning.' A large bouquet of flowers advances across the room towards me. As it's thrust aside, Adam's face appears. He glances around. 'I'm not sure I'm supposed to be here.'

He's obviously expecting to be banished again. I smile faintly. 'It's OK. I had surgery.'

'I know. Alex told me. I thought he'd be here by now.' He pauses. 'How are you feeling?'

'OK.' I gaze past him towards the door as Alex appears. As he comes closer, I can see worry etched into his face. 'Hey.' I reach out my arms as best I can.

'Hi, Mum.' Leaning down, he hugs me and I breathe in the familiar scent of him. He stays there for a moment – boys are never too big for a hug. Then gently he disentangles himself. 'Are you OK? The hospital said you had a bleed on your brain.'

'They haven't actually updated me yet. But the nurse said I should soon be feeling better.'

'Thank goodness.' Alex looks relieved. Then he looks troubled again. 'I'm supposed to have an assessment at uni next week.'

'Then go home,' I say quietly. 'Honestly. You've been so great coming here.' I pause, speaking seeming to take a lot of effort. 'But there's no need to stay now.'

'You're sure?' Alex glances at Adam. 'I can miss the assessment. I'm sure they'll understand.'

'I'm going to be around for a while. I'll keep an eye on your mum,' Adam says. 'I'll keep you posted – I promise.'

'Really?' Alex looks grateful. 'I'm going to stick around for a few more days. But term ends in a month. I can come back and stay for Christmas – if you're still here?'

'Christmas?' I look at him, astonished. 'I've only been here a few days. It can't be Christmas yet.'

'Mum, you've been here nearly three weeks in all.' Alex looks worried again. 'Are you sure you're going to be OK?'

I shake my head. 'But you were here. Yesterday – just before they took me in for surgery.'

Adam says gently, 'Tilly, that was six days ago.'

I'm staggered, truth be told. But what's a few days between friends? I can't get over how lucky I've been.

* * *

With the bleed fixed, I very quickly start to feel better. And though I'm told my brain will take time to heal, very soon, I'm ready to be discharged.

'You have somewhere to stay?' the dark-eyed nurse, Athina – as I now know her name is – says.

'Of course. I have a room in a guesthouse.' I pause. 'At least, I think I do. It's where I was staying before. I'm sure they'll have a room. I mean it is winter.'

But Athina shakes her head. 'Tilly, you must not be alone. What about your friend?'

'You mean Adam?' I blink at her. 'What about him?'

She rolls her eyes at me. 'He has a place. And I think he would be very happy to look after you. He's been here every day for you. You should go there.'

'But I don't need looking after.' I look at her, puzzled. 'Do I?'

'I think...' Athina comes over and sits on the edge of my bed. 'None of us like being looked after. We don't want other people to be... put out, I think you say? But answer me this. If a friend needed help, you would be there for them. It's what we do. Am I correct?'

'Every time,' I say without hesitation. Even if they're not a friend and a total stranger – like Michail. Isn't helping him the whole reason I ended up here?

'So it is the other way around.' She pats my hand. 'Adam wants to help you. Maybe you should let him. Tilly, I think I said before, Adam is a good man.'

I'm stunned into silence. But maybe she has a point. Maybe it wouldn't be so bad if Adam helped me. It's just that I'm not used to being helped.

Athina gets up. 'He is here. Your clothes are in the cupboard.' She gestures towards the bedside table. 'I will get your medication.'

As she walks away, my heart warms as I watch Adam come towards me. 'You don't have to do this,' I say immediately. 'I mean, it's very nice of you. But it's a lot to ask.'

'No one asked. I offered,' he says.

'Thank you, but...' I break off. 'Oh shit. I've just thought I have my suitcase and all my stuff at...' I struggle to remember the name of Nicos's brother.

'At Andreas's place? Don't worry. We can pick it up on the way.'

I shake my head, miserably. 'I can't believe how much trouble I've caused so many people.'

Adam frowns. 'Tilly, you have not caused any trouble for anyone. They want to help you. People love you. They care. It's what happens.' He pauses. 'You should probably get dressed.' Glancing around, he pulls the curtain around my cubicle.

Left alone, I find the clothes I was wearing when I came in, clean and folded in the cupboard beside my bed. I slip out of my hospital gown. My jeans are baggy when I pull them on, my sweatshirt deliciously familiar. 'OK. I'm decent,' I call out, putting on some socks and sliding my feet into my trainers.

Pulling the curtains back, Adam looks at me. 'Shall we go?'

Just then, Athina reappears with a bag containing my medication. She holds it out to me. 'Take care of yourself.'

'Thank you,' I say, a lump suddenly in my throat. 'Thank you for looking after me. And for everything.' Holding my arms out, I hug her.

Taking Adam's arm, we make our way outside. It feels surreal, as if I've been removed from the world – which in a sense, I have, for almost three weeks. But it's left my senses more acute. The air is clean and crystal clear, a weak sun just above the trees. There are glimpses of sea between the white-painted buildings; the sound of voices reaching me, chattering in Greek. Taking it all in, I'm mesmerised. And I want to stay that way, I'm realising. Mesmerised by the magic of being alive.

Adam's car is a small and battered Fiat.

'I've borrowed it. My car is off the road.' He opens the passenger door. 'I can't find anyone to fix it.'

'I like this one. It's cute,' I say.

'I'm glad. Personally, I find it noisy,' he says, getting in and starting the engine.

And I see what he means. I wind the window down and the noise gets louder, but it doesn't matter. I'm feeling the cool air on my skin as if I've never felt it before; the softness of the warm December breeze.

On the way back, when we stop at Andreas's place to pick up my stuff, it feels like weeks ago that I was last here. Then we carry on to Adam's place. It's as he said it was, a few metres from the harbour. Once parked, he helps me out, taking my arm again. Oh, I like the feel of his arm through mine. I like it far too much.

He unlocks a door and shows me into a cool hallway with a tiled floor and a staircase. 'Ah. I can't believe I didn't think about this.' Putting down my bag, he picks me up.

'You can't carry me,' I say.

'I think you'll find I already am.' Before I can say anything else, he carries me up the stairs. Then gently putting me down, he unlocks the door into his apartment and taking my arm, leads me inside. 'Make yourself at home. I'll get your bag.'

Now, I'm kind of oblivious as he says that. You see, when he said apartment, I was expecting a holiday home on one floor with a balcony that's just about big enough for a table. Not anything remotely like this.

The living space is huge and airy, simply furnished with a pair of huge pale sofas arranged to face the fireplace, the light pouring in through shuttered windows that give a view over rooftops of the sea. Tentatively making my way over, I push one of them open and just stand there.

It's like I'm in a dream. Maybe I am. Maybe I did die and this is what heaven looks like. My reverie is interrupted by the sound of the door closing. I turn to see Adam standing there.

'Your place is so lovely,' I say wistfully. 'If it were mine, I'd never want to move away.'

'Thank you. I really want you to treat it like your home.' He comes over and stands next to me. 'It's been empty far too much.' He pauses. 'Shouldn't you be sitting down?'

'I'm enjoying the view,' I say. 'So much. It's weird. Everything feels different since I fell.'

'It isn't surprising, is it?' His eyes gaze into mine. 'After what you've been through...' He breaks off.

'I nearly didn't make it, did I?' I say in a small voice, suddenly feeling vulnerable.

'You came close,' he says. 'But you're still here.' He takes one of my hands and leads me over to one of the big, squishy sofas. 'Why don't you sit down? I'll make some coffee. And lunch – if you're hungry?'

'Thanks,' I say. And I probably should eat something. But I'm not sure how to explain that it isn't food I'm hungry for. It's life.

* * *

This may seem a rather unnecessarily long-drawn-out end to a story that should probably be winding up right now, but it isn't over yet. First, I want to share a little of what unfolds next, because we all need reminding of the magic in this life. It proves that after the darkest times, the sun still shines. That it never really went away; I just lost sight of it, for a while.

Out of the blue, I get a message from Elena. Then she comes out for a couple of days, which is the perfect time for us to have a catch-up.

'It's been quite literally like a crash course,' I tell her. 'It feels like my brain has been downloading all this stuff.' I frown. It's exactly how it feels. 'Whatever. I don't see anything the same way any more.'

'It isn't surprising,' Elena says. 'So much has happened.' She pauses. 'You look different.'

I roll my eyes. 'My hair's dreadful.' Old habits die hard. But some of it was hacked off before I had surgery for my bleed. It's going to take time to grow back again.

'Your hair is fine. And you're lucky. It grows really quickly.' Then Elena frowns. 'You seem really calm.'

'I am now. But El, I had my moments of panic in the hospital. I could hear and I could think. But I couldn't move. More than once, I wasn't sure I was going to make it.' I hesitate. 'El? I saw Lizzie.'

Elena looks shocked. 'What do you mean? You saw her?'

'She was with me.' My eyes are filled with tears. 'She's still there. She told me it wasn't my time.'

'Thank goodness for that,' my friend says. Then she changes the subject. 'While he isn't here, I want to know all about Adam...'

'Well...' A smile crept across my face. 'The thing about us, is the timing has always been out...'

* * *

Even now, though, I'm not sure this is the right time. Adam is friendly, caring, concerned. But I sense a distance. And for my part I can't help wondering if he's looking after me as a good friend would.

'It's so nice of you, to let me stay here,' I say to him one morning.

He looks surprised. 'I wouldn't have it any other way.'

'Are we...' I hesitate. 'I suppose, I'm wondering about us.' I break off, gazing at him. 'I mean, I know I'm still recovering, but I really am happy to be with you.'

'Me too,' he says softly. Coming over, he strokes my hair back. 'You need to heal, Tilly. We don't have to rush anything. Just let me take care of you.'

Emotion sweeps over me. No one's ever said anything like that to me before. Christmas comes and the boys fly out for a few days – Adam's apartment is more than big enough. We spend a wonderful Christmas Day at Nicos's bar, drinking his finest wine and eating delicious food at a table overlooking the harbour.

It's time that's precious, but after they leave again, I can't shake off the cloud that hangs over me. There's the house in England still to be sold. Added to that, I don't know when Adam has to go back to work; I've no idea how long any of this will last.

That evening, I take my courage in both hands and confront him. 'You've been so kind. And this time together has been so...' My eyes are suddenly filled with tears. 'It's been so many things. But I really should think about leaving,' I say gently.

He looks startled. 'I had a feeling there was something on your mind. But I wasn't expecting that.'

I sigh. 'The thing is, this is your life. I still have a house to sort out in England. And I suppose I should meet up with Gareth and at least talk to him.' And the truth is, I'm not sure what my next step is.

'I know you have a lot that's unresolved. But then what?' Adam watches me. 'When the house is sold, what are your plans?'

'I haven't got any,' I say. *I've been a little preoccupied, remember?* 'I suppose I was thinking about buying somewhere small that could still be a home for the boys, when they need it. I haven't really thought much further than that. I know I have to, but until now, I haven't been ready.' I pause. 'What about you? Don't you have somewhere to be?'

'At some point.' He's silent for a moment. 'You know those times, when you find yourself at a crossroads?'

'Only too well.' My words are heartfelt. 'Is that where you are?'

'You could say.' He clasps his hands together. 'I'm due to go back to London with my current job. But I've been offered another – back in San Jose, believe it or not. I could do a year, then come back and carry on working as a travel writer. Maybe base myself here, even.'

'Wow.' I stare at him. 'Those are awesome choices.'

'They are. Believe me, I know that.' He turns towards the window. 'But it isn't helping.'

I can't help wondering if in some way, I'm complicating things for him. 'I should go, shouldn't I?' Staying here isn't helping either of us. 'I'll book a flight in the next few days.'

'That quickly?' He doesn't meet my eyes. 'Where to?'

I shrug. 'I guess England. I can stay at my old house for now. I'm sure I would have heard from Gareth if it had been sold.' Or if anyone had offered close to the asking price. Or maybe Gareth still plans to browbeat me into selling to him. My heart sinks at the thought of what I'm going back to. But I have to face the music at some point.

'Are you up to it?' For a moment, he looks anxious. 'It's quite a trip to make so soon after surgery.'

'I'll be fine. I'll take it slowly. I can ask for help if I need it.' I think how pleased Elena will be to see me.

'You promise you will?' Adam says.

Nodding, already I'm imagining going on one of my nostalgic walks to Selham railway station. Except that oddly, it doesn't have the same appeal. 'I need to go,' I say to him. 'It feels like there are boxes to tick before I'll be properly free.'

He nods. 'I think I know what you mean.'

* * *

I've asked myself over and over, when it comes to Adam, why I'm holding back. And slowly I'm working out what the answer is. Having only just started to find out who I am, I can't risk losing myself again.

Forty-eight hours later, after a rather quiet and poignant farewell dinner at Nicos's, Adam drives me to the airport. Neither of us says much; it feels like every other time our paths have crossed, that it's still not the right time for us, as for the first time I consider that maybe it never will be.

'Take care of yourself,' he says in my ear as he hugs me in the drop-off zone.

'I will.' Pulling away, I gaze into those gorgeous eyes. 'You, too.' I pause. 'The next step... It will work out, you know.' I smile. 'For both of us.'

There isn't much more to say. We've said everything we can. I don't stop to watch him drive away. Just turn and merge with the crowd making its way towards the terminal building, only as I leave him behind finally realising something.

You see, it's taken until these last few moments, but I think I've worked out what I want.

But first, I have to face everything that brought me here.

25

You must ask for what you really want. Don't go back to sleep.

— RUMI

Inside the airport, I drop my bag and make my way through security. Today, even the duty free doesn't exert its usual pull as I head for the gate, stopping to buy a coffee and drinking it along the way.

I'm still questioning the wisdom of what I'm doing. But whatever comes next, I have to make this trip back to England. Even though it's now January and the weather will be appalling; that our family home is not my home any longer. That every fibre of my body is telling me to stay here. To go back, find Adam; that I shouldn't be leaving him like this. But my head is telling me I have to.

The flight is quiet – four long hours of contemplation during which I replay the weeks that have passed since arriving here. How I felt when I got in the taxi in England that first day, dreaming of going to San Jose before the fog changed my plans; to all the stops and signposts, as well as leaps of faith, that eventually led me to Crete.

And now, I'm going back to England. By choice. I can't think of anyone in the world who wouldn't think I'm mad right now, going back to face a cheating husband, a grumpy father and a family home that's going to be sold – in January – when I could have been staying in Greece.

But sometimes, you just have to face things. There's also the small matter of the legality of staying. Oh yes, since Brexit, you can't even do that any more and have to deal with layers of bureaucracy, not to mention mountains of paperwork in order to do so. That, most definitely, is for another day.

As it happens, I'm spared the gloom of January, at least for a few hours; it's dark by the time my flight lands. Outside the terminal, I find the taxi waiting to drive me back to the house.

'Had a nice holiday, love?' the driver asks.

It wasn't exactly a holiday. And I did spend half the time in hospital. But he doesn't need to know any of that. 'Yes, thanks,' I say, gazing out of the window.

One hour later, when the taxi pulls into the drive, the security light comes on and to my surprise, I notice a car parked outside; trepidation filling me as I realise I'm straight into the thick of everything I came back for. Because it's Gareth's car.

My first thought is *Oh no, he's broken up with Olivia and moved back. Worse still, he wants me back.* Paying the driver, I'm wary as I get out. The driver lugs my suitcase towards the house just as the door opens and Gareth comes out. 'I'll take that.'

I follow him in, closing the door behind us. 'I wasn't expecting to see you here,' I say warily.

'I thought I'd come over and make sure the heating was on.'

He pauses, looking at me. 'I heard – about you being in hospital – from the boys. Are you OK, now?'

'I'm fine.' I take off my jacket. 'I really am. I nearly wasn't.' I take my bag through to the kitchen and seeing a vase of flowers on the table, I stop in my tracks. They can't be from Gareth. 'They're lovely,' I say.

'There's some wine in the fridge. I thought you might like a glass – after your journey.'

Frowning, I turn to look at Gareth. 'Why are you being so nice? Or maybe, considerate is a better word.'

He looks taken aback. 'I didn't like the thought of you coming back to an empty house. Is there something wrong with that?'

Oh my God. We're doing it already – overreacting to each other, slipping back into those tedious, pointless, niggling exchanges. 'No,' I say hastily. 'And I appreciate it. Really. I mean it.' I get out two glasses. But for once, I'm not walking on eggshells. I'm trying to break a pattern. 'Why don't you have a glass with me?'

He hesitates. 'Just the one.' Pulling out a chair, he sits down. 'How are you?'

'I'm fine now.' I don't want to share the details with him. Going to the fridge, I take out the bottle of white. It's a wine I used to love. After pouring two glasses, I take them over to the table. I pass one to Gareth and sit opposite him. 'How's Olivia?' She's the elephant in the room – and she probably is quite elephantine by now.

'Really well. The baby is due next month.'

'How does it feel?' I'm curious. 'Getting ready to be a dad again, when you're used to the boys being grown up?'

'All right, I think.' He pauses, a frown crossing his face. 'It's made me realise how badly I behaved – when I found out you were pregnant. And I'd quite like to do things differently this time around.'

This is when my mouth, quite literally, drops open. It isn't exactly news to me – I mean, Gareth did behave atrociously. But as revelations go, to hear him actually say that is quite a shocker. 'You did.' I'm oddly calm. 'We were too young, looking back. But d'you know what the worst thing is?' I pause. 'We never got over it, did we? We let it set the tone for the rest of our marriage.' And that's the saddest truth. 'That's what I regret. Not having the boys, though... They're the best thing by miles I've ever had in my life.'

'Mine, too,' he says. 'I was an arse, wasn't I?'

'You were,' I say. 'But you can't just blame yourself. I let it go on, building up my resentments, when it would have been much more grown up to talk about it.' I shake my head. 'Half the trouble was, it was engrained in me from the start that divorce was strictly no-go. Mad, isn't it?'

He manages a smile. 'When you put it like that...' He looks at me slightly awkwardly. 'Tilly? I do still love you. If you wanted to—'

'Gareth.' I cut him off. Who does he think he is, saying this now, after everything he's done; when he has a baby on the way – with Olivia. 'I think we both know you and I have had our day.'

'Do you mean that? I know how it seems, but—'

I interrupt him. 'I'm really not sure you do.' I shake my head. 'You're having a baby, for Christ's sake. What would Olivia think if she knew you were sitting here having a glass of wine with me, and you'd just told me you loved me?' I can't believe I'm taking Olivia's side.

'Sorry.' Sitting back in his chair, he sighs. 'Since you went away, I've been back here a few times. I've sorted most of our stuff – I guessed you'd taken what you wanted to keep. But all I could think about were the times we've sat around this table over the years – us and the boys. When your mum was still with us. And Lizzie, of course...'

I gaze at the man I spent so much of my life with; wonder *why* I did. 'From where we are now, is there any point in being anything else?' But there are still too many elephants in the room, in my life and we still haven't mentioned the last of them. 'Do you still want to buy the house?'

'I did.' He puts down his glass. 'But I'm not so sure now. On a purely financial level, it would make sense.'

'Only to you,' I remind him. 'You were trying to rip me off.'

'I'm really sorry.' He looks mortified. 'But it would never have worked. This was our house, Tilly. I'm not sure I want to live here with anyone else. Anyway, Olivia thinks...'

Ah, here we go. Just as I'm starting to think there's a shred of decency in him, I find out the real reason for Gareth's change of heart.

'...She thinks it might be nice to move nearer her parents. They live in Oxford. They've given her some money.'

'I see.' So there it is. History repeating itself. Lucky old Gareth benefitting from wealthy in-laws, all over again. But then I stop myself. *Don't be so bitter and twisted, Tilly. It isn't like you want him any more.* 'Sounds as though you've fallen on your feet.'

'You think?' Totally oblivious to the hint of sarcasm in my voice, he goes on. 'Her place is on the market and once it's sold, when you and I sell this house too...' He tails off. 'You probably don't need all the details.' He looks at me. 'So what about you? What are you going to do?'

'I haven't decided,' I say cautiously. 'I'll probably stay here till the house is sold – and I think we should get on with that as soon as possible. But afterwards... I'll probably go away.'

'For good?' Gareth sounds surprised.

I haven't consciously thought about it – until now. But living in England doesn't excite me any more. Whereas Europe, maybe Greece... Mulling the thought in my head, I like how it feels.

'Quite possibly.' Finishing my wine, I put my glass down. 'Won't Olivia be wondering where you are?'

'Yes. Shit.' He leaps to his feet. 'I should get going.' He looks at me. 'I'll speak to the estate agent tomorrow. Hopefully, we can get things moving, now that Christmas is out of the way.' He heads for the door.

'That would be great.' I watch him open it. 'Thanks for the wine.' Suddenly I remember. 'And the flowers.'

'You're welcome.' Then he looks confused for a moment. 'The flowers weren't from me, though. They were on the doorstep when I got here.'

As Gareth walks out to his car, I lock the door, then go over to the flowers. Stuck on the outside is a small brown envelope. Curious, I open it.

> *Dear Tilly, welcome home! I hope you find what you're looking for.*
>   *Love Adam xx*

Well. I haven't even given him my address; he must have asked one of the boys. But who else would send me flowers? A warm feeling fills me as I search the almost empty cupboards – Gareth has done what he said and cleared most of our stuff. But I find what I'm looking for. A big old chunky glass vase that was Mum's. The flowers remind me of Greece – in shades of clear blue, with sweet-scented golden mimosa and leaves I recognise as olive twigs.

I pick up my phone to text Adam.

TILLY

Thank you. The flowers are beautiful.

I pause, wondering what he's decided.

TILLY

> Do you know where you're going yet? Tilly xx

I press send, then instantly regret I didn't type 'love Tilly'. Not because I love him – though maybe I do. It's possible to love someone as a very good friend, after all, and as friends go, they don't get much better than Adam. Then because I'm overthinking things again, I text Elena.

TILLY

> Hi! I'm back!! Fancy a coffee? Or wine?
> Sometime this week? Xxxx

That night, I sleep in my old bed, the house both familiar and alien to me. I awake early the next morning to leaden skies and rain that make me long to be back in Greece. Picking up my phone, I read the message from Elena.

ELENA

> Thank God. I'll come over this afternoon if you're not busy. xxx

I text her back.

TILLY

> Come any time xxx

Then I read one from Adam.

ADAM

> Still undecided. Glad the flowers reached you.
> The sea's stirred up this morning. I think there's a storm on the way. Enjoy your stay. A xx

I can't deny I'm disappointed that he doesn't type 'love Adam'. But then it's not as though I typed 'love Tilly'.

I get up and go to the wardrobes to find that everything of Gareth's has gone. I'm impressed. Then as I go from room to room, I'm suspicious. It's too tidy, too organised, in a way that is most definitely not Gareth's style, which leads me to one conclusion, which is that Olivia has been here.

I imagine her going through our things, under the guise of helping him. Not at all liking how that feels, I think about texting him. But then I calm myself down. I wasn't here, remember? And it's done now. I need to get the hell out and start moving on with my life.

* * *

After getting up, I drive over to my father's house. Now, I will be honest here. Much as I'm looking forward to seeing him, I'm secretly dreading the state I know the house will be in.

As I turn into the drive, I'm unprepared for the nostalgia that wallops me head on. But then it will always be a place of lifelong memories; and it's exactly as it was when I left here – only three months ago, I remind myself.

Once parked, I get out, noticing the flower beds are tidy, that pinprick green shoots are poking through the earth.

As I stand there, the door opens and my dad steps outside, a broad smile stretching across his face. 'Tilly! You should have said you were coming over. I didn't know you were back.'

'Hi, Dad.' I hurry over and hug him tightly. 'It's really good to see you.' He smells of home and my childhood rolled into one.

'Come on in. I'll put the kettle on.'

Now, this is the bit I haven't been looking forward to, expecting the detritus of the months, a thick layer of dust, a grimy kitchen. But as I walk into it, to my utter astonishment, it's neat and clean, one of the windows cracked open onto the garden.

Relief washes over me. 'The place looks great, Dad.'

'Not bad, is it?' He gives it perfunctory glance. 'I have an admission to make. It isn't my doing. It's Rick's.'

'*What*?' Since when has my brother-in-law become my father's cleaner?

'Felt a bit sorry for the bugger, truth be told. He misses your sister terribly. Asked him if he'd like to come and stay. That was before Christmas. He hasn't left. He's not a bad cook, believe it or not.'

I'd always known Lizzie had him well-trained. But I didn't know he was good at housework, too. 'What about his and Lizzie's house?'

'He's putting it on the market. I know what you're thinking, but there are too many memories in that place. It was his idea to move in here for a while – he's not very good on his own, and I've rather got used to him being around. So I thought, why not?'

'I don't know what to say.' I watch him make us cups of tea, marvelling at how Rick being here makes an odd kind of sense. I mean, he and my dad were lonely; now they're not. 'I'm really glad it works for both of you.'

'Strange how things work out, isn't it?' He comes over, frowning as he puts the cups on the table. 'But I was rattling around in this place.'

I pick up my cup and sip my tea. 'I'm really pleased it's working out, Dad. For both of you.'

'Well, it does for now. I'm sure in time, Rick will meet someone else. But in the meantime, it's good for both of us. Now.' Sitting down, he looks at me. 'I want to hear all about what you've been up to.' He hesitates, clearing his throat. 'But first, I have a confession to make.'

I'm taken aback. 'You do?'

He nods. 'You see, when you went away, I have to say I felt quite cross with you. You and Gareth separating, then this...'

'Dad,' I start. This is not what I came here for. But he lifts his hand up.

'Please. Let me just say this, Tilly. I *was* cross. But then I got to thinking how it was Gareth who had the affair. And it isn't just that. I think that all of us had become rather dependent on you. Goodness knows, your mother used to tell me off for taking her for granted. I realised I'd been doing it again. Taking *you* for granted. I'm sure Gareth did, too. Anyway, I apologise.' A look of regret crosses his face. 'I want you to know I love you, Tilly. You're a wonderful daughter, and I really appreciate everything you've done for me.'

'Gosh.' It really is a day of surprises; I'm speechless for a moment. Then I blink away the tears that are suddenly in my eyes. 'I love you, too, Dad.'

It's actually the nicest time I've spent with my dad in as long as I can remember, as I consider that maybe absence really does make the heart grow fonder. It's also one of those life lessons, that without me sticking my oar in trying to fix everything for them, my father and Rick turned out to be perfectly capable of sorting out their own lives. It's just I never would have imagined it. But three months ago, I wouldn't have been able to stop myself.

* * *

'You are sure you're OK now, aren't you?' Elena looks worried when she comes over.

'I'm fine. My head has been scanned almost to death,' I tell her, which isn't the best choice of words, given the circumstances.

'So what now?' She cups her hands around her coffee mug.

'Well...' I look at her. 'I never thought I'd say it, but I'm definitely done with this house. I want it sold. I'm well and truly done with Gareth, too.' I pause for a moment, thinking of last night. 'It's over. In the past.' I try to think how to explain to her. 'All that grief and sadness… it seems to have gone. But nothing seems the same, now. All that time I was lying in a hospital bed, the weirdest thing happened, El. It was like I relived my life all over again.' I frown. 'Actually, not so much lived it… It was like I was observing it. The thing is, I saw things I didn't the first time around. It taught me so much about the choices I made – and about Gareth.'

'He's an arse,' she mutters.

'He knows he's been an arse,' I say quietly. 'He was here when I arrived last night. He'd even put a bottle of wine in the fridge. We had a glass together.'

'*You what?*' Elena's eyes are like saucers.

Then I tell her. 'He asked if I thought there was a chance for us.'

Elena looks shocked. 'Cheeky fucker. I hope you told him where to go.'

'Of course – you wouldn't believe how diplomatic I was. And it was OK, actually. You see, I've decided there isn't any point in rowing with him. We talked about the elephants…'

'Elephants?' Elena frowns.

'Just the stuff we were never able to talk about before – and the mistakes we made. But we both know there's no going back. What happened between us is in the past. He and Olivia are planning to move near Oxford.'

'Good,' she says with feeling. 'At least that makes it easier for you to stay around here. I mean, it is your home.'

'That's the thing,' I say slowly. I love El, and I don't want to upset her. 'It doesn't feel like home here. Not any more.'

She stares at me. 'What do you mean?' Then she looks at my flowers. 'Who are those from?' she says suspiciously.

'Those?' They really are the loveliest flowers. 'They're from Adam.'

But as I tell her how we left things, something happens inside my head. By that, I mean a kind of unravelling of all the confusion starts, and this glorious pattern begins to emerge. I see the shimmering threads of my life interwoven with those of Adam's. From our first meeting to the chance meetings since. The times we've just missed each other, been committed to other people. Culminating in now, when both of us are free – albeit in separate countries.

'So why are you hesitating?' Elena looks perplexed. 'Seriously, Tilly, I don't get it. Here you are in the middle of what seems like some great fated love story – if it's really like it is with Adam and you haven't embellished it...'

'I haven't,' I say firmly. I mean, honestly. What is she thinking? Me, embellish things? 'I suppose my marriage has left me a bit untrusting. Hardly surprising, in the circumstances. And if something's too good to be true, in my experience, it usually is.' I hesitate. 'Don't you agree?'

'Not always,' Elena says. 'Don't forget, Tilly. Life can truly be magical. Only you seem to have forgotten that.'

Once, I would have agreed with her. But as I'm all too aware, it can be magical – I rediscovered that in Crete. In the landscape, the people. In myself. *Oh Tilly. Even now, can't you be honest with yourself?* 'I don't think this is so much about realising how I feel,' I say, somewhat sheepishly. 'It's about finding the courage to admit it to myself.'

There's frustration in Elena's eyes. Right now, there must be a million things my friend could say to me. But mercifully, she keeps it brief. 'You need to call Adam,' she says. 'Immediately, for God's sake.' Leaning across the table, she pushes my phone towards me.

* * *

On this occasion I don't do as she says. I wait until she's gone, while I try to work out what I'm going to say to him. When eventually I do call him, it goes straight to voicemail.

Hi, it's me. Can you call me? I mean, it's Tilly, in case you haven't realised. Thank you.

I keep my phone with me, just in case. But by that evening, I'm anxious when he still hasn't returned my call. Telling myself he could be on a flight, I close the curtains, then warm up some soup and switch on the TV just as the news comes on, my focus sharpening as Greece is mentioned.

Suddenly remembering the storm Adam mentioned, I stare aghast at the images of windswept coast and flooding. *Oh my God.* Forgetting my soup, I pick up my phone to call Adam again. But like last time, it goes to voicemail.

Hi, are you OK? I've just seen pictures of the storm on the news. It looks terrible over there. Please call me.

Starting to panic, I open Google and search for more information on Greek news channels, my fears growing when Chania is mentioned, realising that if the storm is that bad, communications may well be down. I imagine the people I know in Chania – Adam, of course. But also Nicos and Andreas and his wife. Michail, even. All of them battling with the storm that's raging.

Putting down my phone, my mind is racing; my dominant thought, *I should be there.* And this time, it isn't about solving their problems, being Tilly the hub. It's simply because I care about them.

I pick up my phone again. Finding no direct flights, I book a flight to Athens, leaving at five thirty in the morning, followed by another flight from there to take me to Crete. Then like I did the last time, when I was supposed to be going to San Jose, I book a taxi to take me to the airport.

Sleep is impossible that night. Not because of the time the taxi will be turning up. It's the thought of Adam caught up in the storm; the reality that I'm unable to reach him. At 2 a.m. I make myself a coffee, my sleeplessness irrelevant when an hour later, the taxi turns up.

It's another indication of how much has changed in just a few months that unlike last time, I can't get away from here quickly enough. The roads are quiet, the drive uneventful. And even though it's early, the airport is busy, as airports always are. But by a stroke of luck my flight is half full and I have a row of seats to myself. After the aircraft takes off, I try to block out the worst-case scenarios filling my head, because fretting isn't going to help Adam or anyone else. And there's always the chance the storm will have blown through, that nothing is as bad as it looked on TV.

My hopes are short lived, however. After a very turbulent approach, when we land in Athens I'm met by chaos. As well as the damage it's caused, the storm has disrupted flights and led to ferries being cancelled. Finding an information desk, I'm told the airports in Crete are closed and flights are cancelled indefinitely.

I know from the San Jose experience that there's no point in getting worked up about it; that the airlines don't have a hotline to the elements. Finding a chair to sit on while I wait, I try to call Adam again. But yet again, it goes to voicemail. I leave him another message.

I'm in Athens. My connecting flight is cancelled. I don't know how long I'm going to be stuck here. When I knew how bad the storm was, I had to come back.

Sitting in the terminal, I watch the rain lashing against the windows. Outside, no planes are moving. In fact, nothing's moving. Everyone's taken shelter out of the storm. Wondering how exactly I'm going to get to Crete, above the kerfuffle around me, I hear my name called out.

'*Tilly?*'

Leaping to my feet, I turn my head to find out where it's coming from; through the crowd, seeing a familiar face. 'Nicos!' I hurry over to him.

When I reach him, he kisses me on both cheeks. 'What are you doing here, Tilly?'

'I heard about the storm. I had to come back. I've been trying to call Adam but he isn't picking up. Have you seen him?'

'I have not.' Nicos is silent for a moment. 'Everyone who can is leaving. Those of us who haven't, have moved to high ground. The storm...' He shrugs. 'It is the worst in living history. We do not know what we will go back to. I am going to my mother's, here in Athens. You can come with me if you like. My mother will make you most welcome.'

'That's really kind.' I pause. 'But I need to find Adam.'

Nicos nods. 'He is a good man. I think he was sad after you left. You were good for him.'

'He was good for me too.' I gaze at Nicos. 'Maybe I will see you again – back in Crete.'

'I think that is likely.' Taking one of my hands, he kisses it. 'If you do not find Adam, you can go to Andreas's house. Now, I must go to my mother.'

'See you, Nicos.'

I watch him make his way towards the exit, then for the next twelve hours, I wait. It's all any of us can do. There are no flights in or out of Athens; no trains or buses. Instead, all transportation seems to have ground to a standstill.

But the storm passes. Storms always do – my mum was right when she said that all those years ago, even though she wasn't talking about the meteorological kind. The sound of the wind gradually lessens, the intensity of the rain reduces to a drizzle before the clouds lift, thinning out as glimpses of blue appears.

Just before darkness falls, at last the airport reopens. So it is that fifteen hours later than anticipated, I'm on a flight as it takes off for Crete.

26

After Every Storm There Is a Rainbow

You can't see rainbows in the darkness. But I figure that doesn't mean there aren't any. And maybe rainbows are like the wind – just because you can't see them, it doesn't mean you can't feel them. After a rocky approach and my flight lands in Crete, I imagine a giant rainbow arching over the island, underneath which, somewhere, Adam is safe.

The airport terminal is crowded with delayed passengers waiting to leave the island. Making my way outside, the road is littered with debris from the storm as I head for the taxi ranks. And it's mad, really, but until now, I haven't thought any further ahead than actually getting here. I don't even know for sure that Adam's still here.

I give the driver Adam's address. 'It's a friend's house,' I explain. 'Will you be able to wait? If he isn't there, I will stay with another friend.' I try Adam's number again, but the line is dead. It's the same when I try to call Andreas.

'There is no signal,' the driver tells me. 'No electricity, either. The storm has knocked everything out.'

'Oh.' I'm taken aback. There was no indication of any power outage at the airport.

'The airport has generators,' the driver explains, slowing down and stopping at a tree that's blown across the road. 'We will have to take another way.'

Crete is far from how I remember it, the little houses in darkness, no streetlights lifting the gloom. Even the street where Adam lives looks different when we reach it.

The driver stops outside his door. 'You see if your friend is there. I will wait.'

'Thank you.' Getting out, excitement flickers through me as I cross the street and knock at his door. When there's no reply, I knock again, then try the handle. But it's firmly locked.

My heart sinks. But it's late. Too late to hang around. I get back into the taxi. 'He isn't there. Can you take me to this address?' I tell him where Andreas lives.

He sets off. Then as we reach the end of the street, I see a beaten-up Fiat I think I recognise, slowing down before it parks at the roadside. 'Stop,' I cry to the taxi driver.

He slams the brakes on and I leap out of the taxi, running over to the car, trying to work out if it's Adam's or not.

Getting out of the car, he freezes. 'Tilly?' There's amazement in his voice. 'What are you doing here?'

Reaching him, I fling my arms around Adam. 'I've been so worried.' Suddenly I'm aware of tears streaming down my cheeks. 'I'm so glad you're OK.' Pulling back, I gaze at him. 'You are OK, aren't you?'

He smiles, gently wiping the tears off my face. 'I've never been more OK in my life.' He pauses. 'I love you, Tilly.'

A kind of magic weaves itself around my heart as he says that. They truly are the most beautiful words I've ever heard. 'I love you, too,' I say softly. 'I think I've always loved you.'

'You're not going to disappear again, are you? It feels like I'm putting my heart on the line, but you and I... Have you ever wondered why we shouldn't do this?'

'I have,' I say softly. 'Only about a hundred million times.'

'It's just that right now, there isn't anything in the way any more, is there?' He looks slightly anxious.

'There isn't.' It feels like I've waited all my life for this moment.

'You have no idea how that makes me feel to hear you say that.' He gazes into my eyes. 'I didn't finish telling you the story in the hospital, and it isn't that interesting. But the reason something was always missing with Louise was because of you.'

'Oh.' Pulling back slightly, I look at him, shocked. 'Did I do something?'

In the darkness, I can just about make out his smile as he nods. 'I suppose you could say that. You see, you bewitched me, Tilly.' He lets go of me and takes one of my hands. 'From that first day, you put a spell on my heart.'

It feels like my breath has been taken away. For all the right reasons, you understand. It's just that no one's ever said anything quite like that to me before. 'Is that a bad thing?' I say warily.

'It is for me.' He's silent for a moment. 'What it means is...' He takes a deep breath. 'You, Tilly, are the only woman in the world for me.'

Standing there, I soak up what he's saying, this stuff that dreams are made of. 'Wow,' I whisper, suddenly giddy. Then I kiss him.

27

New Chapters

And that is the end – of the old Tilly, at least, God bless her cotton socks. It also marks the start of a brand-new chapter. One set amongst the aftermath of Crete's worst storm in living memory, which is kind of fitting, because only out of such things does a phoenix arise. And in a way, that's how it feels. Stretching my wings and discovering a new way to be.

I know things are on track when a flow starts – otherwise it wouldn't feel like a flow. After spending a week helping clear up the damage of the storm, Adam and I fly, completely uneventfully, back to England. The house sells for almost the asking price; we spend a few days catching up with the boys at their respective universities.

I introduce Adam to my dad – slightly trepidatiously. After all, I'm about to commit the sin of divorce, as Adam already has. But most extraordinarily, they get on like a house on fire. No mention of churches, religion; no sanctity of marriage conversations. It's just as easy when Adam meets Rick.

Elena, as I already know, completely adores Adam. And when you put all of this together, you have proof, that while there will always be ups and downs, happy-ever-after really exists.

Only one thing is a bit weird – but there was always going to be some weirdness. It's when I call Tallulah, and I get her voice-mail. I leave her a message.

Hey, it's Tilly. Just letting you know I've found the flow – and to say thank you again.

Several hours later, she texts me back.

TALLULAH

Dear Tilly,

This is where you and I say au revoir. I'm hoping you've rediscovered sassy Tilly. The one who wanted to fly free – until that dreadful husband of yours clipped your wings. In other words, the Tilly you used to be.

It means you don't need me any more. But to be honest, you never did. You have all the answers you're looking for. You always did have. You just have to trust yourself.

Bon voyage! Have a wonderful life!

Tallulah xx

I read it again, then stare at it in amazement. But Tallulah has always known me better than myself. Or has she? I'm frowning again. She's right. I really must learn to trust myself.

'Thank you,' I whisper to Tallulah, or maybe it's to me, knowing if anyone's watching, it might seem ever so slightly odd. But who cares if I look a bit mad? 'Thank you,' I say to myself – a little louder, this time. 'It's taken you a while, but you're doing OK. You should be proud of yourself.'

* * *

That evening, Adam and I map out the next step. Only the one – it's good not to be too ahead of these things. The best laid of plans... Well, we all know what happens to them. Anyway, back to Adam. Things being what they are, he decides to take the job in San Jose – for a year. After all, that's where I was always headed, which means it feels perfect for both of us.

After that, we'll go back to Greece, which for some reason Adam sounds uncertain about. 'I've been thinking about Crete... Do you think you could live there?'

My eyes widen. 'You mean forever?'

Adam hesitates. 'Maybe. It's just a question at this stage... If you'd rather not, we can go somewhere else.'

'Yes.' I kiss him. 'A hundred times yes.' I could definitely live in Crete forever.

* * *

And so the flow goes on. I eventually get to San Jose, if not quite as planned. Actually, I fall a bit in love with it, even though it's nothing like I'd imagined it would be. But I'm cool with that. It's an adventure, the first of many to come. And I firmly believe that's what life is about.

Who are you? I ask myself in astonishment. *Who is this positive upbeat woman? Where's poor sad Tilly gone?*

This time my smile is broad. You see, I'm starting to get the sense that part of me has gone for good. I conjure a mental picture of her gathering up her sadness, her guilt, her shame, and regret, then hurling them off the edge of a cliff, standing there a moment to watch them sink into the frothing water. *Making room*, as Tallulah would have said, for this brand-new chapter – not that I or anyone else know what that's going to turn out to be. And in her place, I dare to imagine, that as Lizzie once said, there's a rainbow.

Life can be messy, unpredictable. The best laid of plans can fall wildly, devastatingly apart. But as I'm learning, nothing is perfect, and there's always a way through even the darkest times. And that's to fall in love with life all over again.

To take each beautiful day as it comes.

* * *

MORE FROM DEBBIE HOWELLS

The next gorgeous, sweeping romantic read from Debbie Howells is available to order now here:

https://mybook.to/DebbieHowellsNewBackAd

ACKNOWLEDGEMENTS

This book was inspired by the life journeys we all find ourselves on. All of them are different and this one took a bit of a convoluted path, with a few too many elephants – I owe huge thanks to my editor, Isobel Akenhead, for helping smooth that out and for getting this book into shape. Huge thanks also to Niamh Wallace and Issy Flynn, and to everyone who makes up the wonderful team at Boldwood Books for all your hard work in helping get my books out into the world.

A massive thank you as always to my super-agent, Juliet Mushens, and to everyone at Mushens Entertainment, for everything you do and for being such a wonderful home for an author.

And as always, a huge thank you to my family and friends. To Sarah and Freddie for always being so supportive. To my children, Georgie and Tom – I feel blessed every day to have you. And to Martin for being my rock through a year that hasn't been the easiest one.

And lastly, thank you to the wonderful community of bloggers and reviewers, and to you, my lovely readers. You are the reason I'm able to do this. When there are so many books out there, I appreciate each and every one of you for picking up a copy of one of mine. x

ABOUT THE AUTHOR

Debbie Howells is a *Sunday Times* bestseller, who is now fulfilling her dream of writing women's fiction with Boldwood. She has perviously worked as cabin crew, a flying instructor, and a wedding florist! Now living in the countryside with her partner and Bean the rescued cat, Debbie spends her time writing.

Download your exclusive bonus content from Debbie Howells here:

Visit Debbie's website: www.debbiehowells.co.uk

Follow Debbie on social media:

ALSO BY DEBBIE HOWELLS

ALSO BY DEBBIE HOWELLS

The Life You Left Behind

The Girl I Used To Be

The Shape of Your Heart

I'll Stand By You

The Forgotten Girls (or The Boyfriend?)

Time to Take a Chance

The Last Days of You and Me

The Memory Of

This Thing Called Love

For One Moment With You

9 781837 037360